From,

Megan Hands

thank
you ♥

Broken Pieces

MEGAN HANDS

authorHOUSE

AuthorHouse™ UK
1663 Liberty Drive
Bloomington, IN 47403 USA
www.authorhouse.co.uk
Phone: UK TFN: 0800 0148641 (Toll Free inside the UK)
       UK Local: (02) 0369 56322 (+44 20 3695 6322 from outside the UK)

*This is a work of fiction. All of the characters, names, incidents,
organizations, and dialogue in this novel are either the products
of the author's imagination or are used fictitiously.*

Published by AuthorHouse 11/29/2021

ISBN: 978-1-6655-9513-1 (sc)
ISBN: 978-1-6655-9512-4 (e)

Print information available on the last page.

This book is printed on acid-free paper.

Chapter 1 - Monday

‹◆◆◆◆◆›

As Madi's alarm went off. She rolled out of bed and realised what day it was. It was Monday the 30th of May. Her first day at her new school which she had been dreading for weeks now. Madi's in 4th year at school.

Madi's life has not always been easy. She lost both her parents in a car crash and her youngest sister Jessie as well.

Madi is 15 and had 5 sisters before Jessie died but after Jessie, she had 4. Their names were Summer (9), Autumn (7), Lilly (6) and Grace (11 months) who was Jessie's twin. She lived in Garmsby with her parents but moved to Ely when they died.

After Madi's parents died, Madi, Summer, Autumn and Lilly all got put into care. Grace got put into emergency foster care because she was too young to be in a care home. It was hard for Summer and the younger two sisters because they were quite young and struggled with the change.

The next day, all the girls got fostered by Grace's foster parents so that the girls were together. It was hard for Madi to get used to someone other than her parents taking care of her sisters, so she was controlling at some points by mistake.

The day finally came for Madi's first day at her new school Silver Oak Academy which she did not want to go to. Linda the girl's social worker picked up all the girls to take them to school. Linda dropped Summer, Autumn and Lilly off at school.

When they arrived at Madi's school, the head teacher Mr Vandelay welcomed Linda and Madi into his office and were sorting out the paperwork. Then Mr Vandelay came out and spoke to his PA Miss Power and asked her to get Miss Edwards up to his office.

As Mr Vandelay sat down, Madi looked at Linda confused as to who Miss Edwards was.

Madi asked, "Who is Miss Edwards?"

Mr Vandelay replied, "All will be revealed when she arrives."

There was then a knock at the door. Mr Vandelay went to the door and said, "Aah hello Miss Edwards." Miss Edwards entered, and she looked really kind. "Hello, I'm Miss Edwards, you must be Madi."

Madi muttered silently, "Hi."

Mr Vandelay said, "Miss Edwards is your form tutor."

Miss Edwards said, "Yes so if you have any problems you come to me"

"Madi if you would like to go with Miss Edwards and she will get you ready for today," said Mr Vandelay

As Madi was leaving, Linda said "Remember your meeting at lunch.?"

Miss Edwards interrupted "What meeting?"

"Sorry." Linda replied, "It's a meeting to discuss Madi's placement with her foster parents." Madi then said, "I won't forget, meet you in the car park at lunch."

"Come on Madi lets go to my office," Miss Edwards said.

As Miss Edwards and Madi were walking down to her office because Miss Edwards was a deputy alongside Mr Stevenson. As Madi and Miss Edwards arrived at Miss Edwards office she said, "In you come Madi, take a seat." "Okay Miss," Madi replied.

Miss Edwards then came and sat down next to Madi. Madi then asked Miss Edwards politely.

"What is this all about?" Miss Edwards replied.

"Well I'm your form tutor to help you with the loss of your parents, your sister and your anxiety brought on by the crash."

"Okay then Miss," said Madi.

So, then Madi and Miss Edwards talked about what is happening and what not. Miss Edwards then said, "Right I guess it's time for the grand tour,"

Madi then replied, "Miss what about my lessons?"

"Well, Madi you are keen but you have the first half of today off timetable so we can get you settled" Miss Edwards replied.

Madi and Miss Edwards then started on the tour. Miss Edwards then knocked on this door that said Mr Stevenson then came out and in the sweetest voice ever.

"Ah hello you must be our new arrival."

"Yeah, my name is Madi," Madi replied.

"I'm Mr Stevenson the other deputy head and your English teacher I think." Then Miss Edwards interrupted, "Yip Mr Stevenson is your English teacher and I think you will both get on great."

"Right well I better get back to my class" Mr Stevenson said. "Catch you later sir," Madi replied. "Bye," Miss Edwards said with smile.

The tour continued and Madi and Miss Edwards then reached Madi's math class and Miss Edwards knocked on the door and out came Mr Skelton and he said, "Well hello you must be Madi, I'm Mr Skelton."

Madi sort of stuttered "H...hi."

"Well, I look forward to seeing you in my class, do you like maths" Mr Skelton said, "Umm I do but it's not my favourite," Madi said "Well with teamwork and cooperation we will get maths to be your favourite subject" Mr Skelton said.

"Okay sir," Madi replied.

"Bye Madi, Miss Edwards," Mr Skelton said.

"Bye sir." Madi replied, "Bye Mr Skelton." Miss Edwards said.

"Right Madi we only have one more class to visit before lunch" Miss Edwards said. "What class is that Miss?" Madi asked. "Mrs Glen, your history teacher," Miss Edwards replied.

"Uh history" Madi said.

"Now Madi no need to be like that I know you aren't a huge fan of history, but I think you will enjoy it because Mrs Glen makes her lessons interesting and fun," Miss Edwards said.

"Okay miss I'll give it a chance" Madi replied. "Come on then let's go meet her." Miss Edwards said happily. As they both arrived at Mrs Glen's door. Miss Edwards knocked on the door and out came Mrs Glen.

"Oh, hello Miss Edwards and I'm guessing you must be Madi." Mrs Glen said.

"Hey miss yeah I'm Madi" Madi replied.

"Madi is really looking forward to doing history this year" Miss Edwards said, Madi then stared at Miss Edwards with sheer shock in her face. "Aww well that's good Madi I look forward to seeing you in my class, I will catch up with you later Madi" Mrs Glen said.

"Bye miss." Madi replied.

"Bye-bye Mrs Glen," Miss Edwards said before Mrs Glen walked back into her class.

After Madi and Miss Edwards finished with tour they headed back to Miss Edwards office "Done with the main subjects and before lunch" Miss Edwards said. "Just one more thing miss" Madi said with kindness in her voice, "Yeah Madi what is it" Miss Edwards replied,

"Who's my science teacher?" Madi asked

"Well you are looking at her" Miss Edwards replied.

"No way Miss. Really?" Madi said

"Yes honestly, do you like science?" Miss Edwards asked

"Yeah miss it's my second favourite subject after English but I do better in science than English" Madi replied.

The cloak struck half past 12 and Madi's meeting was going to begin soon. "Are you nervous?" Miss Edwards asked Madi "Hell yeah miss" Madi replied. "Listen to me right just relax and breathe okay and come find me when you are back" Miss Edwards said.

"Okay miss where are you most likely to be" Madi asked. "I'll either be here or in my classroom but most likely be in here because I don't have a class but if I'm not here Mr Stevenson is most likely to be so ask him where I am okay" Miss Edwards replied.

"Okay miss, thank you miss right well time for me to go I guess" Madi said. "Bye Madi" Miss Edwards said "Bye miss see you soon" Madi said before leaving Miss Edwards office.

Madi headed out to the car park at the main entrance and met Linda.

"Hey Madi, are you ready?" Linda asked.

"Yeah let's go" Madi replied.

Linda started up the engine. "Right let us go" Linda said "Let's go before I get any more nervous" Madi replied as the car pulled out the gate to the main road.

It was about 20 minutes later and Linda and Madi arrived at the social worker building for the meeting with Olivia and Simon that is the names of Madi's foster parents. Madi and Linda were already in the meeting room waiting for Olivia and Simon, there was a knock at the door it was the receptionist her name was Violet, and she said.

"Linda that's Olivia and Simon here."

"Okay thanks Violet send them through," Linda replied.

"In you go Olivia and Simon," Violet said.

"Thank you, Violet. Hi Linda and Madi," Olivia replied.

"Hi Olivia, Simon" Linda said

"Hey Simon, Hey Olivia" Madi replied.

"How are you doing champ?" Simon asked. "Yeah I'm doing fine Si," Madi replied. "How's the new school?" Simon asked, "I've only been there for half a day but it's good" Madi replied "Have you made any friends yet?" Olivia asked "Yeah hundreds" Madi replied with sarcasm "Was that sarcasm?" Simon asked.

"Yeah" Madi replied with a giggle.

"Right to business" Linda said "Well first can we just say we love having you but your control issues with your sister is just a bit too much" Olivia said.

"Control issues what do you mean control issues?" Madi asked. "Well with certain things you don't let Olivia and

Simon do" Linda replied "Well can you blame me I've looked after all my sisters since they were born" Madi said.

"We are getting off topic but champ, you can't live with us anymore" Simon replied

"Wait what" Madi said with tears in her eyes.

"We are so sorry Madi" Olivia said.

"Would it be okay if I went outside for some air" Madi asked "Yeah on you go" Linda said before Madi grabbed her phone and jacket "Thank you I'll be back soon" before opening the door. She walked down the stairs at the social worker building so she could get outside where she sat down on the bench that was outside.

She looked at her phone and knew that her friends from her old school would be at their lunch, so she phoned her best friends Brooke.

"Hey Brooke, how are you?" Madi said.

"Hey Madi, I'm doing okay how about you?" Brooke replied.

"Yeah I'm fine" Madi said.

"So, any reason you called me?" Brooke asked, "Yeah actually" Madi replied "So what's up?" Brooke asked "Well last time I spoke to you I had just got new foster parents; well they have decided to kick me out" Madi replied.

"What do you mean kicked out?" Brooke asked

"They decided that I am controlling because I don't let them do things, but I let them do plenty" Madi replied "Madi listen it might only be for a short while that you don't live with them okay. I'll come visit you soon and you better come visit me okay we are all missing you so much" Brooke said.

"Thanks Brooke I'm missing everyone as well and of course I'll visit you soon you are my best friend" Madi replied "I'll tell everyone that you are thinking of them" Brooke said

"Yeah thanks right well I'll talk to you later" Madi said, "Speak to you soon."

"Bye Madi" Brooke said.

"Bye Brooke" Madi said before hanging the phone up and heading back upstairs to Linda's office.

"I'm back sorry about that" Madi said "You don't need to apologize, are you okay" Linda replied, "Yeah is there any chance I could go back to school please if we are finished here?" Madi said.

"Yeah let's go" Linda said "Thanks Linda" Madi replied.

"Can you both wait here please I won't be long?" Linda asked.

"Yeah, see you later champ" Simon replied

"Bye Si, bye Olivia" Madi said.

"Bye Madi" Olivia replied.

"We will be back soon if you need anything just ask Violet" Linda said "Okay see you soon" Olivia replied before Linda and Madi headed out the door.

They reached Linda's car and they got in. "So how do you think it went?" Linda asked.

"It could have gone better but quick question" Madi replied.

"What's the question?" Linda said

"Do you think if I learn to less controlling do you think Olivia and Simon would maybe let me stay with them again" Madi asked.

"I'm not sure it's up to them but maybe" Linda replied "Okay can you just take me back to school before my lunch break is over please, I need to speak to Miss Edwards" Madi snapped.

"Okay calm down I need to speak to Mr Vandelay because he needs to know what is happening with you" Linda replied.

"Oh yeah now I'm going to be the school freakshow with no parents and no foster parents, aww yeah that's going to be just great" Madi said.

Linda went to say something then realised anything she said would make her more upset. She said it anyway "You aren't a freakshow and it's not as if anyone know is it besides me, Mr Stevenson, Mr Vandelay and Miss Edwards."

"People will find out," Madi replied. Madi's phone then buzzed.

It was her friends Ruby and Quinn the twins as people called them because they were identical twins. "Hey Ruby, Quinn" Madi said "Hey Mads, Brooke told us what happened are you okay?" Ruby asked.

"Yeah I'm fine, miss you all like mad but" Madi replied.

"We miss you too, come and visit us soon" Quinn said.

"Yeah of course I will" Madi said. "Good you aren't missing much by the way" Ruby replied.

"Anyway, Rubes what are you in next?" Madi said "We are in French next" Ruby said. "Have fun" Madi replied with a giggle, "So what are you in next?" Ruby asked "I think I'm in science next" Madi replied "Well enjoy even though you love science" Ruby said.

"Rubes, Q is it okay if I phone you back later, I've just back to school and I need to go speak to my teacher?" Madi asked "Yeah of course" Ruby replied, "Oh and tell Miss Potts I said Hi" Madi said. "We will, speak to you later" Quinn replied "Bye Rubes, bye Q" Madi said "Bye" Ruby and Quinn replied at the same time before they hung the phone up.

"Right let us go" Linda said "Well I'll speak to you later, have a great conversation with the head" Madi replied before walking into school. Madi reached Miss Edwards office and knocked on the door, "In you come" Miss Edwards said. "Hey, miss its only me can I talk to you please?" Madi replied after opening the door. "Yeah of course let's take a walk" Miss Edwards said.

"Okay" Madi replied.

"You can use the office if you want" Mr Stevenson said, "No it's fine I fancy some fresh air" Miss Edwards replied, "Okay then", "Thanks anyway" Miss Edwards said before grabbing her jacket and phone

"Bye, see you soon" Mr Stevenson replied, "We won't be long" Miss Edwards said before opening the door. They headed towards Miss Edwards class because by her class was a set of stairs outside where no one ever went. "So how did the meeting go?" Miss Edwards asked "Terrible, apparently I'm controlling but I can't help it, I've helped looking after my sisters since they were born" Madi replied.

"What do you mean by controlling?" Miss Edwards asked.

"Well I wouldn't let my foster parents do certain things like give Grace her bottle because she takes a certain way and tucking the girls in, I can't help it" Madi replied. "Hey, listen you have been through a huge trauma in your life and it can't be easy especially difficult for a girl of 15" Miss Edwards said. "Thanks, miss, I just feel bad for my sisters they have been through so much already and now I've probably made them worse" Madi replied.

"Madi listen to me, right now you need to focus on yourself let your foster parents worry about your sisters" Miss Edwards said "But miss where am I going to live now that my foster parents have kicked me out" Madi replied "I think Mr Vandelay and your social worker are working that out" Miss Edwards said "Oh great I'm going back into care" Madi replied "Well Madi we have a schoolhouse there is a huge possibility that you will go there" Miss Edwards said "Oh really" Madi replied.

"Anyway, what's wrong with care?" Miss Edwards asked, "Well when me and my sister first arrived, we got settled in and I got put in this room with this girl her name was Lucy, and she was really nice and obviously this was just after my parents died so all I wanted to do was sit in a corner and cry my eyes out" Madi replied "What happened next and with your sisters?" Miss Edwards asked.

"I made sure my sisters shared because they are young and it's bad enough losing their parents, they don't need to split up from each other, anyway me and Lucy went to check on the girls and Lucy brought her sisters, their names were Bella (8) and Anna (6). I could tell the girls were upset but they were still happy the girls all played together, me and Lucy headed back to our room. There was a knock on the door it was one of the care workers her name was Dani, she was a new care worker, but she was a care kid before that. She said.

Hey Lucy and is it Madi. Lucy replied with Hey Dani and I said Yeah, I am Madi, Dani then said Dinner is almost ready so if you want to get your sisters and head downstairs. Okay Dani thanks, Lucy replied before Dani left. I said, "Lucy can you take the girls downstairs?" I do not want dinner. Lucy replied, "Yeah of course are you sure you don't want anything to eat?" I said back Yeah just make sure the girls eat. Lucy left and I sat down on my bed."

"What happened next?" Miss Edwards asked.

"Well everyone was at dinner then there was a knock at the door, and it was Gina, and she was one of the nicest care workers and she said "Hey Madi are you not coming for dinner?" I replied I'm not hungry before breaking down in tears, she came and sat next to me and she said I know you are hurting but you need to eat and your sisters need you. I replied okay then she then said come on and then we left the room and headed down to the dining room where I sat next to Lucy and Summer. After dinner we went into the living room and I was reading my book that my mum had given me called life or death, it was a really good book and my mum wrote like notes about certain sentences.

Anyway I sat downstairs for about half an hour and I went back upstairs and went into my room and there was a note and a ripped up picture on my bed so first off I opened the note, and it said "You are so attention seeking and do you think Lucy likes you ha-ha you even more stupid than I thought oh and btw mummy and daddy's picture is away." I read the note and tried not to get upset then I picked the ripped-up photo up and I realised it was the only picture I had of me, my mum and my dad together.

I went down to speak to Dani, Gina and Tom who was the lead care worker and they got everyone together for a house meeting and no one fessed up to writing the note, but I decided to say to them just to leave it, it is not that important.

Anyway, after that I went outside for some air and Summer came out and she was really upset because she was missing mum and dad" Madi said before the bell rang.

"Time for class" Miss Edwards replied.

"Okay what class am I in" Madi asked while wiping her tears away "Science and will you finish that story later" Miss Edwards replied.

"Yeah miss" Madi said.

Madi and Miss Edwards stood up and headed into her class, "Sit there" Edwards said while pointing at a chair at the front and handed Madi three jotters, one for each different science "These jotters has all the stuff we have cover so far this year" Miss Edwards said

"Thank you miss and miss see when I tell you the rest about care, can I also tell you about what happened the day of the crash" Madi replied "Yeah that was the next thing I was going to ask you about" Miss Edwards said "Thank you miss" Madi replied.

Some of the pupils were outside and Miss Edwards went to the door and said, "Right you lot, you are so loud now quiet before you come in." The rest of the class arrived "Miss Edwards I left my jotters at home" Jodi said, "How many times Jodi you know where the paper is and everyone, I would like to introduce you to our new pupil Madi" Miss Edwards said.

"Hi" Madi replied.

"Right, everyone biology today so purple jotters" Miss Edwards said. The lesson went on and it was ten minutes before the end of the lesson. "Right your homework do the questions on page 22 and page 23 for Wednesday" Miss Edwards said, "But miss that's loads" Paige shouted out "Paige its only ten questions and I've not set you all homework for a few weeks now" Miss Edwards replied.

The bell rang "On to your next lesson, be brilliant. Jodi, can you wait behind please and Madi please" Miss Edwards said, "What's up miss" Jodi replied, "Jodi do you think that you could possibly be Madi's guide for the second part of today please" Miss Edwards asked "Yeah of course, maths next" Jodi replied, "Bye girls, thanks Jodi" Miss Edwards said before the two girls left.

Madi and Jodi walked down the corridor and down the stairs to maths. "So Madi what's your story why you here?" Jodi said.

"Well if I tell you can you please not tell anyone" Madi replied.

"Yeah of course" Jodi said.
"Well both my parents died in car crash and my foster parents live here so I came to this school but I don't know ow what's going to happen next because my foster parents kicked me out" Madi replied "Oh wow and I promise I won't tell anyone and this is our maths class" Jodi said before Madi and Jodi went inside.

"Hi girls, Madi can you sit there please?" Mr Skelton said before pointing at the desk by his desk "Okay sir" Madi replied. "Here are all your jotters with the notes already in them for you so you have less catching up to do" Mr Skelton said.

"Thanks sir" Madi said.

"Okay everyone let us begin if you could get into pairs, please" Mr Skelton said before there was a knock at the door it was Mr Vandelay.

"Afternoon class" Mr Vandelay said.

"Good afternoon sir" Everyone replied

"Can I borrow Madison McDonald please" Mr Vandelay said "Yip on you go Madi" Mr Skelton replied "Leave your stuff we won't be long" Mr Vandelay said. Madi and Mr Vandelay left the math class and headed towards his office. "So how are you feeling?" Mr Vandelay asked, "I'm fine sir" Madi replied "Good" Mr Vandelay said. They arrived at Mr Vandelay's office and in the office, there was Miss Edwards, Mr Stevenson, Linda and Miss Davis who was the house mistress for the schoolhouse. "Well, Madi this is Miss Davis she is the house mistress for the schoolhouse" Mr Vandelay said.

"Hi Miss Davis" Madi said.

"Madi we have all decided to offer you a place in the schoolhouse" Mr Vandelay said "Really?" Madi asked "Yeah honest" Mr Vandelay "Thanks" Madi said "Me and Miss Davis will walk you back to class" Miss Edwards said "Okay miss, Linda what will I do about my stuff that is at Olivia and Simon's" Madi asked "They said you can go collect it after school" Linda replied "Okay" Madi said.

"Linda would it be possible if me and Mr Stevenson take Madi to pick her stuff up" Miss Edwards asked, "Yeah I don't see a problem with that" Linda replied, "Come on you" Miss Edwards said to Madi "Bye Linda, sir" Madi said "Bye Madi" Linda said.

Miss Edwards, Miss Davis and Madi all left Mr Vandelay's office and towards Madi's math class. "Madi after this class and after your English class. Come to my office" Miss Edwards said, "Okay miss" Madi replied "And you can tell me the rest of your story" Miss Edwards said "Yeah of course" Madi replied.

They arrived at the door of Mr Skelton maths class. "In you go and I'll see you at the end of period 7" Miss Edwards said "See you at the end of period 7" Madi said before walking back into class. She sat down at her desk and noticed a note sitting on her desk and it said.

"New girl ha-ha don't think you are going to make any friends because you aren't because you are a freak and a TP."

Madi read the note then ran out of class dropping the note. Mr Skelton picked it up and read it "Okay who done this," no one confessed. "Darcy can I talk to you outside quickly?" Mr Skelton said.

"Darcy, I need you to do me a huge favour," Mr Skelton said. "Yeah sir" Darcy replied "Can you go to Miss Edwards office and tell her I need to borrow her?" Mr Skelton asked. "Okay sir," Darcy replied.

"I'm trusting you Darcy" Mr Skelton said.

"Yes sir" Darcy said before heading to Miss Edwards office.

She reached Miss Edwards office and she knocked on the door "Come in" Mr Stevenson said before Darcy opened the door. "Hi Miss, Sir, Miss" Darcy said, "Yeah Darcy what can we do for you" Miss Davis said "Umm… Mr Skelton need to borrow you Miss Edwards I think it's something to do with Madi" Darcy replied "Okay I'm just coming are you coming Vanessa? Jason?" Miss Edwards asked.

"I'll stay here in case she comes here" Mr Stevenson said, "Good idea I'll come with you Molly" Miss Davis replied. Miss Edwards, Miss Davis and Darcy all headed towards Mr Skelton's class. They arrived at Mr Skelton's door, Darcy went into the class and Mr Skelton's came outside "I found this on the floor after Madi ran out of class" Mr Skelton "I think I know where she might be, Vanessa you help Daniel find out who done it if no one fesses up get William" Miss Edwards said while walking away.

Madi was sitting on the stairs outside by Miss Edwards class by herself. The door opened and it was Miss Edwards.

"Hey Madi, it's really cold out here now how about you come inside, and we can go to my classroom" Miss Edwards said.

Madi did not say anything she just walked into Miss Edwards classroom. "What's wrong Madi come on talk to me" Miss Edwards asked, "This happened at my last school before my parents crash and went on for the 2 and a half years, I was there but I didn't say anything because I knew these people and they could do a lot of damage not just to me but my family" Madi said with tears rolling down her face "Come take a seat" Miss Edwards said before pointing at one of the desks.

Madi and Miss Edwards sat down on the green chairs at the round desks in her science class "I hate this, why are people so cruel sometimes" Madi said "I know people can be cruel but you just don't let it show" Miss Edwards replied "I'll try miss can I go back to class now" Madi asked.

"If you feel up to it, you only have about 20 minutes before your class is up" Miss Edwards replied "Okay miss you are going to deal with these people aren't you" Madi asked "Yes Madi of course I will but if anything else happens you have to promise me you will tell me or Mr Stevenson or any other member of staff" Miss Edwards replied "Yeah I promise miss" Madi said "Come let's go" Miss Edwards said.

Madi and Miss Edwards left Miss Edwards science class and went down the main staircase that takes them to Mr

Skelton's class. Miss Edwards knocked on the door and Mr Skelton and Miss Davis came out "Madi why don't you go and wash your face and I'll come get you soon" Miss Edwards said.

Madi did not say anything she just walked towards the toilet. Miss Edwards stepped into the class and snapped "You lot shut up, Jodi and Darcy outside please" the whole class went silent but started oohing because Jodi and Darcy had been asked to step outside.

"What's up miss" Jodi said "Is Madi okay miss" Darcy asked.

"I need you two girls to go to the toilets and check on Madi and I need you to make sure she is okay; can I trust you" Miss Edwards replied.

"Okay miss" Jodi said

"Can you see if you can find out what is bothering her" Miss Edwards replied, "Yeah we will try" Darcy said, "But don't make it obvious that you want to know" Miss Edwards replied.

"Yeah of course miss, we won't be long" Jodi said. The two girls left leaving Miss Edwards, Mr Skelton and Miss Davis outside "Did anyone fess up" Miss Edwards asked "Nope" Mr Skelton replied, "I think you know what we need to do" Miss Davis said to Miss Edwards.

"Yip get William involved until someone confesses" Miss Edwards replied. "He's going to go mental you know how much he hates bullies and especially with his new pupil" Miss Davis said, "I know but that girl has been through enough without this did you know that she was bullied the full two and a half years she was at her last school" Miss Edwards replied.

"Oh, I feel so bad for her" Mr Skelton said "Remember just treat her like a normal pupil" Miss Edwards replied "Yeah of course" Miss Davis said.

In the toilets Madi was standing at the sink wetting a paper towel so she could wash her face, she paused and realised her paper towel was wet enough she turned to the mirror that was behind her "Why did this have to happen to me" Madi said to herself before Jodi and Darcy walked into the toilets.

"Hey Madi" Jodi said "It's only us" Darcy said.

"Hey, are you both alright" Madi asked "Yeah we are fine are you okay" Jodi said while walking closer.

"Yeah of course I'm fine" Madi replied before wiping a tear away.

"Come on Madi talk to us" Darcy said "Fine okay you want me to talk, well both my parents died in a crash along with my baby sister oh yeah my aunts and uncles want nothing do with me because they blame me for the crash and my foster parents kicked me out" Madi snapped

"Wow umm... we didn't know" Jodi replied "Sorry for snapping I just get frustrated when I get upset" Madi said "Happens to the best of us don't worry about it" Darcy replied before the bell rang.

"English time" Jodi said "On you both go I'll catch up" Madi replied "Are you sure Madi" Darcy said "Yeah get my bag when you go to get yours, please" Madi replied "Of course will we say to Mr Stevenson" Jodi asked "Just say I'm here he should know what's happened" Madi replied.

Madi, Darcy and Jodi all left the toilets and Madi headed towards Miss Edwards office.

Darcy and Jodi headed to Mr Skelton class to get their bags then they headed to Mr Stevenson, Madi reached Miss Edwards office and she knocked on the door "Come in" Miss Edwards said "Hi miss it's only me" Madi replied.

"Hi Madi, how you are you feeling?" Miss Edwards asked.

"I'm fine I was just wondering if I could talk to you for two minutes" Madi replied "Yeah of course what's up" Miss Edwards said "I was wondering if you could organise for me to have a counsellor" Madi replied.

"Well Madi that's what I'm here for" Miss Edwards said "I just feel like a burden to you miss" Madi replied. "You aren't a burden to me but if you want a counsellor, I'll sort it okay" Miss Edwards said, "Thanks miss" Madi replied. "What class are you supposed to be in?" Miss Edwards asked "English with Mr Stevenson" Madi replied "Come on then I'll walk you up I need to talk to Mr Stevenson anyway" Miss Edwards said before her and Madi left the office and headed up to Mr Stevenson's class.

They arrived at Mr Stevenson and Miss Edwards knocked on the door and Mr Stevenson came out and said, "How you are feeling Madi?"

"Better sir," Madi replied.

"Madi just wait behind at the end of class because I'm heading to the office anyway so you can walk down with me," Mr Stevenson said.

"Yeah," Madi replied.

"In you go Madi," Miss Edwards said before Madi headed into class and sat with Darcy and Jodi. "What happened?"

Mr Stevenson said, "She wants a counsellor" Miss Edwards replied, "No way is it really that bad" Mr Stevenson said, "Oh can I actually borrow Jodi and Darcy" Miss Edwards asked.

"Yeah of course," Mr Stevenson said before walking into his classroom and saying "Jodi, Darcy Miss Edwards wants a word."

Jodi and Darcy headed outside the classroom to where Miss Edwards was "Hi girls come on we will go into Mr Browns classroom it's empty" Miss Edwards said.

Before Miss Edwards, Jodi and Darcy all headed into Mr Browns class next door. "What's up Miss?" Darcy said, "Did you talk to Madi" Miss Edwards asked.

"Yeah miss and to be honest she was really worked up about everything" Jodi replied.

"What do you mean by everything" Miss Edwards asked "Well the crash and that her foster parents kicked her out and I can't remember the last thing" Jodi replied.

"I remember it was that her aunts and uncle have nothing to do with her because they blame her for the crash" Darcy said "Wow she didn't say anything, can you both please keep an eye on Madi especially you Jodi because Madi is moving into the school house tonight" Miss Edwards replied.

"Yeah of course miss, Madi is still keeping a smile on her face" Jodi said.

"I know but she is still struggling so you do need to be sensitive and careful about you say around her" Miss Edwards replied.

"Yes miss" Darcy said, "Right that's all I wanted to talk to you both about now back to class and work

hard" Miss Edwards replied "Yes miss, bye miss" Jodi
said "Bye miss" Darcy said.

The two girls headed back into class and sat next to
Madi then there was another knock on the door, it was
Miss Davis "Hi Mr Stevenson sorry to interrupt but I was
wondering if I could borrow Jodi, Paige, Rebecca, Katie,
Millie, Aiden, Caleb, Hunter, Hudson, Adam, Addison and
Savannah" Miss Davis said "Yip on you all go will they be
long" Mr Stevenson replied "No they should only be about
10 minutes" Miss Davis said "Okay on you all go" Mr
Stevenson replied.

Everyone who Miss Davis wanted to speak to all headed
to the canteen.

"Right everyone, I just wanted to tell all of you that we are
having a new pupil joining the schoolhouse, some of you
may know her. Her name is Madi and I want all of you to
be nice because she hasn't had the best start in life okay"
Miss Davis said.

"Yes miss" everyone replied.

"Miss" Rebecca said raising her hand "Yeah Rebecca" Miss
Davis replied "What do you mean that she hasn't had the
best start in life" Rebecca asked "I can't discuss other pupils'
personal stuff" Miss Davis replied "Okay miss" Rebecca
said "Right everyone back to class expect Savannah, Jodi,
Paige and Addison."

Everyone left the canteen expect Savannah, Jodi, Paige and
Addison "Right girls I need you all to help Madi settle in
and I really shouldn't tell you this but I can trust you not
tell anyone but Madi's parents died in a crash and she has
just been kicked out of foster home where her sisters are but

girls I'm being deadly serious do not say anything to anyone" Miss Davis said.

"Wait what" Addison said "Yeah I know but girls do not say anything to anyone, right now back to class" Miss Davis replied "Bye miss" Savannah said "See you later miss" Paige said "Bye-bye miss" Addison said "Bye girls" Miss Davis said before all the girls left and they headed to Mr Stevenson's class.

Miss Davis headed towards Miss Edwards office to see if she were there to talk to her about Madi. She reached Miss Edwards office and knocked on the door, but no one answered so she peaked her head round the door and into the office and Miss Edwards was not there.

She then headed to Miss Edwards class to see if she was there and she was with a 1st year class, Miss Davis knocked on the door and said "Hey Miss Edwards can I talk to you for two minutes please"

"Yeah, everyone continue with your work in silence" Miss Edwards replied.

Miss Davis and Miss Edwards headed outside the science class "What's up" Miss Edwards said "I just want to say to you that I have told… " Miss Davis said before she got interrupted by the noise coming from the class "Hold on a minute" Miss Edwards said before walking into the class.

"Excuse me you lot I thought I told you work in silence" Miss Edwards said.

"Sorry miss" Everyone said "Silence" Miss Edwards said before walking back out the class, "So as I was saying I've told the kids in the schoolhouse that Madi is moving in but I have only told Savannah, Jodi, Paige and Addison why she is moving in" Miss Davis said.

"Okay do they know not to tell anyone why she is moving in" Miss Edwards asked, "Yeah and they won't say anything anyway" Miss Davis replied. "Is that all" Miss Edwards asked, "Yeah I'll catch up with you later" Miss Davis replied before Miss Edwards went back into her class, Miss Davis headed down to her classroom because she is the Food Tech teacher.

Meanwhile back in Mr Stevenson's class, everyone was working in trios on a poem so Madi was working with Darcy and Jodi "This poem is so confusing" Madi said "I know it isn't it" Jodi said "Done" Darcy said "What wait already how did you do that as quickly" Jodi replied.

"It's easy" Darcy replied "We will just copy you because you know we are working in trios" Jodi said "Yeah" Darcy replied "Madi you are quite quiet everything okay" Jodi asked, Madi just nodded. "You can talk to us whenever you know that" Darcy said.

"Yeah I know" Madi said before her phone rang "Who's phones that" Mr Stevenson asked "Mine sorry sir can I go outside to answer it please" Madi replied "Yeah on you go" Mr Stevenson said.

Madi went outside of the class and answered her phone it was her cousin Payton "Hey Payton what can I do for you" Madi said. "Hey Madi, I just wanted to check in with you and to tell that auntie Kate is coming up for a visit but it's to see what's happening with your parents will, but you did not hear it from me" Payton said.

"Yeah I won't say anything but don't say that I said this she is a gold digger, anyway how's baby Cole" Madi replied.

"Yeah he's fine I'll have to come visit you soon and bring him with me" Payton said.

"Yay I can't wait to see you again and I cannot wait to meet baby Cole he looks so cute in his pictures" Madi replied.

"He is just one of the most amazing babies ever" Payton said "Listen Payt I'm going to go I'm supposed to be in English but I'll give you a phone or a facetime later if that's okay" Madi replied "Yeah of course Mads, you should of said anyway I will speak to you later I love you bye-bye" Payton said "I love you too bye-bye" Madi replied before she hung up the phone.

Before Madi walked back into class she took a deep breath and she went to open the door Mr Vandelay walked past and asked "Everything okay Madi" "Yeah sir" Madi replied "Are you sure" Mr Vandelay asked "Yes sir" Madi replied.

"What are you doing out of class" Mr Vandelay asked "Sorry sir my cousin phoned me about something" Madi replied "It's fine Madi as long as you are okay and remember I'm here if you need to talk about anything okay" Mr Vandelay said "Okay sir, Thanks sir" Madi said before walking into class where Mr Vandelay was going.

"Good afternoon class" Mr Vandelay said, "Afternoon Mr Vandelay" The class replied "Can I have a word with your class Mr Stevenson" Mr Vandelay asked "Yip everyone pens and pencils down and listen" Mr Stevenson replied.

"Right recently I have noticed that bullying has been increasing massive and I will not stand for it so anyone who is caught bullying will face up to a 2-week suspension and maybe even expulsion do I make myself perfectly clear?

If anyone needs to tell me anything about a bullying situation, my door and Mr Stevenson and Miss Edwards door will always be open, but I will say it again do I make myself perfectly clear that I am not standing for any bullying in my school" Mr Vandelay said. "Yes sir" The class replied "Thank you" Mr Vandelay said before leaving the class "Remember what Mr Vandelay said, anyway whose done as we only have about 10 minutes left" Mr Stevenson said.

"We have," Jodi said. "We have sir," Savannah said. "So have we" Rebecca said "Us too" Hunter said "And us" Aiden said, "Good that means no one has any homework" Mr Stevenson replied before the bell rang "Can we go now sir" Rebecca said "Okay you lot, you can go now have a good evening" Mr Stevenson said before everyone expect Madi left the class.

"Are you okay Madi" Mr Stevenson asked "Yeah I'm fine sir, I just nervous in case I upset them more" Madi replied "It will all be okay come on let us go to the office" Mr Stevenson said before he grabbed his jacket and briefcase. Madi and Mr Stevenson headed out of his class and walked towards his office, while they were walking to the office, they saw Mr Newwall who was the PE teacher, Miss Welch who was the French teacher and Miss Halfpenny who was the drama teacher all of whom have not met Madi yet. "Sir who were they" Madi asked "You haven't met them yet" Mr Stevenson replied "No sir I think I was supposed to meet them tomorrow" Madi said.

"Okay and we are here let us see if Miss Edwards is" Mr Stevenson said before he opened the door to the office.

"Thanks sir, hi miss" Madi said.

"Hiya Madi how are you doing" Miss Edwards asked.

"I'm fine miss" Madi replied.

Chapter 2 - Counsellor

+ + + + + +

"Right well let us go" Mr Stevenson said before Miss Edwards phone rang "Actually hold that thought for 5 minutes please" Miss Edwards said before she walked out the office. "Wonder what that's about" Madi said "Me too" Mr Stevenson said "Anyway sir, I haven't asked you how you are" Madi asked "I'm good Madi thanks for asking" Mr Stevenson replied, Madi just smiled.

"Hello" Miss Edwards said, "Hello is this Molly Edwards speaking" Sage asked, "Speaking what's up?" Miss Edwards replied, "This is Sage from the counsellor company you phoned up earlier about a meeting for one of your students and we have a counsellor free tonight, her name is Melony and is experienced in your students situation" Sage said.

"Okay and can she come to Silver Oak Academy schoolhouse please and what time" Miss Edwards replied.

"Yip she can and how does 6:30 pm sound" Sage said.

"Yeah that is perfect, thank you so much" Miss Edwards replied, "Okay bye" Sage said "Bye" Miss Edwards replied before she hung up the phone and walked back into the office.

"Right, we can go now" Miss Edwards said.

"What was that about" Mr Stevenson asked, "I'll fill you in later" Miss Edwards replied.

"Okay whose car are we taking" Mr Stevenson said, "We will take mine, it's bigger", "Okay" Mr Stevenson said.

Madi, Mr Stevenson and Miss Edwards all headed towards the staff car park, they reached Miss Edwards car "Let's go" Miss Edwards said before starting the engine "Have you go your seatbelt on Madi" Mr Stevenson asked "Yeah sir" Madi said before taking her phone out of her pocket "Good right let's go" Mr Stevenson said "Madi what's Olivia and Simon's address" Miss Edwards asked "88 High View Hill" Madi replied before Miss Edwards put it into her Sat Nav, "Now we can go" Miss Edwards said before reversing out of the parking space and headed towards Madi's ex foster parents house.

They reached Madi's ex foster parent's house after about 20 minutes "I'll knock" Madi said "Okay" Mr Stevenson replied before they all got out the car. Madi walked on ahead leaving Miss Edwards and Mr Stevenson still at the car. Madi knocked on the door and Olivia answered and said "Hi Madi come in."

"Hi Olivia, are the girls here?" Madi replied.

"Yeah, you come in and I'll get them to come down," Olivia said before Madi, Miss Edwards and Mr Stevenson walked into the house.

Olivia walked upstairs where the girls were, and they ran downstairs "Hey my girlies," Madi said before the girls ran into her arms expect from Grace who was sleeping. "Madi," Summer said. "Listen girls I'm just here to get my stuff then I'm leaving," Madi said. "What why?" Summer asked "Sum right now I can't live here okay and it's for the best but it won't stop you from seeing me. I'm going to live in the schoolhouse," Madi replied.

"But… you can't leave me here," Summer said before she ran upstairs in tears. "I'll deal with her just give me 5 minutes" Madi said before she ran upstairs into Summer's room.

"Sorry I forgot to introduce myself I'm Miss Edwards and this is Mr Stevenson we are the deputies at Madi's school and I'm also Madi form tutor and her science teacher and Mr Stevenson is Madi's English teacher" Miss Edwards said "Well it's nice to meet both of you can I get you anything to drink" Olivia replied "No I'm fine" Mr Stevenson said "No thanks" Miss Edwards said "Okay take a seat if you want" Olivia said before Miss Edwards and Mr Stevenson sat down on the couch.

Madi knocked on Summer's door and said, "Hey Sum it's only me can I come in" "Yeah" Summer said while wiping a tear away "Come here, give me a hug" Madi said before Summer gave her a hug "Why are you not staying here anymore" Summer asked before Grace started to cry.

"Wait a minute and I'll go get Grace and then I'll tell you" Madi said before she headed into Grace's room and brought her back into Summer's room. "Now can you tell me why you can't stay here" Summer asked "Well basically I don't let Olivia and Simon do stuff and Linda thinks it would be best if we had a cooling off period" Madi replied "But what about us? What about me, Autumn, Lilly and Grace?" Summer asked, "I'm still going to see you it's just I'm not going to be here every single day" Madi replied.

"First I lose mum and dad and Jessie now I'm losing you" Summer said "Listen Sum you aren't going to lose me I'm only a phone call away yeah" Madi replied "Okay" Summer said "Now are you going to help me pack up my stuff" Madi replied "Yeah" Summer said before her and Madi walked into Madi's old room to pack up her stuff. "Who my girly whirly" Madi said to Grace "That's funny Madi" Summer said, "Hey you shut up" Madi replied before tickling her "Stop" Summer said while laughing "There's that lovely smile and laugh I love" Madi said.

Madi, Summer and Grace all headed downstairs with the stuff from Madi's room. "Right, that's me sorted" Madi said "Me and Mr Stevenson will load your stuff into the car, and you can say your goodbyes" Miss Edwards said "Okay miss" Madi replied before the door opened it was Simon. "Hey Si" Madi said "Hey champ, how is you?" Simon asked, "I'm fine how was work today?" Madi replied "It was good" Simon said.

Miss Edwards and Mr Stevenson came back into house "Madi time to go" Mr Stevenson said "Just give me 5 minutes please sir" Madi replied "We will go into the kitchen and give you girls some space" Olivia said before the adults went into the kitchen.

Madi and all the girls sat down on the couch "Madi" Autumn said, "Yeah Almond" Madi replied "Where are you going?" Autumn asked "Listen I'm going to live at my schools schoolhouse because it's too much for me to live here" Madi replied "But what about us" Autumn said "You are still going to see me it's just not going to see me every single day okay" Madi replied "I'm going to miss you Madi" Lilly said "I'm going miss you too Lil" Madi replied before hugging Lilly and wiping a tear away.

"Right girls as much as I love you, I need to go" Madi

said "No stay with us" Lilly replied "Lil I can't" Madi said before shouting on the adults, "I don't want you to go" Summer said "I know Sum I don't either but this is the best for everyone" Madi replied "Please don't go Madi" Autumn said "Listen to me Almond, I know you don't want me to go but I love you all of you so much and you have one set of amazing foster parents" Madi replied.

"Madi it's time to go" Miss Edwards said.

"Okay miss, girlies selfie" Madi replied.

"Yeah" Summer said before Madi took a selfie with all the girls, "Bye girls" Madi said.

"Bye Madi" The girls said "Actually before you go, we have a present for you" Olivia said.

"You didn't have to get me anything" Madi replied.

"Here you go" Olivia said before she handed Madi a bag.

"Thank you" Madi said before opening it "So do you like it champ" Simon replied.

"I love it, I forgot you took this picture of me and the girls" Madi said before giving Simon and Olivia a hug. "Now it's time for me to go, bye girlies" Madi said "Bye" the girls said before Madi, Miss Edwards and Mr Stevenson walked out the door back to the car. Madi, Miss Edwards and Mr Stevenson all got back into the car and Miss Edwards started the engine "Are we good to go" Mr Stevenson asked "Mhm" Madi replied, as Miss Edwards put the car into gear and started to drive away.

Olivia, Simon and the girls stood at the door and waved as Miss Edwards pulled away. Miss Edwards investigated the mirror to check on Madi and she noticed her wiping away a tear but didn't say anything about it because she didn't want to upset Madi even more "Oh Madi listen remember how you asked for a counsellor, well there is someone coming at 6:30pm tonight and her name is Melony" Miss Edwards said "Okay miss" Madi replied.

They reached the schoolhouse and Miss Edwards parked in one of the spaces and waiting outside at the door was Jodi and Miss Davis. "Hi Madi" Jodi said, "Hi Jodi" Madi replied "Madi, Jodi is going to take you to your room, and I'll come up shortly to check on you" Miss Davis said, Madi didn't say anything her and Jodi just went into Madi's room leaving Miss Davis, Miss Edwards and Mr Stevenson.

"So how did it go" Miss Davis asked "One of her sisters had a meltdown about her leaving, she is really upset about leaving her sisters and I can see why they look up to her so much" Miss Edwards replied "It was quite awkward, I can tell she looks up to Simon I think his name was but I think she doesn't like Olivia that much" Mr Stevenson said "That's what I picked up as well and Madi's councillor is coming tonight at 6:30pm" Miss Edwards replied.

"I'll keep the kids out the way the best I can because I know how cruel kids can be but I doubt any these kids what say anything" Miss Davis said "Thanks Vanessa I'm going to check on Madi and see how she is doing" Miss Edwards replied.

Miss Edwards went upstairs and into Madi's room where Madi and Jodi were "Hey girls how are you?" Miss Edwards asked.

"I'm good miss thanks how are you" Jodi replied.

I'm fine miss" Madi said.

"I'm great thanks Jodi" Miss Edwards replied.

"Right let's start unpacking so I can get this room sorted" Madi said "Okay Madi let's do it" Jodi replied, "I'll help you as well" Miss Edwards said "Thanks miss umm… what time is it?" Madi replied.

"It is 30 past 5 so we have around an hour" Miss Edwards said "Okay miss" Madi replied "What do you mean you only have an hour" Jodi asked "Umm… you won't tell anyone will you but I've got a counsellor coming at half 6 tonight so I want to set my room up so it's done but please don't tell anyone" Madi said "Oh okay and I won't say anything you can trust me" Jodi replied "Thank you Jodi" Madi said before hugging Jodi "Right come on we are losing valuable organising time" Jodi said "I know let's get a move on, Miss Edwards you start on that set of boxes and Jodi you do them" Madi said while pointing at the boxes "Let's do this" Jodi replied.

Time went on and Madi's boxes were emptying quickly "Right girls can you do the rest yourself" Miss Edwards asked, "Yeah miss we will be fine" Madi replied "I'll give you a shout when Melony arrives" Miss Edwards said.

"Okay miss" Madi replied.

As Miss Edwards was leaving she noticed a picture on the floor and it was an ultrasound from what she thought was one of Madi's sisters, "Madi whose this" Miss Edwards asked "That is my brother" Madi replied "Wait brother" Jodi said "Yeah he died when he was around four days old" Madi replied without making eye contact with Miss Edwards and Jodi.

"What was his name?" Miss Edwards asked "His name was Jack" Madi replied "That's such a nice name" Jodi said "It is, is it" Madi replied "What age would Jack be now?" Miss Edwards asked "He would have been 11 so Summer didn't meet him but I always told her about him, well what I remember" Madi replied.

"Anyway, I'm going to go downstairs to meet Melony" Miss Edwards said.

"Okay miss" Madi replied.

Miss Edwards went downstairs leaving Madi and Jodi upstairs "How is she?" Miss Davis asked, "I don't know, I've just found out she had a brother who died anyway here comes Melony I think" Miss Edwards said, "She looks nice and I'll go get Madi" Miss Davis replied before going upstairs.

"Hi, you must be Melony" Miss Edwards said.

"Yip and you must be Molly Edwards" Melony replied.

"Yeah Jason if you could show Melony into the dining room and Madi will be down in one minute" Miss Edwards said before Mr Stevenson and Melony went into the dining room.

Miss Davis and Madi came downstairs "Madi listen to me, the woman in there is Melony and she is the counsellor, but listen to me just tell her everything she is qualified to deal with the stuff you have been through okay" Miss Edwards said "Okay miss, you can go if you want" Madi said. "No, I'm going to stay here until you are finished with Melony" Miss Edwards said "Miss can you actually come in with me I don't know if I can do it myself" Madi said to Miss Edwards "Yeah of course let's go" Miss Edwards replied before her and Madi went into the dining room.

"Madi this is Melony and Melony this is Madi" Miss Edwards said before she and Madi took a seat. "Hi" Madi said.

"Hi Madi, I am here to help you so just get everything

off your chest" Melony replied. "Okay I'll talk to you about what happened the day of the crash" Madi said "Okay" Melony replied "So basically every few months me and my sisters have a sister bonding day" Madi said before Melony interrupted and said "What do you mean sister bonding day?" "Well it's a day dedicated to just me and my sisters so we can spend more time together" Madi replied.

"Do you want a cup of tea?" Miss Edwards asked to Madi and Melony.

"Yeah 1 sugar and milk please" Melony replied.

"Yes, please miss and 1 sugar and milk as well" Madi said

"Okay you keep talking I'll be back in 5 minutes" Miss Edwards said before she went into the kitchen and made three cups of tea.

"Here you go" Miss Edwards said before putting two cups of tea on the table and going back into kitchen to grab her cup "Right Madi what happened next?" Melony asked. "Well me and my sisters went downstairs into the living room with some board games which were Jenga, Kerplunk and Battleships and we also had jigsaws for the younger girls.

We played them for about two hours and then we decided to watch a movie so I got Summer, Autumn and Lilly to go upstairs into my bedroom and grab the pillows and blankets off my bed, anyway me and the girls all snuggled together and I heard my parents arguing in the kitchen.

I turned the movie up so the girls wouldn't hear but I think they did, I then noticed that Jessie was boiling so I told Summer that I would be back in two minutes so I lifted Jessie up and headed into the kitchen where my mum and dad were and as I walked in they stop arguing. I said to them that Jessie had a really bad temperature so they decided to book a doctor's appointment and luckily they had a cancellation so the doctors could see Jessie today, my mum and dad said to me that they were going to be gone for about an hour or so but they would get the neighbour to check in with us."

"Right so what happened next?" Melony asked "My parents left to go to the doctors, and we were watching Little Mermaid as it was the girls favourite movie, it's not anymore so we finished watching that movie and I just put another movie on. Then we finished that movie, I put on another movie it was about 3 hours later and my parents still weren't back.

There was a knock on the door and I just thought it was the neighbour and I opened the door and standing there was a social worker and two police workers and they asked to speak to us, they came in and told us that my parents got into a really bad collision with another car and everyone involved died" Madi said before taking a deep breath.

"Madi just take your time we are here to help okay" Miss Edwards said.

"Can I really quickly run to the toilet please?" Madi asked.

"Yeah go on" Melony replied.

"I'll be 5 minutes okay" Madi said.

"Okay just take your time" Miss Edwards replied before Madi walked off to the toilet.

It was around 5 minutes later and Madi wasn't back yet, so Miss Edwards said to Melony "I'll be right back I'm going to check on Madi" "Okay" Melony replied before Miss Edwards went upstairs and checked in Madi's room to see if she was there which she wasn't. She then knocked on the toilet door where Madi was washing her face "Madi it's Miss Edwards are you okay?" "Yeah I'm fine miss" Madi replied before opening the toilet door "Let's go back downstairs to finish this appointment", "Okay miss" Madi replied before her and Miss Edwards walked back downstairs and into the dining room where Melony was.

"Sorry about that, I haven't actually told anyone about what happened on the day of the crash" Madi said while taking a seat. "Listen Madi it's fine I'm here to help" Melony replied, "Where was I?" Madi said.

"The social worker came round and told you and your sisters that your parents had died" Melony replied "Yeah so I, Summer, Autumn and Lilly were really upset like they had massive floods of tears and I just didn't know how to react because I didn't want to upset my sisters even more if they saw me upset if that makes sense" Madi said. "Yip makes perfect sense continue" Melony replied, "So the social worker Linda told us to go upstairs and gather some stuff together as we will be going into a care home and told me to get stuff for Grace as she was going into an emergency foster place because of her age. Me and the girls went upstairs, and I grabbed their suitcases and told them to put their teddies, books and toys in there and I would get their clothes in a different suitcase," Madi said.

"Okay keep going," Melony said.

"You are doing really well Madi," Miss Edwards said.
"As I was in my room I could hear the girls sniffling in their bedrooms as the wall were quite thin, I was trying so hard not to cry because I knew the girls would hear me but I couldn't hold my tears back any longer I just wanted my

mum and dad and my sister back. There was then a knock at my door and it was Summer and her eyes were so red from crying and she came in and said that she missed mum and dad and I told her I know you are upset, so am I, but I need you to be strong for your sisters because they need us and she said I know and gave me a hug"

"Are you okay Madi?" Melony asked.

"Yeah I'm fine I just needed to take a breath there," Madi replied.

"You are doing amazingly" Miss Edwards said with a smile on her face.

"Summer went back into her room and I went into my mum and dads room to tidy up a bit so that it doesn't look as messy when my aunts and uncles come to get stuff that they want from my parents room if that makes sense" Madi said "Yeah makes perfect sense" Melony replied.

"Well, it's been an hour so I think times up because it's getting late" Miss Edwards said "Yeah" Madi replied "Well I'll be in touch about when your next appointment is" Melony said "Thank you Melony" Madi said before she, Melony and Miss Edwards walked towards the door "Thank you Melony, bye" Miss Edwards said before Melony got into her car and drove off.

"So, do you feel better?" Miss Edwards said.

"Yeah thanks miss" Madi replied before she walked upstairs and into her room.

"Well I think it's time we go" Mr Stevenson said

"Yeah but Vanessa can you keep an eye on Madi please" Miss Edwards replied

"Yeah of course, now on you go home" Miss Davis said

"Bye I'll see you in the morning" Miss Edwards said

"Bye see you in the morning" Miss Davis replied as Miss Edwards and Mr Stevenson got into Miss Edwards car and shut the door, Miss Davis then went upstairs and into Jodi's room to talk to her.

"Hi Jodi, can you do me a massive favour?" Miss Davis asked, "Yeah miss of course" Jodi replied, "Can you please keep an eye on Madi, I think she is really struggling" Miss Davis asked. "Yeah, would it be okay if I go make tea for me and Madi and get biscuits please" Jodi replied, "Yeah of course" Miss Davis said "Thanks miss" Jodi said before she headed into Madi's room.

"Hey Madi, do you want some tea and we can have a good girly chat" Jodi asked, "Yeah Jodi" Madi replied "How do you take your tea?" Jodi asked. "1 sugar and milk" Madi replied "Okay, I'll be back in 5 minutes and I'll bring biscuits as well" Jodi said "Thanks Jodi" Madi replied before Jodi went downstairs and into the kitchen and made two cups of tea and grabbed the packet of shortbread and went back upstairs.

"Here you go, one cup of tea and some shortbread now let's have a girly chat" Jodi said while passing Madi her cup of tea and sitting on Madi's bed "Thanks Jodi you really don't need to do this you know" Madi replied "I want to, you are one of us now the schoolhouse kids and we look out for each other" Jodi said "Thanks Jodi" Madi replied. "Right what happened at the appointment?" Jodi asked "Well the appointment was the very first time I have ever talked about my parents and wow it was hard" Madi replied "Well guess what you have talked about it and it's going to get easier honest" Jodi said.

"Yeah that's true do you fancy doing our science

homework so it's done" Madi replied "Yeah as long as you are okay and you know that you can talk to me whenever" Jodi said "Yeah I know, now go grab your jotter" Madi said "Okay what jotter is it?" Jodi replied. "It's the purple one for biology" Madi said "Okay I'll be right back" Jodi said before walking out of Madi's room and into her own room and grabbed her purple jotter.

"Right I'm back let's do this" Jodi said.

"Can you remember what page it was?" Madi asked.

"Yeah, I put it in my diary it's pages 22 and 23" Jodi replied.

"Okay let's do this; do you need a pencil?" Madi said "Yeah please" Jodi replied before Madi passed her a pencil. The girls began working and finished about 15 minutes later "Wow that was quick, I thought that was going to take longer" Madi said. "That's the thing about Miss Edwards she doesn't give hundreds of work unlike some of the other teachers" Jodi replied "Anyway that's done even though it isn't due into Wednesday" Madi said. "Yeah we will probably get loads of work tomorrow" Jodi replied.

"Right tell me all about the teachers that I haven't met" Madi said "So then ones you haven't met yet are:

Mr Newwall who is the PE teacher he's nice,

Miss Welch who is the French teacher she isn't that strict but will have a go at you if you forget to do your course work or homework and,

Miss Halfpenny who is the drama teacher and our head of year and she is just one of the kindest teachers ever to me anyway" Jodi replied.

"We have double English first tomorrow" Madi said. "Oh, by the way you have Mr Stevenson for the first half, and you have Mr Brown the second half" Jodi replied. "What's Mr Brown like?" Madi said "Well let's just say he is the world grumpiest teacher" Jodi replied with a giggle, "Seriously" Madi said "Yeah he is so grumpy, word of advice do not, and I repeat do not get on his bad side" Jodi replied. "Right I won't get on his bad side, I will just sit in the class quietly" Madi said "I have been in trouble by him at least 4 times and I was sent to detention every single time" Jodi replied "Tut-tut naughty" Madi said with a giggle.

There was a knock at the door "Come in" Madi said before the door opened. "Hi it's only me just wanted to say lights out at 9:30pm, which is in an hour and a half" Miss Davis said, "Okay miss" Madi replied with a smile on her face.

"It's nice to see a smile on your face Madi" Miss Davis said.

"Thanks, miss it's nice to have a smile on my face" Madi replied.

"Good, good" Miss Davis said.

"Oh, miss what's for dinner tomorrow?" Jodi asked.

"I was thinking we could have pizza to celebrate our new arrival" Miss Davis replied.

"Yay miss" Madi said.

"Yass miss" Jodi said.

"Right now, Jodi another hour then into your own room so you have half an hour down time to yourself" Miss Davis said. "Oh, miss what it be okay if I went downstairs quickly to phone my cousin and I like fresh air before bed?" Madi asked "Yip of course Madi just take your time" Miss Davis replied. "Is that okay Jodi?" Madi asked "Yeah of course I'm going to read my book for my coursework and listen to music for an hour" Jodi replied "Okay thanks Jodi, thanks miss" Madi said.

Madi then walked downstairs and opened the door and sat on the step outside and she phoned Payton "Hey Payt" Madi said "Hey Mads what's up you sound like you have been crying?" Payton replied "I have been crying it was because I was talking about mum and dad and Jessie" Madi said.

"Oh, Mads I promise I'll come visit you soon maybe Friday or Saturday" Payton replied. "You don't have too but Saturday would be better because I'm at school on Friday and by the time I get to the schoolhouse it will be late and I'll only be able to spend like 2 or 3 hours with you" Madi said.

"Listen Mads you are my favourite cousin and auntie Anna and uncle Michael were my favourite auntie and uncle so of course I will visit so Saturday it is, I have a plan for us to do something special" Payton replied. "Thanks, Payt, I love you so much" Madi said "I love you more Mads; Coles being fussing I better go deal with him bye" Payton replied. "Bye, love you" Madi said before she hung up the phone, she sat outside for about 10 minutes thinking about everything that has happened so far then she went back upstairs and back into her room.

She sat down on her bed then decided to get into her pink pyjamas which her cousins Gwen and Derek bought her for her birthday, she then climbed into bed and put her phone on charge and read her book that her gran bought her for her Christmas. There was a knock on the door, it was Miss Davis.

"Lights out in fifty minutes Madi" Miss Davis said.

"Okay miss" Madi replied.

"Can I come in for two minutes" Miss Davis asked.

"Yeah miss, in you come" Madi replied.

Miss Davis came into Madi's room and sat on the bottom of Madi's bed "How are you feeling?" Miss Davis asked "I am feeling a lot better to be honest and miss would it be okay if my cousin comes up on Saturday, I haven't seen her since my parents and sister died" Madi replied.

"Yeah of course is that who you were on the phone to earlier" Miss Davis said.

"Yeah miss, she's my oldest cousin she is 19 and has a little 6 month old baby called Cole he's so cute here's a picture for you" Madi replied before grabbing one of the photo frames and handing it to Miss Davis "Oh my god he's beautiful" Miss Davis said. "I know I think my cousin is bringing him up on Saturday" Madi replied "Okay Madi well you still have forty minutes till lights out so you can do what you want within reason for forty minutes" Miss Davis said "Okay miss and thanks" Madi replied.

"You don't have to thank me I'm just glad you are feeling better" Miss Davis said before standing up and walking to the door "I do feel a lot better" Madi replied "Night Madi" Miss Davis said with a huge smile on her face "Night miss" Madi replied before Miss Davis left.

Chapter 3 - Tuesday

+ + + + + +

T he forty minutes past and it was lights out, Madi
fell asleep. The next morning everyone was waking
up at 7 o'clock and they headed downstairs to get breakfast,
Madi sat with Jodi and Morag one of the other schoolhouse
kids who was really good friends with Jodi to have breakfast.
Madi had toast and jam then she went upstairs to get ready
for school as she was getting ready her phone rang it was
her auntie Kate.

"Hey auntie Kate how are you" Madi said.

"Hi Madi, I'm good how are you" Kate replied.

"I'm fine I'm just getting ready for school" Madi said.

"Okay, this will only take two minutes I just wanted
to tell you that I am

coming up tomorrow for a meeting with your parents
lawyer and I am coming

to see you and your sisters, I am bringing Kendall,
Kevin, Kennedy and Kass"

Kate replied.

"Okay auntie Kate I'll speak to you later I just need
to get ready right now I'm

running behind" Madi said.

"Okay bye Madi I'll give you a call when I'm heading up" Kate replied.

"Bye auntie Kate" Madi said.

There was a knock at the door it was Jodi "Come in" Madi said "Only me just wondered if you wanted to walk to school with me, Morag, Addison, Savannah and Paige" Jodi replied "Yeah sure thanks" Madi said.

"What's up" Jodi asked "My auntie Kate is coming up tomorrow I don't want to see her and I'm pretty sure my sisters don't want to either, they know that our aunts and uncles hate us" Madi replied. "Listen Madi, don't let it get to you" Jodi said "I'll try not to but it's just hard" Madi replied. "Anyway, are you organised?" Jodi asked, "I think so, what do we have today again?" Madi replied.

"We have double English, history, PE and double food tech" Jodi said. "Right okay" Madi replied "Have you got your PE kit?" Jodi asked "Yeah I've got my navy blue t-shirt, my leggings and my black trainers" Madi replied "Okay we are leaving in 15 minutes" Jodi said "Okay I'll meet you downstairs" Madi replied "Yeah okay, see in 15" Jodi said "Okay" Madi replied before Jodi left and headed into her room.

The 15 minutes past and Madi grabbed her bag and her jacket and walked downstairs to meet Jodi, Morag, Addison, Savannah and Paige. "Right let's go" Jodi said before the girls left the schoolhouse, "Why do we have to have double English, I don't mind Mr Stevenson but why do we need to have Mr Brown he hates me" Paige said "You know he only hates you because you answer him back and you are cheeky" Addison replied. "That's not true" Paige said, "Yeah it is" All the girls except Madi said "Fine it is, it's not my fault he starts it" Paige replied, "You know we are right" Savannah said "I know" Paige replied sharply.

"Are you alright Madi? you are really quiet" Addison said, "Yeah sorry I've just a lot on mind right now" Madi replied "Do you want to talk about it?" Addison asked "No it's fine thanks anyway" Madi replied "We are always here if you need to talk to us" Addison said. "Thanks, Addi" Madi said. "Come here" Addison said before she gave Madi a hug "I needed that, thanks" Madi replied "No bother" Addison said before the girls reached the school "Well I'll see you in double English" Madi replied "Where are you going Madi?" Morag asked "I'm just going to the toilet I need to make a phone call" Madi replied "Okay see you in double English" Morag said.

Madi headed to the toilet and Jodi said to the girls "I'll catch all of you up."

"Where are you going?" Savannah asked.

"Nowhere I'll be back soon," Jodi replied.

"Okay," Savannah said before Jodi walked off.

"Wonder where she is going," Paige said.

"Me too Paige," Addison replied.

"Are any of us going to check on Madi," Morag asked.

"I'll go," Savannah replied.

"Okay Sav" Morag said before Savannah walked towards the toilet.

Jodi left the girls and walked towards Miss Edwards office and knocked on the door. "Come in" Miss Edwards said before Jodi walked in "Hi miss, sir" Jodi said, "Hi Jodi" Mr Stevenson said, "Jodi what can we do for you?" Miss Edwards asked.

"I think Madi is a bit stressed out the now" Jodi replied

"How do you mean?" Miss Edwards asked "Well you didn't hear this from me, but her auntie Kate is coming to visit I think tomorrow but she definitely is visiting" Jodi replied "Okay Jodi, I will catch up with her and some point" Miss Edwards said. "Okay miss, but please don't say it was me who told you" Jodi replied "I won't, now go catch up with your friends" Miss Edwards said "Okay bye miss, sir" Jodi replied before walking out of Miss Edwards and Mr Stevenson's office.

Savannah headed towards the toilet to see how Madi was "Madi it's me Savannah" Savannah said to Madi who was in the toilet cubicle, "Hey Sav are you okay" Madi replied as she was walking out the cubicle "Yeah I'm fine, are you?" Savannah said, Madi nodded with tears in her eyes. "Tell me what's wrong" Savannah said "I…just can't do this anymore" Madi replied before breaking down in tears "Hey come here what do you mean you can't do this anymore" Savannah said before giving Madi a hug.

"If I tell can you please not say anything to anyone, please Sav I'm trusting you" Madi replied.

"Yeah of course Mads" Savannah said "It's just not fair I am constantly scared of everything like if someone has an argument it just takes me back to the day of the crash and with my auntie visiting I just can't do it, I don't want to see her and I'm pretty sure my sisters don't either and I can't see my sisters every single day and it just kills me that I can't" Madi replied. "Oh, Mads listen if you ever feel like this again you can trust me and tell me okay" Savannah said. "Thanks Sav, and does it look like I have been crying?" Madi replied "No honestly it doesn't" Savannah said before the bell rang.

"Right well time for double English" Madi replied "Let's go, come on we will walk up together and trust me I won't say anything to anyone" Savannah said "You can tell Addi and the girls but none of the girls outside the schoolhouse" Madi replied "Okay we are going to be late come on" Savannah said "Let's go" Madi replied before her and Savannah walked out of the toilet and towards Mr Stevenson's class.

The girls reached Mr Stevenson class; they were five minutes late "Girls nice of you to join us" Mr Stevenson said, "Sorry sir" Savannah said "Sorry sir" Madi replied "Take a seat" Mr Stevenson said before Savannah and Madi sat down at their seats.

"Now we can begin, right everyone in your trios" Mr Stevenson said before everyone got into their trios, "Are you okay?" Jodi asked Madi "Yeah" Madi replied "Today we are going to work on the poem again" Mr Stevenson said "Why aren't we finished with this poem yet" Rebecca asked "Rebecca we have only been doing it for two weeks, we have at least another two week left unless we finish it early" Mr Stevenson replied, "Okay" Rebecca said before there was a knock on the door. It was one of the other English teachers "Everyone work quietly, I will be 5 minutes" Mr Stevenson said walking towards the door.

"Sir what have we to do?" Jess shouted out.

"I want you to think about what the poet is trying to tell you" Mr Stevenson said before walking out the class to talk to the teacher. "Mads are you sure you are okay?" Jodi said "Yeah I'll fill you in tonight" Madi replied "We are here whenever you need to talk us yeah" Darcy said "Yeah and Jodi do you think Miss Davis would mind if me, you,

Darcy and some of the other girls from the schoolhouse have a girly night in" Madi replied "I don't think she would have a problem with it but we can ask her at break or lunch or when we are food tech" Jodi said.

"We will ask her in food tech" Madi replied before Mr Stevenson walked back in.

"Who has an answer, what do you think the poet is trying to tell us?" Mr Stevenson said before Madi, Savannah, Darcy, Aiden, Caleb, Jess, Hunter and Katie put their hands up. "Yip Madi" Mr Stevenson said "I think the poet is trying to tell us that life can throw us curveballs but there is always a way around them if that makes sense" Madi replied "That is spot on Madi well done" Mr Stevenson said before Madi smiled. "She is such a suck up" Rebecca whispered to Jess, and Tiffany, Jess and Tiffany started laughing.

"Girls care to share the joke" Mr Stevenson said.

"No sir" Jess replied while laughing.

"Girls stop laughing or else you will be in detention for the rest of the week" Mr Stevenson said.

"Okay sir" Rebecca replied before the girls stopped laughing.

"Good" Mr Stevenson said before the bell rang.

"Right everyone next door to Mr Browns class" Mr Stevenson said "Bye sir" Katie said "Bye sir" Darcy said "Bye sir" Madi said "Oh Madi, can I quickly talk to you please?" Mr Stevenson asked "Yeah sir" Madi replied before everyone else in the class left "So I just wanted to check how you were" Mr Stevenson said. "I'm okay" Madi replied "Is there anything bothering you" Mr Stevenson asked "No sir honest" Madi replied "Are you sure" Mr Stevenson asked "Yes sir" Madi replied "Okay I'll come with you tell Mr

Brown that I was talking to you" Mr Stevenson said before him and Madi headed next door to Mr Browns class.

"Mr Brown this is Madison McDonald but she likes to be called Madi, I was talking to her that's why she was a tiny bit late sorry" Mr Stevenson said "Okay, come in Madi there is an empty table by the door" Mr Brown said before Madi took a seat at the empty desk by the door.

"Mr Brown can I talk to you outside for two minutes?" Mr Stevenson asked "Yeah, everyone get your jotters out so I can check the homework and anyone who has not completed it will be in detention for a week" Mr Brown said before walking out the door.

"You need to be careful with Madi, she is a really sensitive girl and she has not long lost her parents" Mr Stevenson said "Wait what she has lost her parents?" Mr Brown replied. "Yeah me and Molly are going to be filling everyone in at the staff meeting after school" Mr Stevenson said "Right well I will go easy on her" Mr Brown replied. "No, we want you to treat her like everyone else, but she is just a bit sensitive, so you just have to be careful of that" Mr Stevenson said.

"Okay thanks Jason" Mr Brown replied before walking back into class.

"Right homework, the one person who should not have completed the homework is Madi" Mr Brown said before walking around the class to see who the homework has done "The homework was so hard" Jess whispered to Rebecca. "Yeah I know" Rebecca replied.

"EXCUSE ME GIRLS DID I TELL YOU TO TALK!" Mr Brown shouted, as Madi covered her ears "Sir we weren't talking" Jess replied.

"ARE YOU ANSWERING ME BACK NOW!" Mr Brown shouted before Madi ran out of the class. "Darcy go tell Mr Stevenson that Madi has ran out of class and Jodi go tell Miss Edwards" Mr Brown said.

"Okay sir" Darcy replied before walking out of class "Okay sir" Jodi replied before walking out of class "YOU GIRL GET TO DETENTION NOW!" Mr Brown said, "No sir why should I" Jess replied "Right umm… Addison go fetch Mr Vandelay now" Mr Brown said before Addison walked out the class and towards Mr Vandelay office "Ha-ha has to get the headteacher involved can't even deal with the class by himself" Jess said.

"RIGHT I WANT YOU OUT MY CLASS NOW!" Mr Brown shouted "No" Jess replied before Mr Vandelay walked in "Jessica Burton out now" Mr Vandelay said "Fine" Jess replied before grabbing her stuff and walking out the class towards Mr Vandelay's office.

"Where's Madi" Mr Vandelay asked Mr Brown in a hushed voice.

"She ran out the class, Darcy and Jodi are getting Jason and Molly" Mr
Brown replied in a whisper.

"Right okay, I'll deal with Jess you just get back to teaching your class"
Mr Vandelay said in a whisper before leaving.

Darcy and Jodi headed to Mr Stevenson's and Miss Edwards office "Do you think Madi will be okay?" Darcy said "She's one strong girl, she should be okay" Jodi replied before Darcy and Jodi reached Mr Stevenson's and Miss Edwards office.

Darcy knocked on the door "Come in" Mr Stevenson shouted before Jodi and Darcy walked in.

"Girls what can we do for you" Miss Edwards replied.

"Mr Brown sent us Madi ran out of the class" Jodi replied.

"Right girls thanks you can go back to class" Miss Edwards said.

The girls left the office and headed back to Mr Brown class. "Right well you go see Alan to see if you can find out what went on and I'll go try and find Madi" Miss Edwards said "Okay it's Alan anything can happen in his class you know what he's like" Mr Stevenson replied. "Right now he's not that bad" Miss Edwards said before she started to head out of the office.

"Do you want me to fill William in?" Mr Stevenson asked

"Umm… how about wait until we see what is happening with Madi then we will decide what
to do" Miss Edwards replied

"Okay will we meet back here" Mr Stevenson asked

"I'm going to go find Madi and bring her back here" Miss Edwards replied

"Right let's do this" Mr Stevenson said before he and Miss Edwards left the office.

Miss Edwards headed towards the toilet and Mr Stevenson headed towards Mr Browns classroom, Miss Edwards reached the toilet and said "Madi are you in here?" "Yeah miss" Madi replied before opening the toilet cubicle "What's wrong?" Miss Edwards said "T…he" Madi tried to say.

"Come here" Miss Edwards said before Madi gave her

a hug, Madi took a deep breath. "Right are you okay now?" Miss Edwards said, "Yeah miss" Madi replied "Let us go to my office" Miss Edwards said. "Okay miss" Madi replied before her and Miss Edwards headed out of the toilets and towards Miss Edwards office. They reached Miss Edwards office and went in and took a seat.

"Right Madi are you going to tell me what's wrong" Miss Edwards said.

"Mr Brown was shouting at Jess, I just get really panicky and worked up when people started shouting at each other and I just didn't know what else to do expect to just run out the class, sorry" Madi replied.

"You don't have to apologise but listen to me I know its hard right now but trust me it will get easier" Miss Edwards said.

"But will it miss" Madi replied "Yeah honestly I haven't been teaching for long but my older sister is a teacher in a different school and she had a pupil go through a similar thing and it took them a while to get over the grieving stage but with help they eventually got there" Miss Edwards said.

"But how long is a while miss" Madi replied "I don't know Madi everyone is different" Miss Edwards replied before the door opened, it was Mr Stevenson.

"Madi how are you" Mr Stevenson asked Madi "I'm fine sir" Madi replied, "Miss Edwards can I talk to you outside" Mr Stevenson asked "Yeah, Madi we will be 5 minutes" Miss Edwards replied. "Okay miss" Madi said before Miss Edwards and Mr Stevenson left the office and stood outside looking in the window that was on the door.

"What did you find out from Alan?" Miss Edwards asked, "Well Madi ran out after Alan started shouting at

Jess" Mr Stevenson replied, "Yeah that's what Madi said to me because she gets worked up and panicked when people start shouting" Miss Edwards said. "Okay, well I have an idea for Madi" Mr Stevenson replied, "What is it" Miss Edwards asked "How about we persuade her to join one of the clubs" Mr Stevenson replied "That's a good idea" Miss Edwards said before Mr Stevenson and Miss Edwards walked back into the office.

"Madi we have a good idea how about you join a club?" Miss Edwards said.

"What clubs are there" Madi replied.

"What about we check the notice board at Lunch to find out" Miss Edwards said.

"Yeah" Madi replied "How are you feeling now" Miss Edwards asked.

"Yeah a lot better miss" Madi replied.

"Right the bell is going ring in about ten minutes so you can either stay in here for ten minutes or you can head back to class" Miss Edwards said. "Can I just stay here for the ten minutes please" Madi replied "Yeah of course do you want to help me or you can help Mr Stevenson if he has anything that he needs help with" Miss Edwards said "I don't have anything you can help with" Mr Stevenson replied "Madi can you sort out these papers it's a test for my 2nd years" Miss Edwards said before giving Madi a pile of papers.

10 minutes later the bell rang.

"Right Madi go get your friends and I'll catch you up at lunch" Miss Edwards said "Okay miss, bye miss bye sir" Madi replied before leaving the office. Madi headed towards the lockers where Jodi and the other girls hung out and the girls were there.

"Hey Mads" Jodi said "Hi" Madi replied.

"How are you" Addison asked "I'm a lot better now" Madi replied.

"Good, what are we in next" Jodi said.

"History, do you do the essay" Savannah replied.

"What essay" Jodi asked.

"The one about why history should be on the curriculum" Savannah replied.

"Umm… no I kind of forgot oops" Jodi said "Jodi you numpty Mrs Glen is going to kill you" Addison replied "What do I tell her" Jodi said "Just tell her you forgot about it the worst that will happen is detention" Savannah replied. "Anyway, Mads what do you want to do for lunch, go to the canteen or go to a classroom" Addison asked "Well I'm going to speak to Miss Edwards at lunch at some point but probably the canteen" Madi replied. "Okay what are we in before lunch" Jodi said "Maths" Madi replied "And we did not have any homework for that did we" Jodi asked "No we didn't" Addison replied "Okay that's good" Jodi said "What are you like" Savannah said "I'm so forgetful honest" Jodi replied "We know that" Addison said before all the girls giggled.

The bell for the end of break rang "Right history time" Paige said before the girls headed off to history, they reached the history class they were the first ones there.

"Hi girls in you come" Mrs Glen said.

"Hi miss" Jodi said.

"Hi Jodi, how are you?" Mrs Glen replied.

"I'm good, how about you?" Jodi said.

"I'm fine thanks for asking" Mrs Glen replied.

"And this is Madi" Jodi said.

"Yip I know, how are you Madi?" Mrs Glen replied.

"I'm fine miss, where will I sit" Madi said.

"Why not you sit next to Darcy" Mrs Glen replied.

"Okay miss" Madi said before taking her seat next to Darcy.

The rest of the class arrived "Right everyone come in quietly please" Mrs Glen said before the class walked in. "Silence please, today we are going to do something different I am going to pair you up with someone from the class that you might not know that well" Mrs Glen said.

"Miss, Madi doesn't know that many people" Jodi said, "Yes I know" Mrs Glen replied "Just wanted to make sure" Jodi said. "Oh, before that homework who has done the homework, I set 2 weeks ago. Put your hand up if you haven't done the homework" Mrs Glen said before Jodi, Madi, Rebecca, Jess, Conner, Alex and Brogan put their hands up "Miss do you want me to collect the homework in" Darcy asked "Yip thanks Darcy and can you all go stand outside" Mrs Glen replied "Miss will Madi come outside" Jodi said "No you can sit down Madi" Mrs Glen replied as Jodi, Rebecca, Jess, Conner, Alex and Brogan walked outside the class "Okay miss" Madi said before sitting down.

"Right why isn't my homework complete" Mrs Glen said "I've started it but I forgot all about miss, I'm sorry I'll get it done for you for tomorrow" Jodi replied "Not good enough but okay" Mrs Glen said. "Well miss I didn't know what to do so I didn't do it" Jess said "Jess that is not a reason why the homework isn't complete you have had this set for 2 weeks you could have asked for help" Mrs Glen replied.

"WHY ARE ALL THE TEACHERS PICKING ON ME" Jess shouted.

"Jess I am not picking on you because if I was you would be out here by yourself, I am just telling you that if you didn't know what to do is not an excuse" Mrs Glen said.

"WHY DID YOU NOT TELL JODI OFF FOR FORGETTING" Jess shouted.

"Because she started it but forgot" Mrs Glen said, "I'M NOT LISTENING TO THIS" Jess replied before walking into class and grabbing her stuff and walking out, "I'll deal with you all later get back into class" Mrs Glen said before everyone walked back into class.

"Right time for partners, so we will have Aiden with Hope, Madi with Hunter, Darcy with Hudson, Jodi with Rebecca, Conner with Millie, Alex with Paige, Brogan with Addison, Savannah with Ryder, Katie with Jess, Adam with Izzy, Morag with Tiffany, Lucas with Scarlett, Stella with Jamie, Anna with Milly and finally Sage with Reagan" Mrs Glen said.

"Mads we are paired up with the twins" Darcy said "What's Hunter like?" Madi asked "He's really nice" Darcy replied "Okay I'll take your word for it" Madi said. "Move next to your partner and I'll give you your task" Mrs Glen said before everyone moved next to their partners.

"Hi Hunter, I'm Madi" Madi said.

"Hi Madi, I'm Hunter" Hunter replied.

"Right silence everyone, the reason I have put you in partners because we are going to do posters" Mrs Glen said before the class cheered. "I love doing posters" Jodi said before there was knock at the door "Come in" Mrs Glen said before the door opened it was Miss Power "Mr Vandelay would like to see you in his office next period" Miss Power said "Okay, thanks Lucy" Mrs Glen replied before Miss Power left.

"So, each pair is going to get a different topic to do a poster on, you might have the same topic as another pair" Mrs Glen said "So miss you are going to give each pair a topic and we need to research it but another pair might have the same topic" Jodi replied "Exactly" Mrs Glen said "That makes sense" Jodi replied.

"Right so Aiden and Hope, Conner and Millie, Adam and Izzy, Katie and Jess and Anna and Milly are going to do World War One.

We will have Madi and Hunter, Darcy and Hudson, Jodi and Rebecca, Savannah and Ryder and Alex and Paige do World War Two.

Brogan and Addison, Morag and Tiffany, Lucas and Scarlett, Stella and Jamie and Sage and Reagan are going to do the Atlantic Slave Trade" Mrs Glen said.

"Miss are we doing the posters on A4 or A3" Jodi asked "Umm… let's do it on A3, can Madi and Darcy go borrow some off of Miss Edwards or Mr Stevenson or another teacher if they don't have any" Mrs Glen replied "Okay miss" Darcy said before she and Madi headed out the class.

"Where will we go first?" Madi asked "Umm… let's try Miss Edwards first" Darcy replied as the girls headed upstairs to Miss Edwards class. "Will I knock, or will you?" Madi asked "I'm not bothered if you want to knock and I'll speak, or I'll knock, and you speak" Darcy replied "Can I speak" Madi asked "Yeah of course" Darcy replied. "Thanks, Darcy, for everything even though I've only known you for a day I feel like I've known you for years" Madi said "I know it's weird, anyway here we are" Darcy replied as the girls reached Miss Edwards class.

Darcy knocked on the door "In you come" Miss Edwards said before the girls walked in "Hi Miss" Madi said "Hi girls what can I do for you?" Miss Edwards asked, "Do you have any A3 paper" Madi replied "Yeah I think so" Miss Edwards said before checking the drawers behind the door "It's fine if you don't it's just because we are doing history posters" Madi replied. "Here you go" Miss Edwards said before handing Madi some paper "Thank you miss sorry for interrupting you" Madi replied "No bother girls" Miss Edwards said before the girls left.

"Let us go back to history now" Darcy said before the girls headed back to history, "Here you go Miss, Miss Edwards gave it to us" Madi said "Thank you girls can you gave everyone a piece?" Mrs Glen said "Yip miss of course" Darcy replied before her and Madi handed each pair a piece of paper.

"Right everyone we have 20 minutes left so I'm going to tell you more about the posters and you can either start them tonight and get a head start or wait till tomorrow but that means you will have more work" Mrs Glen said. "Miss mine and Jodi's partnership isn't going to work" Rebecca said "Why?" Mrs Glen asked "It's a bit sensitive" Rebecca said "How about you go outside, and I'll come and talk to you in a minute Rebecca" Mrs Glen replied before Rebecca headed outside.

"What is the problem? why can't you work with Jodi" Mrs Glen asked

"I don't want to get her into trouble, but she has been bullying me and I'm afraid that if I work with her that it's going to get worse" Rebecca replied. "Right well how about you go back into class and I'll talk to Jodi" Mrs

Glen said before her and Rebecca walked into class, "Darc I don't trust Rebecca I think she's deliberately trying to get Jodi in trouble" Madi whispered while standing at Darcy desk. "Don't get involved as much as we like Jodi don't get involved because she wouldn't want you getting in trouble" Darcy whispered back "Madi back to your seat please and Jodi can I talk to you outside please" Mrs Glen said before Jodi headed outside.

"Mads don't worry about it" Darcy whispered to Madi. "Right what's the problem, why can't you work with Rebecca" Mrs Glen asked "I don't have a problem with Rebecca, she's the one who has a problem with me" Jodi replied. "Well she's claiming that you are bullying her" Mrs Glen said "Me I've been bullying her miss do you seriously believe that" Jodi replied, "I don't know" Mrs Glen said.

"Miss seriously I'm not that type of person you know I aren't" Jodi replied "Just wait here I'm going to get Rebecca" Mrs Glen said "Okay Miss" Jodi replied before Mrs Glen walked into class. "Rebecca, can I speak to you outside?" Mrs Glen asked, "Yeah Miss" Rebecca replied before heading outside "Right what is seriously going on between you?" Mrs Glen asked.

"Miss, I told you she's bullying me" Rebecca said.

"Stop saying I'm bullying because you know I'm not" Jodi replied.

"See what I mean miss" Rebecca said.

"What I haven't done anything" Jodi replied.

"Jodi go to detention you aren't in trouble just go to cool down" Mrs Glen said

before Jodi walked off.

Mrs Glen and Rebecca walked back into class, "Sorry

about that everyone so posters, you all have your topics so you will have a week to complete them and then you will present them to the class so you can make flashcards and I want your posters to be as colourful as possible" Mrs Glen said. "Miss do we really have to present them" Madi asked "Yes and also can I speak to Paige for two minutes" Mrs Glen said "Yeah Miss" Paige replied before walking outside.

"Right would you mind if I switched your partner" Mrs Glen asked "Yeah depends on who it is but" Paige replied, "As much as this poster project was supposed to be a kind of bonding exercise, I might have do to this the once" Mrs Glen said "Miss who is it" Paige asked "Jodi" Mrs Glen replied "Yeah Miss that's fine" Paige said "Thank you, you can go back in now" Mrs Glen said before her and Paige walked in.

"We have 10 minutes left so does everyone know what topic they are doing?" Mrs Glen said "Miss what about my poster partner" Rebecca asked "Paige is going to be Jodi's partner and you are going to be with Alex" Mrs Glen replied. "What topic am I doing then" Rebecca asked "The same one you were originally supposed to be doing" Mrs Glen replied "World War Two" Rebecca said "Yip" Mrs Glen replied "So miss all we need to do is make a poster and present it" Rebecca said "Yes, now everyone you can start packing up now" Mrs Glen replied.

"Hunter, do you want to start ours tonight to get a head start" Madi asked "Yeah of course" Hunter replied before the bell rang "Right everyone on you go enjoy the rest of the day" Mrs Glen said before everyone left.

"PE time" Darcy said before the girls headed to PE, "Get changed everyone then I'll tell you what we are doing"

Mr Newwall said before everyone headed into the changing rooms and walked to the wall outside the hall "Becca I've forgotten my kit" Jess whispered "I have as well don't worry about it" Rebecca whispered back. "Sorry I'm late sir I was in detention" Jodi said "Okay get changed quickly" Mr Newwall replied "Umm… sir I've forgot my kit" Jess said "Me too sir" Rebecca said.

"Girls not good enough you know what happens detention now" Mr Newwall replied before the girls walked off "You okay Jods" Madi asked "Yeah and what's happening in history have I got a new partner or am I still with Rebecca" Jodi replied "You are with me now" Paige said "Okay" Jodi replied. "Okay I think that's everyone, so today we are going to be doing running" Mr Newwall said before people sighed "Why does everyone hate running?" Madi asked "Because we need to run around the track for the whole period" Jodi replied "Running is well good" Madi said "Right I'll do the register then we will go outside" Mr Newwall said before he took the register and then everyone headed outside to the track.

"Run around the track till I tell you to stop" Mr Newwall said "I can't wait to beat you" Jodi said "You wish" Madi replied "3…2…1 go" Mr Newwall said before the class started running. Mr Vandelay came out "Hiya Will everything alright" Mr Newwall said. "I'm fine Miles any chance I could borrow Jessica Burton" Mr Vandelay replied "Yeah she's in detention alongside her sidekick Rebecca" Mr Newwall said "What have they done now?" Mr Vandelay replied "Forgot their kit again" Mr Newwall said "I'll add that into the many things in need to talk to her about" Mr Vandelay replied.

"Go on Madi, come on you lot" Mr Newwall said "She's really fast" Mr Vandelay said "I know she's good do you think she would be a good addition to the running club" Mr Newwall replied "I think she would why not you ask her at the end of class" Mr Vandelay said "I will, so yeah Jess is in detention" Mr Newwall said "Right thanks I'll catch up with you later" Mr Vandelay replied "Bye" Mr Newwall said before Mr Vandelay walked back into school.

"Come on you lot" Mr Newwall said "Sir I can't" Paige said while trying to catch her breath and walking off the track "Right if anyone else can't run anymore off the track" Mr Newwall said before Libby, Hunter, Darcy, Jodi, Millie, Addison, Savannah, Adam, Morag, Tiffany, Lucas, Scarlett, Stella, Sage and Reagan came off the track out of breath "That is something no human should do" Savannah said while trying to catch her breath "I am so surprised that all of you gave up as quick" Mr Newwall said. "Sir I couldn't do it anymore" Savannah replied "Come on you lot" Mr Newwall said "Come on Mads" Darcy and Jodi shouted.

"And you can stop" Mr Newwall said before Aiden, Madi, Hudson, Conner, Alex, Brandon, Ryder, Katie, Izzy, Jamie and Anna stopped running and tried to catch their breath. "Well done Mads" Jodi said to Madi "I told you I would beat you" Madi said while trying to catch her breath. "Right you lot you have 10 minutes to get changed so quickly get changed" Mr Newwall said before the class headed inside "I need a drink of water I'm out of breath" Morag said "Me too" Madi said. "Madi can I talk to you for two minutes please?" Mr Newwall asked, "Yeah but can I get my water bottle first?" Madi said "Yip" Mr Newwall said before Madi went into the changing room and grabbed her water bottle.

"Mads are you not getting changed?" Jodi asked "Mr Newwall wants to talk to me first then I'll get changed" Madi replied as she was headed to the door of the changing rooms, "Okay" Jodi said before Madi headed to Mr Newwall's office. Madi knocked on Mr Newwall's office door "Come in" Mr Newwall said before Madi walked in.

"What did you need to talk to me about sir" Madi said.

"I won't keep you long, but I just wanted to tell you that you done the most laps

out of the full class" Mr Newwall said.

"Did I" Madi replied.

"Don't sound so surprised but how you feel about joining the school running

team and it's not just running around the track we do games and go to

competitions against other schools" Mr Newwall said.

"Can I think about it sir and I'll get back to you" Madi asked.

"Yeah of course, on you go get changed" Mr Newwall replied before Madi walked out the office and to the changing rooms.

"What did Mr Newwall want" Darcy asked "Nothing really just to tell me that I had the most laps in the class" Madi replied, "Well done and are we going to the canteen for lunch" Darcy said "Yip and I also need to go see Miss Edwards at lunch" Madi replied as she was getting changed.

"Okay" Darcy said, "I'll be five minutes" Madi said, "Okay I'm going to wait outside" Darcy said before headed outside. The bell rang before Madi finished getting changed

"Mads we will meet you in the canteen if that's okay?" Darcy said, "I will be two minutes" Madi replied "Okay meet us in the canteen", "Okay" Madi said as the girls walked off.

Madi then headed to the canteen and found where the girls were sitting. "Hey Mads this is Brogan, her sister Abby, Hope and her twin Millie" Jodi said.

"Hi" Madi said

"Hi Madi, how are you" Brogan said

"I'm fine thanks for asking" Madi replied as she sat down next to Paige and Darcy.

"Mads do you want to grab lunch" Paige said "Yeah let us go" Madi replied before her and Paige went to grab lunch. The girls got their lunch and ate it "What have we got next?" Paige asked "Double food tech" Darcy replied.

"Why do we only have food tech once a week" Madi asked "It's so we have more time for our other subjects" Addison replied, "Aww that makes sense" Madi said "What do you think we will be doing this week?" Savannah asked. "No idea" Paige replied "Umm...I'll be back soon guys" Madi said.

"Where are you going" Darcy asked, "I just need to go see Miss Edwards, I won't be long" Madi replied "Okay do you want any of us to come?" Darcy asked "No I won't be long honest" Madi replied "Okay" Darcy said before Madi walked away.

Madi walked to Miss Edwards office and knocked on the door "Come in" Miss Edwards said before Madi walked in "It's only me Miss" Madi replied "In you come Madi take a seat" Miss Edwards said before Madi took a seat.

"Miss see how you and Mr Stevenson said I should join a club well I think I might join the running club" Madi replied, "Do you like running?" Miss Edwards asked "It's one of my favourite things to do it helps me clear my head and with everything that has happened so far it's just you know good" Madi replied. "What are your other favourite things to do?" Miss Edwards asked "Well my top favourite thing is dancing, then it's running, and I really like singing that's about it" Madi replied.

"You do know we have a dance studio" Miss Edwards said "No I used to do competitive dance but then you know my mum and dad died and I couldn't keep doing it because we moved away" Madi replied "Well there is two dance coaches who come in for the girls to do dancing and they also have a team outside of school that they are always looking for people to join" Miss Edwards said. "What do you need to do to use the studio?" Madi asked "If you go see Mr Newwall he has a sheet for you to book a spot" Miss Edwards replied, "Right thanks Miss" Madi said "No bother Madi, you can go if you want" Miss Edwards replied "I'll catch up with you later Miss" Madi said "Bye Madi" Miss Edwards said before Madi left the office.

Madi headed back to the canteen to meet back up with the girls "I'm back" Madi said "Hey Mads everything okay?" Jodi asked "Yip and can you come with me to see Mr Newwall" Madi replied. "Yeah what for" Jodi said "He asked me to join running club and I said I would think about it, but I thought about it and I want to join" Madi replied "Yeah of course lets go" Jodi said before her and Madi headed to Mr Newwall's office.

The girls reached Mr Newwall's office and Madi knocked on the door "In you come" Mr Newwall said before the girls walked in "Hi Sir" Madi said "Girls what can I do for you?" Mr Newwall asked. "I've made a decision about running club and I would like to join" Madi replied "That's great Madi, we train on a Monday Wednesday and Friday and I'll catch up with you about dates for competitions and stuff" Mr Newwall said. "Okay sir thanks" Madi replied "Oh Sir, when is Miss Georgia and Miss Farrah coming in" Jodi asked "As far as I'm aware they are coming tomorrow and Friday" Mr Newwall replied, "Okay Sir thanks" Jodi said "Thank you Sir bye" Madi said "No bother girls bye" Mr Newwall replied before the girls left Mr Newwall's office.

"Who's Miss Georgia and Miss Farrah" Madi asked Jodi "The girls get to do dancing every couple of days a week and they are the dance teachers that come in to teach us and they also have a dance team outside of school that many of the girls are a part of" Jodi replied.

"Fun fact for you I used to do competitive dance before my parents died" Madi said "Are you any good?" Jodi asked "I should think so with me doing it since I was 3 years old so I should think I'm good" Madi replied "Well how about tomorrow we book a studio spot and you can show me" Jodi said "Deal" Madi replied before the girls started giggling. The girls headed back to the canteen to meet back up with the rest of the girls "We are back what you all talking about" Jodi said "We are talking about Jess and her outbursts" Paige replied "It's not nice to talk about people sorry for sounding like a Debby downer but trust me it's not nice to be spoken about, people done it to me at my old school" Madi said.

"Sorry we won't talk about it anymore" Addison replied "Oh by the way Miss Georgia and Miss Farrah are supposed to be coming in tomorrow and Friday" Jodi said before the girls cheered "Yay I love it when we have dancing I feel like we haven't done dancing for ages" Savannah said before Madi's phone rang "Sorry I need to take this I'll be right back" Madi said "Okay we will be here" Jodi said before Madi walked out the canteen and sat on the stairs by her math class.

"Hi Aunt Kate" Madi said "How are you Madi" Kate asked "I'm fine what can I do for you" Madi replied "You know how I am coming up tomorrow do you think you could get the afternoon off school and do you think your sisters could get the afternoon off as well, just so me and your cousins can spend time with you" Kate said. "I can't sorry I've got a huge science test in the afternoon and you will need to ask the girls foster parents and our social worker if you could spend time with them" Madi replied.

"Okay you all have a set of foster parents" Kate said "I don't the girls do" Madi replied, "Why don't you" Kate said "Me and my social worker and my teachers decided it would be better if I lived in my schools schoolhouse" Madi replied. "Okay so can you text me your social workers and the girls foster parents number so I can ask them please?" Kate said "Yeah I will soon I have to go get lunch and talk to one of my teachers about a club I'm doing" Madi replied "Okay I'll let you go then" Kate said "Bye Aunt Kate" Madi said "Bye Madi" Kate replied before Madi hung up the phone. Madi then phoned Linda her social worker. "Hiya Madi what can I do for you" Linda asked.

"Umm… this is probably going to sound a bit weird but one of my aunts are coming up to see about my parents will because the lawyer is up here, none of my family like me or my sisters so when my auntie calls can you tell her that it is up to the foster parents.

I am going to call Olivia after this to tell her to say no because the girls can't deal with it, I know they can't" Madi replied. "Yip okay" Linda replied "Sorry if that sounds weird but I'm just trying to protect my sisters" Madi said, "I completely understand that, and do you have any good news because you know how much I love good news" Linda said. "Yeah I am officially part of running club" Madi replied "Aww well done that is good news and any bad news" Linda said "No" Madi replied "Okay good listen I'm going to go I've got a meeting, so I'll catch up with you later" Linda said. "Okay I'll catch up with you later bye" Madi replied "Bye-bye Madi" Linda said before she hung up the phone. Madi then phoned Olivia.

"Hi Olivia" Madi said.

"Hey Madi, what's up" Olivia said.

"So this might sound a bit weird, but my Aunt Kate is coming up to meet with the lawyer about my parents will and she wants me to see if I can get the afternoon off, I said I can't because I can't bear seeing her and my cousins as bad as that sounds I just can't. She also wants to spend the afternoon with the girls, but can you please tell her no because the girls know our whole family hate us and I honestly don't think they could bear it if that's makes sense" Madi replied.

"That makes perfect sense Madi and the girls have been a bit upset recently so I think it would be best if they didn't meet up with your Aunt as well" Olivia said "Thank you so much Olivia and sorry for you know being controlling I didn't mean it you know I didn't" Madi replied. "It's no bother Madi and do you fancy coming for dinner at some point during the week?" Olivia said "Yeah of course" Madi replied "How about Thursday" Olivia said "Yeah because I don't have running club" Madi replied "Okay I'll tell the girls and I'll give you a text or a call later" Olivia said. "Okay well I'll let you go, and I'll speak to you soon" Madi replied "Okay Madi I'll speak to you soon bye", "Bye Olivia" Madi replied before hanging up the phone.

Madi then sat on the stairs for about 5 minutes until Jodi and Darcy came and sat with her.

"Everything okay?" Jodi asked

"Yeah I'm not going to see my Aunt and I get to have dinner at Olivia and

Simons on Thursday, I can't wait because I get to see the girls again" Madi replied

"That's great and do you want to go see if we can find Miss Davis and ask her if

Darcy can come over and if we can have a girly night in" Jodi said

"Let's wait until next period" Madi replied

"Okay now let's go get the rest of the girls" Jodi said before the three girls headed to the canteen.

Chapter 4 - Dancing

—◆◆◆◆◆—

"What can we talk about" Darcy asked "How about we go see Mr Newwall to see if the dance studio is free" Jodi replied. "Yeah let's go" Addison said before the girls started walking towards Mr Newwall's office and Jodi knocked on the door, "Come in" Mr Newwall said before Jodi walked in.

"Hi Sir, me again is the dance studio free" Jodi asked "Yeah and please can you please make sure it's the same way you found it when you leave?" Mr Newwall replied "Yip Sir thanks" Jodi said before walking out the office and with the other girls walking to the dance studio.

"Madi two options we can start teaching you the dance for tomorrow or you can show us a solo" Jodi said "How about I show you my solo that I done before I left my dancing?" Madi replied.

"Yes I can't wait" Darcy said "Give me two minutes I'm going to put my leggings on" Madi replied before walking into the changing rooms and put on her leggings. "Madi use to do competitive dance before she came here" Jodi said before Madi walked back in. "Give me your phone and I'll connect it to the speaker" Addison said to Madi before Madi handed over her phone "What song you using?" Savannah asked "Wait and see" Madi replied.

"There you go all connected" Addison said before handing Madi her phone back "Thanks Addi" Madi replied "Do you want me to do the music?" Darcy asked "Yeah it's that one" Madi replied while pointing at a song "What's the song called?" Morag asked "It's called when the war is over, it was the last song I done at my studio" Madi replied "Tell me when to start" Darcy said "Go" Madi replied before Darcy started the music.

"Go on Madi" Jodi said while Madi started dancing "Go get Mr Newwall he would love to see this" Darcy whispered to Savannah. "Okay" Savannah replied before running to get Mr Newwall "Keep it up Mads" Jodi said before Mr Newwall walked in with Savannah "I never knew she danced" Mr Newwall said to the girls.

"Woah go on Madi" Savannah said

"Great energy Madi" Mr Newwall said before Madi's solo finished

"Oh my god Madi that was amazing" Jodi said

"Thanks" Madi replied as she was trying to catch her breath

"I am shocked that was just amazing" Darcy said

"Thanks Darc" Madi replied

"Well done Madi you should proud I've never seen anyone do a dance with so much emotion" Mr Newwall said "Thank you sir" Madi replied "You should be very proud and you will definitely have to show Miss Georgia and Miss Farrah that they will love it, if you give me a minute I'll make a phone call to see if they can come in after school so you can show them" Mr Newwall said. "That would be great sir" Madi replied "Give me two minutes" Mr Newwall said before walking out the hall "I am just amazed Mads" Jodi said "Thanks Jods" Madi replied.

Mr Newwall walked back in. "Right Madi, Miss Georgia and Miss Farrah are both free after school and would love to see your solo" Mr Newwall said. "Yes of course" Madi replied "Well just come here after period 6 and I'll be here and girls you can come if you want" Mr Newwall said.

"Yeah of course we will if it's okay with Mads?" Jodi said "Of course it's alright" Madi replied. "Right girls there is 5 minutes left of lunch so Madi get changed and the rest of you make sure the studio is tidy please" Mr Newwall said before Madi went into the changing rooms and the rest of the girls went into the studio to make sure it was clean.

The bell rang for period 5 "Let us go" Jodi said, "Umm… guys slight problem I have no idea where I'm going" Madi replied "Follow us" Jodi said as she giggled. The girls reached the food tech class "Afternoon girls in you come" Miss Davis said "Miss" Jodi said "Yes Jodi", "Can Darcy come over tonight and can we have a girly night in please" Jodi asked "Yeah of course girls and also congrats on getting into the running club Madi" Miss Davis replied.

"Thank you miss" Madi said "Another thing miss you should see this girl dance she is amazing" Jodi said while pointing at Madi, "I'm not that good" Madi said "Well miss, the dance teachers are coming in after school to watch Madi do her solo why not you come" Jodi said. "If it's okay with Madi I would love to come" Miss Davis said, "Yeah miss I would love it if you came and do you think Miss Edwards would like to come as well?" Madi replied.

"How about one of you girls go ask her" Miss Davis

said, "I'll go" Darcy said "Me too" Savannah said "Okay girls on you go" Miss Davis said before the girls headed to Miss Edwards class.

The two girls came back from Miss Edwards class as Miss Davis was starting the class "Quickly girls I'm just about to tell you what we are doing today" Miss Davis said "Sorry miss" Darcy said as her and Savannah ran over to the table "Right so today we are going to be making smoothies" Miss Davis said "What type of smoothies?" Jodi asked.

"The ones with fruit, I've got loads of fruit so you just pick what fruit you want and blend it but you are working in pairs so find a partner" Miss Davis replied "Mads you and me" Jodi said "Yeah" Madi replied "6 people per table so everyone go to the table and decide what fruit you want" Miss Davis said before Madi, Jodi, Darcy, Paige, Savannah and Addison went to the table by the front of the class. "So, what did Miss Edwards say?" Madi asked Darcy and Savannah "She said she would love to come" Darcy replied "Are you all still coming?" Madi asked "Yeah of course we wouldn't miss it" Addison replied.

"Miss?"

"Yes Rebecca" Miss Davis said.

"They aren't working" Rebecca said while pointing at Madi's table.

"We are discussing what we are doing" Jodi said

"No you weren't" Rebecca replied

"Right girls stop, Madi's table go get your fruit and Rebecca's table decide what

fruit you want and write it down" Miss Davis said

"Okay miss" Madi said before her, Jodi, Darcy, Paige, Savannah and Addison grabbed their fruit

"Thank you girls, now Rebecca's table go" Miss Davis said before Rebecca, Jess, Hope, Millie, Brogan and Katie grabbed their fruit "Right boys come get your fruit and then you go and then you go" as she pointed at the tables.

"Okay miss" Hunter said before he, Hudson, Aiden, Conner, Alex and Ryder went to grab their fruit "Hunter come here a minute please" Madi said "Okay" Hunter said before walking over to Madi "So I think I have to bail tonight, because I'm showing the dance teachers my solo and I promise the girls I would have a girly night in" Madi said. "Okay that's fine and umm… if you want I could start the poster and then we can finish it later" Hunter said, "Yeah that would be fine and if you want you can come see my solo" Madi replied "I would love to Madi" Hunter said "That's all I wanted to say" Madi said "Okay" Hunter said before him and Madi walked back to their tables.

"He likes you" Jodi said

"No he doesn't" Madi replied

"He does" The girls said in sync

"He does not" Madi replied

"Hudson come here and bring the blueberries" Jodi said before Hudson walked over to the girls table "What's up and here's the blueberries?" Hudson said as he placed the blueberries on the table "Sure your brother likes Madi" Jodi said. "Yes, he does" Hudson said "No he doesn't" Madi said "See since you started here, he always talking about you" Hudson said "I don't believe you all" Madi said.

"Fine then don't believe us but we are right" Jodi said "Is that all" Hudson said "Yeah thanks for the blueberries" Jodi replied before Hudson walked back to his table. "Anyway, let's start these smoothies" Madi said "So strawberries, raspberries, blueberries and milk" Jodi said "Yeah" Madi replied as her and Jodi put the stuff in the blender. "What about banana?" Jodi said "Yeah and Jodi do you think Miss Davis will let me go practise my solo" Madi replied "Once we have finished, we can ask her" Jodi said "Okay" thanks as Madi switched the blender on "That looks amazing" Jodi said as Madi switched the blender off.

"Miss what do we do now" Madi said "Pour it into the glasses and try it then write the recipe up" Miss Davis said "Okay miss" Jodi said. "You pour it into the glasses, and I'll write the recipe up" Madi said. "Okay then we can ask if we can go to the dance studio to practise your dance" Jodi said as she was pouring the smoothie into the 6 glasses at the side.

"We used strawberries, blueberries, raspberries, banana and milk, right?" Madi said "Yeah," Jodi replied as Madi noted it down. "Right got it done," Madi said. "Miss," Jodi said "Yeah, Jodi?" Miss Davis said. "Me and Madi are done," Jodi said. "Like completely done?" Miss Davis asked. "Yip." "Okay I'll be there in two seconds," Miss Davis said. "Okay" Jodi said before Miss Davis walked over to the table where Madi and Jodi were working.

"Right let me try your smoothie and let me see what you put in it" Miss Davis said as Jodi handed her the smoothie and Madi gave her the list of ingredients "Miss is there any chance me and Madi can go to the dance studio so Madi can practise her solo" Jodi said. "Why don't you go see Mr Newwall and if he's okay with it I don't mind" Miss Davis said "Okay" Jodi said before she left the class "Your smoothie is really nice Madi well done" Miss Davis said "It wasn't all me" Madi replied "I know, can you start tidying up please" Miss Davis said "Okay miss" Madi said before grabbing the cloth at the side of the sink "Thank you" Miss Davis said before the bell rang for period 6.

"We are finished miss as well" Darcy said "And us" Savannah said "Okay everyone if you are done I want you to pour your smoothie into the 6 glasses and write down the ingredients you used and then tidy up the mess" Miss Davis said before Jodi walked back into the class. "Sorry for taking ages miss" Jodi said "It's fine is it free" Miss Davis said "Yip can me and Madi go now" Jodi said "Yeah on you go girls" Miss Davis said "Thanks miss" Jodi and Madi said before they left the class "Miss where are they going" Rebecca said "That's none of your business Rebecca just focus on your work" Miss Davis said.

Madi and Jodi were walking down the corridor with their bags to the dance studio "Excuse me girls" Mr Brown said as the girls stopped walking "Yes sir" Jodi replied "Why are you girls out of class?" Mr Brown asked "We are going to the dance studio" Jodi replied "Do you have a note?" Mr Brown asked "No sir, but Mr Newwall and Miss Davis said it was okay" Madi replied "I will be asking them but on you go" Mr Brown said "Okay sir, thanks" Madi replied before Madi and Jodi continued walking to the dance studio.

"Let's let Mr Newwall know that we are here" Jodi said "Okay let's do that" Madi said before her and Jodi walked up to Mr Newwall's office and knocked on the door "Yip in you come" Mr Newwall said before the girls walked in "Only us, we just wanted to let you know we are here" Jodi said "Okay girls and Madi can I borrow you for two minutes?" Mr Newwall said "Yeah of course" Madi said before Jodi walked out the office and towards the dance studio.

"So here is the list of all the competitions for the running club and I will definitely organise something for you and the team so you can bond" Mr Newwall said as he handed Madi the list "Thank you sir" Madi replied "Now go practise your solo I want you to impress Miss Georgia and Miss Farrah" Mr Newwall said "Okay sir thanks again" Madi replied before she left the office and walked down to the dance studio.

"Jods give me two minutes I'm just going to get changed into my pe stuff" Madi said as she poked her head round the side of the door of the dance studio "Okay" Jodi replied as Madi walked away and into the changing rooms. Madi got changed and walked back into the dance studio "Give me your phone so I can connect it" Jodi said before Madi handed her phone. "Remember it's that song" Madi said while pointing at the song "Yes I know, now I want the same energy then earlier but more energy if that makes sense" Jodi said "That's makes perfect sense" Madi replied. "Are you ready?" Jodi asked.

"Just give me two seconds to warm up because the last thing I need is an injury" Madi replied "Okay" Jodi said before Madi done a quick warm up "Right now I'm ready, start the music" Madi said as she walked into the middle of the dance floor "On you go Madi" Jodi said as she started the music. The music started and Madi began her solo "Woo go on Madi, love the energy" Jodi said.

Madi continued dancing as Miss Halfpenny walked in "Hiya Jodi", "Oh hey Miss" Jodi said, "I was looking for you" Miss Halfpenny said, "What do you need miss?" Jodi said, "So I've heard some rumours going about that you have been bullying Rebecca, is it true" Miss Halfpenny said.

"No why does no one believe I'm not that type of person you should know this miss" Jodi said "Don't get angry please Jodi I just want to get to the bottom of it with me being your head of year" Miss Halfpenny said before Madi's solo finished "Well done Madi and I promise you miss I am not bullying anyone" Jodi said "Hi I'm guessing you are Madi we haven't properly met yet but I'm Miss Halfpenny your head of year" as she shook Madi's hand "Sorry that I'm a bit sweaty I'm just practise my dance to show some people after school but it's nice to meet you" Madi said as she was catching her breath.

"Well Jodi I want you to come to my office tomorrow lunch time and I'm going to get to the bottom of this and if I find out you are lying you are facing a very serve consequences okay" Miss Halfpenny said "Yes" Jodi replied. "Madi I will arrange a meeting for me to get to know you I like to do that with all the new intakes but me, Miss Edwards, Mr Stevenson, Mr Vandelay and your social worker all decided it would be best if Miss Edwards dealt with you" Miss Halfpenny said "Okay miss" Madi replied before Miss Halfpenny left the dance studio.

"What was all that about" Madi asked.

"The rumours of me bullying Rebecca which I have not been" Jodi replied

"Listen I know you haven't been bullying Rebecca there is something dodgy about her, but I don't know what but Jodi as long as you go to that meeting tomorrow and tell the truth then if the school don't believe you then it's their loss" Madi said. "Why do you have such good advice" Jodi asked "When you basically brought your sisters up and your friends always rely on you, you get some pretty good advice out of it" Madi replied with a giggle.

"Do you miss seeing your sisters everyday" Jodi asked "I do miss them but after everything that happened with my mum and dad I know that it's time for me to let them live with another family without me wreaking it" Madi replied. "What about your parents do you miss them" Jodi asked "Of course I do, the minute I found out what had happened to them, I thought this is it my family is never going to be the same again and I was right and the worse thing about that day was seeing my sisters faces when I had to explain to them that mum and dad weren't coming home and neither was Jessie, also having to make the phone calls to the rest of my family members" Madi replied.

"How do you still manage to keep a smile on your face?" Jodi asked "There is no point in being sad when I know my parents would want me to be happy" Madi replied "I'm glad we became friends I know we have only been friends for two days but honestly I feel like I've known you for years" Jodi said "I know" Madi replied "Anyways can you show me a dance that you have done at your studio" Jodi said. "Okay do you want me to show you a hip hop one or contemporary one" Madi asked "Hip hop" Jodi replied "Okay let me look at my music to see if I remember one of mine because I haven't done hip hop for a good few months" Madi said "Okay" Jodi said as Madi checked the songs on her phone "Found it" Madi said.

Madi's phone rang and she disconnected it from the speaker so she could answer it. "Hello" Madi said "Hiya Madi it's Linda here, I have some news for you but I didn't want to tell you until I was entirely sure but there is a family who is interested in fostering you, I have given them your number and they are going to phone you once I'm off the phone to you but I think you will really like them" Linda said. "Okay" Madi said "I'll will go the now and I will catch up with you after you have spoken to them" Linda said "Okay Linda I'll speak to you later bye" Madi said "Bye-bye Madi" Linda said before she hung up the phone.

"Who was that?" Jodi asked, "My social worker there is a family interested in fostering me, they are going to phone me in a few minutes" Madi replied "What are they like do you know?" Jodi asked "Nope" Madi replied before her phone started ringing "Is that them, answer it" Jodi asked "I think so" Madi replied "Go on answer it Mads" Jodi said "Okay" Madi replied before answering the phone.

"Hello this is Madi McDonald may I ask who is calling" Madi said "Hi Madi my name is Dawn and me and my husband Chris have an interest in fostering you" Dawn said "Oh hiya Dawn, why do you have an interest in fostering me" Madi replied. "Well the kids we have fostered so far have been through a similar thing as you and also we want to complete our family with another kid but we do have some ground rules" Dawn said "Okay what are the rules" Madi asked.

"We know you have sisters who are living with a different family well you would not be allowed to see them, you will have to move schools so that you are in the same school as the rest of the kids and also you will not be allowed to go to any clubs inside or outside the school" Dawn replied.

"That is not fair do you know what I don't want to be fostered by you thanks for the offer but no" Madi said "Well with your history I don't think anyone will be interested in fostering you" Dawn said "I'm not listening to this anymore goodbye" Madi said "Bye" Dawn said before Madi hung up the phone.

"What happened?" Jodi asked "I don't want to be fostered by them, if I moved in with them they won't let me see my sisters." "That isn't fair," Jodi said "That's not even the best of it, I would have to move schools again and I wouldn't be allowed to join any clubs inside or outside school." "Did they say anything else?" Jodi asked "That with my history that no one will probably want to foster me," Madi replied. "Just ignore them, they aren't worth your time or effort anyway show me this dance," Jodi said.

"Can you just give me two minutes so I can make a phone call" Madi asked "Yeah of course" Jodi replied "I'll be two minutes" Madi said before walking out the dance studio and sat on the floor. "Come on pick up, pick up" Madi said as her phone was ringing so she could speak to Linda "Hiya Madi everything okay" Linda asked "No" Madi replied "What's happened?" Linda asked "That foster family you paired me with is a definite no-no, I bet they didn't tell you about their rules" Madi replied. "Wait what rules" Linda said "That I would not be allowed to see my sisters that I would have to move schools and that I would not be allowed to do any clubs inside and outside school" Madi said as she was getting more and more frustrated.

"Right calm down you don't need to be fostered by them" Linda said in a relaxed voice "That's not even the best of it they said that with my history that I will be lucky if anyone else is interested in fostering" Madi replied "I will deal with it but please Madi just take a deep breath and relax" Linda said "Okay Linda I'll speak to you later" Madi said "Bye-bye Madi" Linda said before Madi hung up the phone.

Madi walked back into the dance studio "Are you okay?" Jodi asked "Yeah I think so, can you connect my phone back to the speaker, and I'll show you this dance" Madi replied as she gave Jodi her phone "Yip" Jodi said as she was connecting Madi's phone to the speaker. "It's that song" Madi said while pointing at the song "Okay and done" Jodi replied as she placed the phone on the bench "Just watch me" Madi said as she started the song "What's this song called again?" Jodi said "Hurricane" Madi replied as she started to dance "Go on Madi" Jodi said before Mr Newwall walked in with Miss Georgia and Miss Farrah.

"Hi Jodi" Miss Georgia said

"Hi Miss Georgia, Miss Farrah" Jodi replied

"Hi Jodi, how are you?" Miss Farrah said

"Yeah I'm good how about you?" Jodi replied

"I'm good" Miss Farrah said

"That is Madi" Mr Newwall said while pointing at Madi

"She is good at hip hop" Miss Georgia said

"She's almost finished this solo I think" Jodi replied

"Okay" Miss Georgia said as Madi finished her solo.

"Madi this is Miss Georgia and Miss Farrah" Mr Newwall said "Hi Madi" Miss Georgia said "Hi" Madi replied as she was trying to catch her breath "Here's your water bottle" Jodi said as she handed Madi her water bottle. "Thanks" Madi replied before she took a drink "That was a good hip hop solo from the part we seen" Miss Farrah said "Thank you" Madi said. "Where did you learn that solo" Miss Georgia asked, "Delight in Dance" Madi replied "We compete against them at some of the competitions we go to they have some amazing dancers" Miss Farrah said.

"Do you know Miss Victoria the studio head" Madi asked "Yes she's really kind and an amazing choreographer" Miss Georgia replied "That's true" Madi replied before her phone rang "Mads your phone is ringing" Jodi said as she disconnected it from the speaker "Okay, sorry I'll be right back" Madi said as she grabbed her phone off the bench and headed outside. Hello" Madi said "Madi it's me Summer" Summer said "Hey baby what's up?" Madi asked "There're some kids picking on me at school" Summer replied.

"Why are they picking on you" Madi asked "It's because I don't have a mum and dad" Summer replied "I don't know if Olivia has told you but I'm coming for dinner on Thursday so we can sit down and talk about it then" Madi said. "Yay, and also no one wants to be my friends because I'm the new girl and also I don't have any parents" Summer replied, "Listen Sum, kids can be very cruel just ignore them and a friend will come along soon trust me" Madi said "Okay Madi" Summer replied "Look baby I need to go" Madi said "Okay sissy bye-bye" Summer replied "Bye Summer" Madi said as she hung the phone up.

She just stood there thinking about everything so far that has happened in her life, her mum, dad and her sister dying in a crash, having to move into a care home, getting fostered, getting kicked out her foster home, starting a new school, moving into the schoolhouse, making new friends and discover her passion for dancing and running again.

"Hey, are you coming back in?" Jodi said as she stuck her head round the side of the dance studio door "Yeah" Madi replied before she started walking towards the studio doors

"Who was that?" Jodi asked "One of my sisters Summer" Madi replied "How many sister do you have?" Jodi asked.

"Well I have Summer who's 9, Autumn who's 7, Lilly who's 6 and Grace who's 11 months and I should have one more sister Jessie who is Grace's twin but she unfortunately passed away" Madi replied "Are you the oldest?" Jodi asked "Yeah" Madi replied. "It must be great to have loads of sisters" Jodi said "Yeah but it has it's downfalls sometimes like the arguments" Madi replied with a giggle "Trust me, we are our fair share of arguments in the schoolhouse" Jodi said "I'll feel right at home then because we were always arguing in my house" Madi replied before the bell for the end of the day rang.

"I will be right back I need to go fill my water bottle up" Madi said as she grabbed her water bottle "Okay be quick" Mr Newwall said before Madi ran out of the dance studio and towards the water bottle fountain.

Miss Edwards, Savannah, Addison, Darcy, Paige, Hunter and Miss Davis all arrived at the dance studio "Hi Miss Georgia, hi Miss Farrah" Addison said, "Hey Addison how are you?" Miss Georgia replied "I'm good how are you?" Addison said "I'm great, thanks for asking" Miss Georgia replied, "Where's Madi?" Miss Edwards whispered to Mr Newwall "She is filling up her water bottle she should be back soon" Mr Newwall replied before Madi walked in. "Hi Mads you okay?" Darcy asked "Yeah, yeah I'm perfectly fine" Madi replied "Right are you ready Madi?" Mr Newwall asked "Yip sir, let's do this" Madi replied as she placed her water bottle done and passed Jodi her phone "Just tell me when to start the music" Jodi said "Okay" Madi said as she walked into the middle of the dance floor.

"Start" Madi said "Okay" Jodi said as she started the song and Madi started to dance "Go Madi" Darcy said "Woo go on Mads" Addison said "Keep it up Madi" Jodi said. "She is amazing" Miss Georgia said "I know" Miss Farrah replied "Do you think that she would be a good asset to the team?" Miss Georgia asked "She would be perfect" Miss Farrah replied "Come on Madi" Miss Edwards said "Told you she good" Mr Newwall said "She is a great dancer" Hunter said to the girls "We know" Paige said. Madi finished dancing "Wow that was amazing" Miss Farrah said, "That was great Madi" Miss Georgia said "Thanks" Madi replied as she was catching her breath. "Well done Madi" Hunter said "Thanks" Madi replied "That was just amazing" Savannah said "Thanks, listen I'll catch up with you" Madi replied before the girls headed out the dance studio "I'll see you later" Hunter said "See you later Hunter and thanks for coming to watch" Madi replied before Hunter left.

"Madi we would like to offer you a place on our competitive dance team" Miss Georgia said, "I would love to join the dance team, when do we rehearse" Madi replied "We train everyday but the only ones that are compulsory are the Tuesday, Thursday, Saturday and Sunday" Miss Farrah said. "Umm… I can't do this Thursday I'm going for dinner at my ex foster parents house with my sisters" Madi replied "Okay then well if you want you can come tonight for rehearsal or wait until Saturday" Miss Georgia said. "No, I'll come tonight but can one of the girls come with me just for the first rehearsal" Madi replied "Yip that's perfect, well we will see you tonight" Miss Farrah said "See you tonight"

Madi replied "Bye Madi, see you tonight" Miss Georgia replied before her and Miss Farrah left the dance studio.

"Well done Madi" Miss Davis said

"Thank you miss" Madi replied

"I'll catch you up later" Miss Davis said

"Bye miss" Madi replied before Miss Davis left

"Good job Madi" Mr Newwall said

"Thanks sir" Madi replied before Mr Newwall left the studio

"Oh my god Madi that was amazing" Miss Edwards said

"Thanks miss" Madi replied

"You are going for dinner at your ex foster parents?" Miss Edwards said

"Yeah I'm excited but I'm scared" Madi replied

"Listen you will be fine come here" Miss Edwards said before she gave Madi a hug

"I needed that thanks miss" Madi replied.

Jodi was waiting outside the dance studio for Madi "Hey I didn't want to leave you by yourself, the other girls are away home" Jodi said "Hi, I am so tired but let's have a girls night in" Madi replied. "We don't need to do girls night in if you don't want to we can do it another night" Jodi said "No I want to because I have a pretty busy schedule from next week" Madi replied.

"I know" Jodi said "Oh shoot, I need to go to the dance studio tonight come with me" Madi replied before her and Jodi ran up to Mr Newwall's office to see if Miss Georgia and Miss Farrah were still there. "Woah girls where's the fire" Mr Newwall said as he laughed "Huh, never mind anyway Miss Georgia, Miss Farrah what time is rehearsal?" Madi asked "It starts at five and finishes at seven" Miss Georgia replied "Okay thank you miss; I will see you tonight" Madi said. "We will see you tonight Madi and which friend are you bringing" Miss Farrah replied "Probably Jodi or Savannah" Madi said "Okay, well we will see you tonight" Miss Georgia said "Bye" Madi replied "See you later" Miss Farrah said "Bye girls" Mr Newwall said before Madi and Jodi walked away.

The girls headed out of school and walked to the schoolhouse. They arrived at the schoolhouse "What time is it?" Madi asked "It's quarter to 4" Jodi replied "Okay where are the girls" Madi said. "They are probably upstairs if they aren't in the kitchen or living room" Jodi replied "I'm going to put my bag in my room are you coming?" Madi said "Yeah let's go" Jodi replied before the girls walked upstairs and into Madi's room.

All the other girls were in Madi's room waiting for her "Surprise!" The girls shouted "What" Madi said "Well we decided when you left food tech that we were going to surprise you with all your favourite sweets, well the ones we knew anyway" Savannah said "Oh thank you girls honestly it means the world to me" Madi replied. "So, what movie do you want to watch?" Addison asked.

"Umm…well I have dance at five" Madi replied "Oh yeah I forgot I have dance as well" Addison said "Me too" Paige said "Me three" Savannah said "And me" Morag said "We have a hour and about 10 mins so we can start watching a movie and finish it later" Addison said. "Yeah but guys I'm not kidding you I am busy every single day this week" Madi replied "We know, you're running club and dance and the fact you have no time to rest" Savannah said. "It's fine I love the fact that I'll be busy I won't be thinking about anything" Madi replied "That's true.

"What movie are we watching" Addison asked

"Can we just not watch a movie, how about we just talk" Madi replied

"Yeah" Savannah said.

The girls all sat in a circle on Madi's floor with the sweets in the middle "Madi question" Savannah said "Yeah go for it" Madi said as she put a sweet in her mouth "See when your parents died how did you tell your friends that you were moving" Savannah asked. "So my teacher already knew so it was sort of easy to tell my friends, I wasn't in school for about a week or two and all my friends were texting me but I didn't answer because I just did not want to tell them over text.

So, a few days before I was due to move schools and that, I came into school to speak to everyone about me leaving" Madi replied "What did you say to them?" Jodi asked "I said listen everyone two weeks ago I lost my parents and baby sister Jessie in a car crash, and I will be moving so that I can live in a care home but that unfortunately means that I will be moving schools but all I can remember from that day besides what I said was seeing all my friends sobbing their hearts out and I felt so bad because my friends have been there since we were in primary one" Madi said. "That must have been a hard day" Addison replied "It was but I've had harder ones" Madi said before she put a sweet in her mouth.

Time went on and on and the girls had a massive conversation and a great laugh "So I think it's time to get dressed for dancing" Madi said, "Yeah we better get a move on because that's twenty to five" Addison replied. "Listen why don't you get organised and me and the other girls will tidy up" Jodi said "Are you sure?" Madi asked, "Yip it's fine" Jodi replied "Thanks Jods" Madi said before she and the other girls sorted their stuff for dancing.

"Madi who is coming with you?" Darcy asked.

"Savannah can you come with me" Madi replied "Yeah I'm going to dancing anyway" Savannah said "Thanks" Madi replied before she lifted her bag and headed out with the other girls for dancing.

"What's the dancing team like" Madi asked "Oh they are so nice I think you will absolutely love them" Savannah replied "Oh no Sav, I just realised Miss Georgia and Miss Farrah said the last time that the next time we are in dancing we are doing drills" Addison said. "Addie why did you say that" Savannah replied "Sorry" Addison said "I'm going to ask if I can teach Madi the dance or rehearse my solo because you know competitions coming up" Savannah replied.

"That's not fair just because you are good dancer and exercise all the time doesn't mean you get out of drills" Morag said "It's normally me who is leading the drills" Savannah replied "That's true" Paige said "Thanks Paige" Savannah replied. "Well, Madi here we are" Morag said, "Are we not a bit early?" Madi questioned "Well we have 10 minutes before dancing starts so not really" Savannah replied "Okay then let's do it" Madi said before the girls walked in.

"Hi girls" Miss Georgia said "Hi Miss Georgia" The girls said "Evening girls" Miss Farrah said "Hey Miss Farrah" The girls replied. "Miss what are we doing today" Morag asked "We are going to be doing drills" Miss Farrah replied.

"Umm… can I teach Madi the group dance and practice

my solo" Savannah asked "Yeah why not, we were going to ask you to run drills anyway" Miss Georgia said "Okay thanks Miss" Savannah said. "Miss Georgia, Miss Farrah would you mind if I practiced one of my dance while we wait for everyone else" Madi asked "No of course not, just tell us the name of the song so we can put it through the speakers" Miss Farrah replied, "The song is called Summertime" Madi said "Okay is it that one?" Miss Georgia asked, "Yip that's it" Madi replied "What style is it" Miss Farrah asked "It's hip hop" Madi replied "Okay tell us when you are ready" Miss Georgia said "Okay I'm ready" Madi said before Miss Georgia started playing the song.

Madi started dancing as other girls walked in, they whispered to each other. Miss Georgia and Miss Farrah were so glad that they could get Madi to join the team, Madi finished dancing and everyone that was there clapped. "Okay everybody, this is Madi and she is new to the team now some of you will know her, others won't but let's give her a big Dancefloor Divas welcome" Miss Georgia said before everyone clapped and cheered, "Right everyone today we meant to be doing drills but I thought instead we could do some games and rehearse because we have just got an email through to say that we have a competition two weeks on Saturday" Miss Farrah said before the girls all cheered again.

"Girls" Miss Georgia said before all the girls were quiet "So does anyone want to suggest a game to play?" Miss Farrah said before some of the girls raised their hands including Madi "Madi what's your game?" Miss Georgia asked "I don't know if anyone has heard of this game but it's called memory moves" Madi replied "Nope how do you play it" Miss Farrah asked before Madi explained it "Okay let's play that" Miss Georgia said.

It reached seven o'clock and dance club finished "Right everyone see you tomorrow or Thursday" Miss Farrah said, "Bye Miss Farrah, bye Miss Georgia" The girls said, "Bye everyone" The two teachers replied before all the girls left. "What did you think?" Savannah asked "Yeah it was good, see for the competition do you guys compete against Delight in Dance" Madi replied "Yeah how" Addison asked "That's my old dance team and I haven't spoken to them since I left" Madi replied.

"Oh well that's awkward" Addison said "God sake Addie can you not see the girl is worried about it and doesn't need you making comments about it" Morag said, "Sorry" Addison said "It's fine honest let's just get home" Madi replied before her and the girls headed back to the schoolhouse.

The girls reached the schoolhouse "Umm...I'll catch you up, I need to make a phone call" Madi said "Okay" Savannah said before the other girls headed into the schoolhouse. Madi pulled out her phone and called Quinn "Hey Q it's Mads", "Hey Madi what's up, is everything okay, is your sisters okay" Quinn replied with worry in her voice "We are all fine. I just had a question, you cannot say anything to anyone promise" Madi said, "Yeah of course I promise" Quinn replied "Well you know how we used to love dance comps when I was at DID with you and the other girls," Madi said.

"Yeah what about it?" Quinn replied. "I have joined a team here and we have comp two weeks on Saturday and I don't know if you are coming" Madi asked "We are coming and trust me the team is so much better, I think after you left Miss Victoria realised how much of a strong dancer you were and how much the team actually needed you and well she replaced nearly half the team." "Do you think Miss Victoria will answer me if I phone her" Madi asked "Well you can only try but honestly she misses you and I think she is starting to stress without you and your help with the juniors and baby ballet and the office help" Quinn replied.

"Well I'm going to go give her a call and I'll speak to you later but please, please, please I beg you don't mention this to anyone please" Madi said "I won't I promise" Quinn replied "Bye Q", "Bye Mads" Quinn replied before Madi hung up the phone.

Madi sat on the steps contemplating whether to phone Miss Victoria or not, she eventually decided to do it. The phone rang and rang and just before she was going to hang up Miss Victoria answered "Omg Madi, how are you?" Miss Victoria asked. "Yeah I'm fine, I was just phoning to see how you are and how the dance studio is, is it still standing without me" Madi said before she laughed "Yeah it's still standing but I forgot how stressful it was without you because you helped me with absolutely everything and everyone is missing you, especially your juniors and baby ballet class" Miss Victoria replied. "I'm missing everyone as well, I should be coming to visit soon because I need to see all my friends again and you" Madi said "Have you found another dance studio" Miss Victoria asked.

"Umm... that was sort of another reason why I phoned you. I am with Dancefloor Divas and we have comp two weeks on Saturday and I'm just wondering if you will be there" Madi said "Yip, we will be going and honestly, I want to see you like so much I just miss you so much" Miss Victoria replied. "Well I'm going to go the now Miss Victoria because I need to finish some homework" Madi said "Okay sweetie I will talk to you later bye" Miss Victoria replied "Bye-bye" Madi said before hanging up the phone. Madi headed into the schoolhouse and went upstairs to check if she had any homework but she didn't so she decided to facetime her cousin Payton "Hey Payt" Madi said "Hey Mads you okay" Payton asked. "I suppose, I just want to come home I want everything to go back to the way it was, I want my mum and dad and Jessie and the girls back" Madi replied while crying "Oh Madi don't cry, you will make me cry. Listen I know it's hard the now but think about when they died. I know it isn't the same thing but we weren't that old and it was difficult to deal with but we got through it and trust me Mads you will get used to it. I promise you I will visit you soon" Payton said "Okay Payton, guess what" Madi replied as she wiped away the tears "What Mads" Payton asked "I've got a dance comp in two weeks' time" Madi replied "Oh my god sweetie that's amazing I need to come and see it" Payton said.

"Listen Payt I don't know if you realise what day it is tomorrow but it Grace and Jessie's first birthday" Madi replied "Oh no I never ever realised, I know this will be hard but your sisters love you and you still get to see them and that don't you" Payton asked. "Yeah I'm seeing them on Thursday I cannot wait because I'm having dinner at Olivia and Simon's and it was their idea plus I think they know I'm missing the girls" Madi replied, "Yeah listen Madi you are amazing and I love you so much and your sisters will fine you know they will" Payton said.

"I know, I love you too Payton" Madi replied "Well I'm going to go sort baby Cole for bed and I will speak to you tomorrow, what are you in tomorrow" Payton said "Umm… I'm in double French, drama, PE and double science" Madi replied "Right okay well I will talk to you tomorrow" Payton said "Okay Payt I'll speak to you tomorrow" before hanging up the phone.

Madi did not move, she sat on her bed so still. She didn't feel like moving and then there was a knock "Hiya Madi, it's Miss Davis can I come in" Miss Davis asked "Yeah" Madi replied before Miss Davis walked in to see that Madi was crying "Hey what's wrong" Miss Davis asked. "It's my sisters first birthday tomorrow and my mum and dad aren't here and Jessie isn't here and I don't get to be with them" Madi replied before getting more upset, "Listen Madi, I know it's hard but think of it like this if your parents hadn't died then you won't be here and none of the girls would have met you" Miss Davis said "I know, but I want my mum and dad and my sisters" Madi said before Miss Davis cuddled Madi and just let her cry.

Miss Davis cuddled Madi for a good 20 minutes before asking "Do you feel better now?" Madi looked at her "Yeah a lot, thanks miss" Madi replied "No bother, that's what I'm here for and also do you want pizza for dinner?" Miss Davis said, "Yes please" Madi replied "Okay come downstairs and we will get everyone else down" Miss Davis said before she and Madi headed downstairs. They got downstairs and Miss Davis shouted on everyone, they all came downstairs "Right everyone listen I have been thinking and how does pizza sound for dinner" Miss Davis said. "Miss, honestly that is the best idea you have had for ages now, like no offence or anything" Jodi said before everyone laughed. "Okay Jodi thank you for that, what type does everyone want?" Miss Davis said, "Miss why don't you do what you did the last time and just get like 5 large pizzas" Savannah said "Yeah that works Savannah, what kinds" Miss Davis said "2 cheese, a pepperoni, a meat feast, and a ham and pineapple" Jodi replied.

"Are you sure that will be enough?" Miss Davis asked "It was the last time because we got wedges" Jodi replied "So we did, so 5 large pizzas and how many boxes of wedges?" Miss Davis asked "How about 10 boxes of wedges because you barely get any wedges in a box so like 10 should be enough" Jodi replied. "Yeah okay so I am getting 2 large cheese pizzas, a large pepperoni, a large meat feast, a large ham and pineapple and 10 boxes of wedges is that right" Miss Davis asked "Yip" Jodi replied before Miss Davis went to order it. Jodi pulled Madi aside, away from everyone else.

"Mads you okay" Jodi asked

"Come into the living room and I'll tell you" Madi replied before her and Jodi

went into the living room

"What is it?" Jodi asked

"It's my baby sisters birthday tomorrow Grace's and Jessie's and I can't be with

Grace and Jessie isn't here and my mum and dad aren't here" Madi replied

"Aww Mads, listen things will get better you know they will, but for just now let's get pizza" Jodi said as Madi wiped her tear away. They walked back into the kitchen "Right everyone I need you to all get your juices organised because I didn't order any juice because we have plenty of juice in the fridge" Miss Davis said, "Yeah that's fine miss" Savannah replied.

"Okay well the pizzas and that shouldn't be long so if everyone wants to go sort out juice that would be great and Jodi can I borrow you for two minutes please" Miss Davis said "Yeah, yeah miss" Jodi replied before her and Miss Davis walked into the living room. "Right listen, I don't know if Madi has told you about her sisters" Miss Davis said "Her baby sisters' birthday" Jodi replied. "Yeah, so she's a bit emotional the now so I need you to keep an extra eye on her because I know how much you care for her if that's okay" Miss Davis said, "Yeah I will Miss, I just hate that this is her life" Jodi replied "I know Jods it isn't fair but it isn't as if she planned it" Miss Davis replied before the door went.

"That will be dinner hopefully" Miss Davis said as her and Jodi went to the door and it was the dinner "Thank you" Jodi said as she got the pizzas off the pizza guy, "Madi can you come help us please" Miss Davis asked before Madi came to help with the pizzas. Miss Davis, Madi and Jodi all got the pizza and wedges and walked into the kitchen and placed the pizzas and wedges down. "Right, everyone do you have plates and juice" Miss Davis asked "Yip" Everyone replied "Miss, we put juice and a plate out for you" Paige said "Aww thank you" Miss Davis replied "Come on, let's eat I'm starving" Addison said before everyone laughed.

Everyone finished eating "That was amazing Miss, thank you" Savannah said "Honestly you lot, I think you all deserve a treat, you have been the most amazing kids lately and I'm so happy to be your schoolhouse mum" Miss Davis replied. "Miss, I don't think we could have a better schoolhouse mum" Jodi said. "Now you lot, whose turn is it to clean up"

Miss Davis asked, "It is Rebecca and Paige's turn" Morag replied "Right everyone else can have free time, go do some homework, watch a movie, read a book just do something" Miss Davis said before everyone expect Paige and Rebecca left the kitchen.

Madi, Jodi and the other girls headed upstairs and into Madi's room "Hey Mads, you good?" Addison asked "Yeah I'm fine, listen guys I need to finish some stuff for my social worker" Madi replied "Okay, we will let you do it. If you need anything give us a shout" Savannah said before all the girls expect Jodi left the room. "Mads, do you want to be on your own because I don't mind staying" Jodi asked "Yeah Jods I'm fine honest, go do your own thing" Madi replied. "Okay only if you are sure" Jodi said before Madi nodded "On you go I'll be fine" Madi replied before Jodi left.

Madi thought about what to do and decided to wrap Grace's presents, she found the presents in her suitcase that was sitting under her bed, she also found pink sparkly unicorn paper and wrapped her present for her sister. Then she put it in the wardrobe and then lay on her bed facing her ceiling, she lay for about 10 to 20 minutes then there was a knock at the door "Madi, it's Addie. All of the girls are having a movie night care to join us" Addison said. "Yeah, just give me two mins" Madi replied "Bring a blanket if you want" Addison said before Madi opened the door, "I'll be down in two minutes" Madi replied "Hey, Mads you sure you good?" Addison asked "Yes I'm fine Addie" Madi replied before she grabbed her pink blanket off her bed.

Madi and Addison came downstairs, "Mads come sit with me" Savannah said "No Madi come sit with me" Paige said, "No me" Morag said "Sit with me Mads" Addison said before Miss Davis intervened and said "Listen Madi why don't you come and sit with me", "Yeah please" Madi replied before she sat next to Miss Davis and cuddled into her with her blanket "You feeling better" Miss Davis whispered to Madi "Yeah" Madi whispered back.

"Right you lot what we watching?" Miss Davis said "Miss, really quick question" Jodi said "Yeah Jodi, what is it" Miss Davis replied "Can we watch more than one movie?" Jodi asked "Well has everyone done all the homework that they needed to get done" Miss Davis asked "Yip Miss" Everyone replied "Well I suppose that I will leave the decision up to Madi considering it is her first proper night here" Miss Davis said "Really Miss" Madi asked. "Yeah" Miss Davis said "Okay, thank you Miss and yeah can we watch 5 movies please" Madi asked "Yeah of course, what 5 will you watch" Miss Davis replied.

"How about sing, the croods, Paddington, rise of the guardians and the smurfs" Madi said "OMG, they are the best 5 movies ever" Everyone said before Miss Davis put the movie song on.

The first movie finished, "Who wants popcorn?" Miss Davis asked "Me" Everyone replied "Okay, Madi and Jodi want to come help me" Miss Davis asked "Yeah" Jodi replied "Yeah" Madi said before her, Jodi and Miss Davis headed into the kitchen. "Miss, can I ask you a question?" Jodi asked, "Yeah go for it" Miss Davis replied "Well its two questions actually. One did you always want to become and teacher and two why did you become a schoolhouse mum" Jodi asked.

"One I did not actually always want to become a teacher, I originally wanted to be a lawyer but once I had spoken to my teachers and done a bit of research, I found out how beneficial being a teacher would be and two. I don't know why I became a schoolhouse mum, I just love you lot" Miss Davis replied. "Umm…Miss is it okay if I go to bed, please" Madi asked "Yeah of course, everything okay" Miss Davis replied, "Yeah I'm just really tired" Madi said "Okay sweetie" Miss Davis replied before she gave Madi a hug.

Madi headed upstairs, she was not really tired, she just wanted to be alone, she couldn't handle being around everyone. She reached her room and she just lay on her bed, Madi hated everything right now, she hated being at school, she hated that she was not at home, she hated her parents were dead and she hated that she wasn't with her sisters.

There was a knock at her door, she got up and answered it, it was Rebecca "Hey Rebecca what's up?" Madi said "Nothing much, I just wanted to check in and make sure you were okay" Rebecca replied "Yeah, I'm fine but if you don't mind I would like to get to bed" Madi said as she started to close the door, Rebecca pushed the door open.

"Listen to me, you little attention seeker, nobody in this house likes you, we are only pretending to like you so we can get treats because you are special with your dead mummy and dead daddy and dead sissy, do you know your sisters are better off without you, because all you would do is destroy them like you are doing here." Rebecca said before she stomped off leaving Madi with tears rolling down her face, Madi shut the door and went and lay on her bed with her face in her pillow so her crying would be muffled. Everyone else finished watching the 5 movies and headed to their beds. The house was quiet, it was that quiet you could probably hear a pin drop.

Chapter 5 - Wednesday

- - - - - - -

The next morning Miss Davis came around all the rooms knocking on the door and telling everyone to get up. She reached Madi's room and went in "Hey Madi, time for school" Miss Davis said. "Miss, I don't feel well, can I please stay home" Madi asked "Yeah as long as you promise that you won't just lie in bed all day, you will get up and do some jobs around the house" Miss Davis replied, "Yeah, I will, I promise Miss" Madi said "Okay then sweetie, I'll write you a list as to what has to be done" Miss Davis replied.

"Okay Miss" Madi said before Miss Davis left her room and headed downstairs. Everyone else was downstairs getting breakfast, "Here Miss where's Mads" Jodi asked "Madi isn't feeling too well so she's staying off today, what is she in first" Miss Davis replied, "We are in double French" Jodi said "Okay I'll let Miss Welch know that Madi isn't in" Miss Davis replied.

"Come on you lot" Miss Davis said as everyone finished their breakfast and left the house. Madi heard everyone leave and headed downstairs to see the list of jobs Miss Davis had left for her. She had to tidy the living room, make her bed, tidy the kitchen, do the dishes and tidy her room, Miss

Davis also wrote a note on the bottom of the list which read "If anything and I mean anything is bothering you Madi you come tell me okay", Madi knew she wouldn't never be believed if she told Miss Davis about Rebecca because she is just the new girl, she has no status, she the bottom of everyone.

Madi decided to do her jobs so that they were done. It was about lunch time and Madi had tidied her room, made her bed, the living room, the kitchen and did the dishes. Then there was a knock at the door, Madi who was still in her PJs went to answer, it was Miss Edwards.

"Hi Miss" Madi said

"Hey Madi, you okay" Miss Edwards replied

"Yeah, do you want to come in" Madi asked

"Yeah" Miss Edwards replied before she and Madi walked into the living room

"Do you want a drink Miss" Madi asked

"No thanks Madi

We need to have a talk, so come sit down" Miss Edwards said before Madi sat down "What's up Miss?" Madi asked "Madi, I have only known for a few days and I have spoken to your social worker and she has told me that even when you weren't feeling well, you would still be at school, so what is the problem?" Miss Edwards asked.

"Honestly Miss I'm just having a really bad off day" Madi replied on the verge of tears "Madi come on, you can trust me if something is bothering you I want to know" Miss Edwards said and just as she said that Madi broke down in tears, Miss Edwards had seen Madi cry before but never like this so she knew it must be serious.

"Come on Madi, calm down, I'm here to help" Miss Edwards said "I'm sick of being the new girl" Madi replied through her tears "How what's happened now?" Miss Edwards questioned "Rebecca has been picking on me" Madi replied "Has she now" Miss Edwards asked. "I know it makes me seem childish getting upset about getting picked on but you know my history with getting picked on" Madi replied "I know and it is not acceptable, is that how you didn't want to come to school" Miss Edwards said, "Yeah Miss" Madi replied.

"Right do you want to go get dressed and we will go to school and tell Mr Vandelay and Miss Davis what is happened" Miss Edwards said "Do I need to wear uniform?" Madi asked "No" Miss Edwards said before Madi ran upstairs and into her room to put her PE kit, that was already ironed. She ran back downstairs to see Miss Edwards "You ready?" Miss Edwards asked "Yeah" Madi replied "Okay then let's go" Miss Edwards said before her and Madi headed out "Oh hold on, I need to grab my keys to lock the door" Madi said "Come on then quickly" Miss Edwards replied before Madi grabbed her keys off the table at the door and locking it "Done" Madi said "Jump in the front" Miss Edwards said "Okay" Madi replied before jumping in the front seat of the car.

They set off to school. When they reached school, Miss Edwards parked in her space. "Okay, let us go" Miss Edwards said "Miss, thanks for this" Madi replied with a smile on her face "Madi, it's what I'm here for, we will speak to Miss Davis, Mr Vandelay, Mr Stevenson and Miss Halfpenny" Miss Edwards said "Okay" Madi replied before her and Miss Edwards headed into the school and straight to Mr Vandelay's office. Miss Edwards knocked on the door "Come in" Mr Vandelay shouted "It's just me and Madi, you got two minutes" Miss Edwards asked "Yeah, yeah in you come" Mr Vandelay replied.

"Madi, why don't you go get Mr Stevenson, Miss Halfpenny and Miss Davis" Miss Edwards said "I'll give you a note for them Madi" Mr Vandelay said before handing Miss Edwards a note to hand to Madi "I'll be back soon" Madi said, "They may have classes but just give the note" Mr Vandelay said "Okay sir" Madi replied before she left "Shut the door" Mr Vandelay said to Miss Edwards.

Madi headed off to Miss Davis's class first, she knocked on the door and Miss Davis shouted "In you come" before Madi entered "Hi Miss, only me, I've got a note for you" Madi said "Oh hey Mads, you feeling better and let me read it." Miss Davis said before Madi handed her the note, the note read "Dear Miss Davis, Miss Halfpenny and Mr Stevenson, when you get two minutes could you please come to my office to discuss an issue including Madi that involves Rebecca and would like to get your opinion on how to proceed as you are all involved with Madi on some level", after Miss Davis finished reading the note she handed it back to Madi.

"Okay, thanks for that Madi" Miss Davis said before Madi left and Miss Davis followed but went the other way to Madi to go to Mr Vandelay's office, Madi headed towards Mr Stevenson's classroom and he had 2nd years. Madi knocked on the door "Enter" Mr Stevenson shouted "Sir, I've got a note for you" Madi said after she had entered the class "Give it here" Mr Stevenson replied before Madi handed him the note and he read it and handed it back. "It's from Mr Vandelay I don't know if he wrote that it was from him" Madi said "Yeah he did and also Madi, my 2nd years are doing that poem you done and remember you gave me that absolutely amazing answer, can you tell the class it" Mr Stevenson asked before he passed the note back to Madi.

"Oh I love that poem and it was no matter what curveballs life throw at you, you will always get passed them" Madi replied "You've had some curveballs in your life haven't you Madi, would you mind sharing them with the class" Mr Stevenson asked "No I don't mind. Okay so not that long ago, my parents and my youngest sister died in a car crash, leaving me and my sisters orphans. Now I'm still trying to get used to life without them but with the help of the teachers and my friends I'm getting there, and also, I've not long moved to this school because this was the nearest foster family and social worker that would take our case on because we have quite a complicated history.

So that was my curveball, any questions" Madi asked before a few of the 2nd years raised their hands "Vanessa, on you go" Mr Stevenson said, Vanessa was the smallest and the youngest in 2nd year, "Umm…Madi, are you still with your foster family?" Vanessa asked "I am actually not, I live in the schoolhouse" Madi replied "Oh cool, where do your sisters live" Kit asked, she was another 2nd year who was so sassy "Listen guys, I didn't realise the time and I need to go finish something but I promise you guys I'll answer any questions another day okay" Madi said before she headed out the classroom and towards Miss Halfpenny's classroom. She reached Miss Halfpenny's classroom and knocked on the door "In you come" Miss Halfpenny shouted "Hi Miss, got a note for you from Mr Vandelay" Madi said before she handed her the note. "Thank you Madi and why weren't you in my lesson today?" Miss Halfpenny asked "I had an issue this morning, I thought Miss Davis told you" Madi replied "Okay and she did, I just wanted to hear it from you" Miss Halfpenny said as she was reading the note and she handed back to her.

"Is it okay if I go now Miss" Madi asked "Yeah, yeah on you go, where are you going to go?" Miss Halfpenny asked "I was going to go see Mr Stevenson's 2nd year class" Madi replied "Okay, go straight there and if he says no, then come to Mr Vandelay's office" Miss Halfpenny said "I will Miss" Madi replied before she and Miss Halfpenny left the classroom. Madi headed up to Mr Stevenson's classroom and she knocked on the door "Enter" Mr Stevenson shouted before Madi entered "Me again sir, is it okay if I sit in your class because I have nowhere else to go expect Mr Vandelay's office where I would just be sitting outside" Madi asked "Yeah of course Madi, you can help this lot out with their poem" Mr Stevenson said "Thanks sir" Madi replied.

"Can you watch this lot so I can go see Mr Vandelay" Mr Stevenson asked Madi "Yeah course sir" Madi replied before Mr Stevenson left the class. Vanessa raised her hand "What's up Vanessa?" Madi asked "I'm stuck with this question" Vanessa replied "Okay let me read it" Madi said as she came over to Vanessa's desk "It's question 5" Vanessa replied "Okay, using your own words as far as possible explain how the poet shows that change in your life can be good" Madi read aloud.

"Umm...Madi I'm stuck with that one as well" Kit said, "Is everyone stuck on that one?" Madi asked before everyone replied with yeah. "Okay, can I borrow your poem Vanessa"

Madi asked "Yeah of course Madi" Vanessa replied before Madi took Vanessa poem and headed to the front of the class where the whiteboard was. Madi grabbed one of the whiteboard pens "Right you lot, what is the first thing the poet says that you think is important. Just shout out" Madi asked. "Curveballs shouldn't change your life but they still do" Kit shouted out "Perfect, so how will we change that into our own words" Madi said before Mr Stevenson walked in "Oh Madi, what you doing?" Mr Stevenson asked "I was helping the class, are you finished with Mr Vandelay" Madi replied "No" Mr Stevenson said

"Well sir, if you want I will watch this lot, they will behave, won't you" Madi said before the class replied with yes "Okay, any problems, tell one of the teachers okay" Mr Stevenson said "I will sir, don't worry" Madi replied before Mr Stevenson left the class.

"Okay, where were we?" Madi said. "How we would change curveballs shouldn't change your life but they still do into your own words," Carly shouted out. "Thank you, what's your name?" Madi said "Carly." "Okay Carly, so first we need to focus on each of the words," Madi said "Madi could we change curveballs into obstacles?" Vanessa asked. "That is perfect, well done V" Madi replied.

"Could we change shouldn't change your life to shouldn't affect your lifetime" Kit asked "That is superb, well done Kit, last bit of the sentence who is going to change it" Madi replied "Me" said the boy at the back of the classroom who had raised his hand "Yeah on you go, what's your name?" Madi asked. "Jackson" he said "Okay, change but still do into your own words please" Madi asked "So we could change it to however they nevertheless still do" Jackson replied "That is splendid, well done Jackson" Madi said.

"So wait is it that easy" Kit asked "Yip, I know the questions can be worded strangely but choose key phrases in the questions and in the passage and you will be able to do these questions amazingly" Madi said. "Honestly Madi, I'm just going to say what everyone is think, why can you not be our teacher more often" Kit said "Guys I'm only 15, I'm not much older than you lot, I don't even have a teaching degree" Madi replied "So not fair" Kit said before Madi laughed.

"You lot are just fabulous and see if you lot have any worry or problems with English or thing in general, please remember I'm here for you" Madi said before Miss Edwards walked in "Madi, there is someone down in my office for you" Miss Edwards said.

"Oh umm... what will I do with this lot" Madi asked "I'll get Miss Jefferson to watch them" Miss Edwards replied "Okay, I'll see you lot later" Madi said before she left and headed down to Miss Edwards and Mr Stevenson's office.

Chapter 6 - An offer

◆◆◆◆◆

She arrived at the office not having a clue who was in there. She opened the door and low and behold it was her Aunt Cassandra "OMG I'm dreaming, Aunt Cassie" Madi said on the verge of tears "Hey mini marshmallow, how have you been" Cassandra replied (Mini Marshmallow is what Madi's Aunt Cassandra nicknamed her since she was younger).

"I'm so much better now, how about you?" Madi said with tears in her eyes "I'm good but come give me a hug" Cassandra said before Madi ran over and gave her a hug "I've missed you so much Aunt Cass" Madi said "I've missed you more and come take a seat" Cassandra said before her and Madi took a seat. "So is everything okay, is Aunt Kelly and Aunt Lexie and Aunt Amelia okay" Madi asked before Miss Edwards walked in "Yeah, yeah they are fine, I actually had something important to ask" Cassandra said "Yeah ask away" Madi replied "Okay, I don't want you to freak out or anything but would you like to move to Frostford to live with me" Cassandra asked and Madi froze and then she just ran out the office having no clue how to react.

Miss Edwards ran after Madi who had ran straight to the toilet "Wow Madi, I have never seen you ran as fast and unable to know how to react" Miss Edwards said "Miss I just have no clue what to say, I want to go stay but I've only just got used to life here, like what am I supposed to do and what about my sisters" Madi replied. "Listen Madi, isn't this what you have always wanted to live with your family again, and I know she isn't your mum but she is the closest thing to your mum" Miss Edwards said, "But Miss, I've only just started settling down here and then I'm going to have to do it all again" Madi replied.

"Madi, this might be what you need and I know you don't want to do it again" Miss Edwards said "Miss what about my sisters?" Madi asked "Why don't we speak to your Aunt Cassandra about that" Miss Edwards replied "Okay, did you tell Mr Vandelay about Rebecca" Madi asked as her and Miss Edwards walked out if the toilets and back to the office "Yip I did and he is going to get Rebecca's side of the story and get yours, well I'm getting Rebecca's and Miss Halfpenny is getting yours" Miss Edwards said.

"Okay, when is she coming to get my side" Madi asked "I'm not entirely sure, she might do it after school because do you not have running after school" Miss Edwards replied "I completely forgot, Miss do you have any water because I don't have my water bottle" Madi replied "I've got spare ones in my office" Miss Edwards said as they reached her office. "Sorry about that Aunt Cass, I just needed a moment, and I would love to stay with you but what about Summer, Autumn, Lilly and Grace" Madi asked "Well what I was thinking was that we could have you until you get settled in and then we can move your sisters over" Cassandra replied. "Aunt Cassie I would love that so much, can we trial it for a month and then I can decide whether I want to stay or move back here" Madi asked. "Madi, we can take as long as you need I'm not going to rush you into anything" Cassandra replied "I love you Aunt Cass" Madi said "I love you mini marshmallow" Cassandra replied.

"Miss Edwards is it okay if I take Aunt Cass to meet Mr Newwall because I need to go talk to him anyway" Madi asked "Yeah of course" Miss Edwards replied "Aunt Cass want to come with me" Madi asked "Yeah lets go" Cassandra said before her and Madi headed out of Miss Edwards office and towards Mr Newwall's office. "Ah Madi, just the girl I've been looking for, can I borrow you for a second" Miss Halfpenny said "Hi Miss Halfpenny, this is my Aunt Cassandra and can I come find you in about ten minutes?" Madi replied. "Yeah of course, Hi Cassandra I'm Isobel Halfpenny, I'm Madi's head of year" Miss Halfpenny said "Hi, umm…Madi why don't you speak to Miss Halfpenny and I'll wait for you" Cassandra said.

"How long should it take Miss" Madi asked "No longer than ten, twenty minutes" Miss Halfpenny replied "Okay and Aunt Cass can you please come with me?" Madi asked "Of course I will honey" Cassandra replied "Okay let's go in my office" Miss Halfpenny said before her, Cassandra and Madi entered the office.

"Okay explain what happened with you and Rebecca" Miss Halfpenny asked "So last night at the schoolhouse we were having a movie night and pizza to celebrate my first official night at the schoolhouse, so we were watching 5 movies but after the first one I just needed some space because I couldn't handle being around everyone. I was just lying on my bed and then there was a knock at my door and I thought it was Jodi or Savannah or that but when I answered it was Rebecca" Madi said. "Okay so let me get this straight, the schoolhouse were having a movie and pizza party to celebrate your first night but you didn't want to be there so you left and went to your room where you were doing nothing and then Rebecca knocked on your door" Miss Halfpenny said with cheek in her voice.

"Excuse me, my niece is trying to explain what happened to her with Rebecca, she doesn't need attitude off someone who is supposed to support her" Cassandra said. "Thank you Aunt Cass, wait do you know what happened" Madi asked "Yeah Miss Edwards told me" Cassandra replied "Okay sorry for my cheek but I don't believe Rebecca would do this" Miss Halfpenny said. "Okay let me continue, so after I opened the door Rebecca was asking me if was okay and I said that I was fine but I wanted to get to bed and I went to shut the door but she shoved it open and said and this was her exact words listen to me, you little attention seeker, nobody in this house likes you, we are only pretending to like you so we can get treats because you are special with your dead mummy and dead daddy and dead sissy, do you know your sisters are better off without you because all you would do is destroy them like you are doing here" Madi said.

"Okay I still don't believe that Rebecca would say that" Miss Halfpenny replied. "Are you saying my niece is lying or something, have you any clue what she has been through the past few months, because no one can. She is a young girl that requires a bit of support and understanding from people around her, especially you considering that you are her head of year" Cassandra said, "No and I am so sorry if it came across that way" Miss Halfpenny said "Okay,

Madi let's go" Cassandra said before her and Madi left Miss Halfpenny's office.

"Where we are going" Madi asked "To get Miss Edwards to go see Mr Vandelay about how she has just spoke to you, I'm not having it she is supposed to be a figure of authority and is supposed to be one of the main teachers helping you with this" Cassandra said. "Okay Aunt Cass you need to breathe" Madi said as they reached Miss Edwards office. Cassandra knocked on the door "In you come" Miss Edwards shouted before Cassandra and Madi entered the office "Molly, can you come with me to see William so I can tell you both how Isobel Halfpenny has just spoke to Madi" Cassandra said, "Yeah of course but you need to calm down before you go to speak to him" Miss Edwards replied before her, Madi and Cassandra went walked to Mr Vandelay's office.

They reached Mr Vandelay's office and Miss Edwards knocked and walked in, followed by Cassandra and then Madi "I would like to make a complaint against a member of your staff" Cassandra snapped. "Which member of my staff is the complaint against" Mr Vandelay asked, "Isobel Halfpenny" Cassandra replied "What is the complaint for?" Mr Vandelay asked "Not believing my nieces side of the story and speaking very cheeky to my niece and I'm not having that because my niece and had plenty happen to her in the past few months and the last thing she needs is a figure of authority that is support her not believing her" Cassandra snapped.

"Miss Edwards I'm going to go see if the dance studio is free okay" Madi said "Okay, you okay" Miss Edwards asked but Madi just looked at her before she left the office and headed to the dance studio. Madi headed up to Mr

Newwall's office to ask if she would be able to use the dance studio, she knocked on the door "In you come" Mr Newwall shouted before Madi walked in, he could tell that she wasn't right.

"Umm…I forgot what I was coming to ask, oh umm… can I use the dance studio please" Madi asked "Yeah of course, is anything bothering you" Mr Newwall questioned. "No sir, I'm fine" Madi replied "Okay if you are sure, remember I'm here if you need to talk or rant" Mr Newwall said "Thank sir" Madi said before she left the office and headed down to the dance studio. She connected her phone to the speaker and looked through her dance playlist to see what song she could freestyle to, she found the song Inside Out which her juniors used for a duet competition. She pressed play on it and started to freestyle. She was so upset about how Miss Halfpenny spoke to her and she was so overwhelmed with the decision of moving to Frostford, she did not know if she could handle having to moving further from her sisters and not being able to see them as often. She would if she was here, having to be a new girl again. Its times like this when Madi is really overwhelmed and upset that she needed dance and her friends and her parents.

Madi finished dancing and she just stood there until Jodi walked in "Mads, you okay?" She asked, Madi did not answer, Jodi walked over and tapped Madi. Madi just started crying, she could hold it back anymore. "Woah, Mads calm down" Jodi said as Madi kept crying. Jodi left Madi crying so she could get Miss Edwards. Miss Edwards ran in and said "Madi, come on, it's okay, take a deep breath" before Jodi stood beside Madi holding her hand.

"I…I….can't…breathe" Madi said "Look at me Madi,

okay breath with me, in and out, in and out" Miss Edwards said as her and Madi was taking deep breaths, "That's better, I can breathe" Madi replied "Madi, you really scared me, I didn't know what to do" Jodi said "Sorry Jods" Madi replied. "It's fine, I should know what to do" Jodi said "Anyway Miss Madi, was that about the way Miss Halfpenny spoke to you" Miss Edwards asked.

"Yeah and my Aunt Cassandra asking me to move to Frostford to live with her" Madi replied "Wait what, you are moving to Frostford but you can't, you have only just moved here" Jodi said. "I'm trialling for a month then decided to whether it is permanent or not, Jodi this gives me a chance to live with the closest thing to my mum. I can't pass up on an opportunity like that" Madi replied, "You won't forget us will you" Jodi asked before Miss Edwards laughed "How could I forget you Jodi, my guide that took me to my first class, you forgot your science jotters, forgot your history essay, I could never forgive you Jodi" Madi replied.

"Anyway, you two, let me see those smiles and Madi, there has been a complaint against placed against Miss Halfpenny and it is very possible that she could be facing a disciplinary hearing because it was completely out of line the way she spoke to you, and Rebecca will be facing a two week detention period which means she won't be in any classes for two weeks" Miss Edwards said. "Okay that is good Miss isn't it" Madi asked "Yeah" Miss Edwards said.

"Finally Rebecca is getting what she deserves" Jodi said "Now Jodi, that's not nice but Jodi why don't you and Madi stay in here until the bell rings and then you can head along to my office or stay here and do some work" Miss Edwards said. "We'll stay here if it's okay with you Miss" Madi replied

"Yip, yip that's okay, have you got stuff to be getting on with" Miss Edwards asked "No" Jodi replied.

"I'll bring something for you to do" Miss Edwards said before she left. "So Mads, you really going to move to Frostford" Jodi asked "Jods, this is my one chance to be with my family, I can't pass up on an opportunity like that" Madi replied. "I know but I don't know how I'm going to be used to school without you again" Jodi said "Jodi listen I'll still keep in touch and I need to come back to visit my sisters" Madi replied, "But like what if you and your Aunt decide that your sisters are moving too" Jodi said, "Jodi listen to me, you are the only one that knows so please don't tell the girls yet, and it will be a while before we decide to move the girls. They deserve to settle with a family and Olivia and Simon are amazing foster parents" Madi replied.

"Okay, when are you planning to tell the girls" Jodi asked "I think I'm going to see if I can tell them tonight and that way, they have time to accept it and come to terms with it" Madi replied before Miss Edwards walked in.

"Okay, I've got a few different worksheets for you, some are science, some are history, some are English, some are maths, it was whatever was in my drawer for 4th years" Miss Edwards said as she handed Jodi and Madi the worksheets and a pencil each. "Thank you Miss" Jodi said "Mr Newwall is going to come sit with you girls because I want someone here in case Madi has another panic attack but I have your class waiting to be taught so I'll go and catch up with you two later" Miss Edwards said before she left.

"What subject will we start with" Jodi asked before Mr Newwall walked in "Why don't we do four science worksheets, then do the two English, then do the one math

117

one and the three history ones" Madi replied. "Yeah sounds good" Jodi said "Did Miss Edwards tell you two I was going to be here to supervise you?" Mr Newwall asked "Yeah sir, she did" Jodi replied "Madi come here for two seconds" Mr Newwall said before Madi walked over. The two girls were sitting in the middle of the floor and Mr Newwall was sitting on the bench at the side. "Are you okay Madi?" Mr Newwall asked "I am now, is running on tonight" Madi asked "Yeah it is but you aren't coming" Mr Newwall replied.

"Wait Sir, are you kicking me off the team?" Madi asked "No Madi, but you have a lot of things happening and they need to take priority over running" Mr Newwall replied, "But running is what helps me take my mind off those thing" Madi said "I know Madi, but I want you to sort out your family issues and friend issues and that" Mr Newwall replied.

"But sir" Madi said.

"But Madi, nothing.

I need you to take priority of your health and your issues especially family ones because they are the one family you get and you have already lost a big part of your family, so you need to sort those issues out first then think of other things" Mr Newwall replied "Ugh fine sir but I'm not happy with this decision" Madi said "I know but issues take priority" Mr Newwall replied before Madi heading back to where Jodi was sitting. "I'm going to the toilet be right back" Madi said before she left and headed to toilet. She reached the toilets and it just so happened that Rebecca and Jess were in the toilet too "Hey Madi" Jess said "Hi Jess, Hi Rebecca" Madi replied

"So Madison, thanks for getting me two weeks detention" Rebecca said "Please don't call me Madison and it wasn't me that made the decision but you had no right to say what you did say" Madi replied. "Oh shut up you attention seeker" Rebecca said before Madi ran out of the toilets and straight to Miss Edwards classroom.

She reached Miss Edwards class and knocked on the door "Enter" Miss Edwards shouted before Madi opened the door. Madi didn't say anything, Miss Edwards just walked outside where Madi was waiting and shut the door "I can't be here anymore" Madi said while wiping a tear away from her face "Hey, what's happened now?" Miss Edwards asked. "I just had a run in with Rebecca and she called me a attention seeker again" Madi replied "Listen Madi, she will be hard on you right now because she got in trouble for what she done but I need you to be happy, these are your last few days at school and I want you to enjoy them okay" Miss Edwards said.

"Okay" Madi replied before Miss Edwards gave her a hug "Why don't you go to my office because your Aunt is there so you can spend time with her" Miss Edwards said. "Okay Miss" Madi replied "Okay" before walking away and down to Miss Edwards office.

"Aunt Cassie" Madi said while fighting tears back "Mads come in, come sit down" Cassandra replied before Madi walked over to the couch where her Aunt Cass was sitting "When can I move in with you?" Madi asked before she lay down on her Aunts leg "What's happened?" Cassandra replied "Rebecca calling me an attention seeker again" Madi said "I was thinking that you could move in not next week but the week after" Cassandra replied "Thank god, I hate it here" Madi said while wiping away a tear "You don't you just hate the people here" Cassandra replied "Yeah, listen I'll be two minutes" Madi said before walking out and towards the dance studio.

"Umm…Sir I'm with my Aunt in Miss Edwards office" Madi said "Okay Madi" Mr Newwall replied "Can Jodi come with me please so my Aunt can meet her?" Madi asked. "Of course, on you go Jodi" Mr Newwall replied before Jodi walked out to where Madi was. "We have one more place to stop before you get to meet my Aunt" Madi said.

"Where is that" Jodi asked "Miss Edwards class, I want to tell everyone because not next week but the week after I'm gone" Madi replied "No that soon" Jodi said with real sadness in the voice. "Yeah Jods" Madi replied before they reached Miss Edwards class. Madi knocked on the door "In you come" Miss Edwards shouted "Me again, Miss can I borrow you for two seconds?" Madi asked "Yeah of course" Miss Edwards replied before heading outside to speak to Madi. "Miss would it be okay if I could speak to the class and tell them all about the move, please" Madi asked "Yeah, let's go" Miss Edwards replied before her, Madi and Jodi walked in.

"Right everyone Madi has something to tell you all so listen to her please" Miss Edwards said "Thanks Miss, umm…so I just thought I would let you all know that not next week but the week after I'm leaving and moving to Frostford" Madi said "Wait Madi, are you being serious" Darcy asked with tears in her eyes. "Yeah, my Aunt Cassandra asked me if I would like to and I really can't pass up on an opportunity to live with the closest thing to my mum" Madi replied with a tear streaming down her face.

Everyone in the class looked shocked and there was a fair share of tears, Jodi was crying, Morag, Addison, Savannah, Paige, Darcy, Hunter, Hudson, Brogan, Scarlett, Stella, Jamie, Anna, Sage and Reagan were all crying. "Now guys, I know you all love Madi but this is what is best for Madi" Miss Edwards said while wiping a tear "Miss, are you crying?" Caleb asked "Yeah, Madi has been a big part of my life so I will really miss her a lot, like you all" Miss Edwards replied "Madi, you won't forget us will you" Savannah said "Of course I won't guys" Madi replied "Good" Addison replied

"Right I'll go because I want to catch up with the second years in Mr Stevenson's class but I will see some of you lot tonight" Madi said "See you soon Madi" Paige replied before Madi and Jodi left. "Right come on, Mr Stevenson's classroom. I need to say bye to the second years, that lot are so funny and kind" Madi said. "Yeah especially that Vanessa and Kit" Jodi replied before they reached Mr Stevenson's classroom. Madi knocked on the door "In you come" Mr Stevenson shouted "Hi Sir, it's us, I was wondering if I could talk to you for two minutes" Madi asked "Yeah of course" Mr Stevenson said before he and Madi and Jodi walked out. "Have you spoken to Miss Edwards" Madi asked "Yeah, I can't believe that you are leaving" Mr Stevenson replied.

"My question is can I talk to your second years please" Madi asked "Yeah of course" Mr Stevenson replied "Great more tears" Madi said before her, Mr Stevenson and Jodi walked into the class. "Right my lovely lot, Madi has something she wants to tell you so please listen up" Mr

Stevenson said, "Okay I couldn't really wait to tell you but I am leaving and moving to Frostford to stay with my Aunt" Madi replied "So is this a curveball for you" Vanessa asked with tears in her eyes "Yip this is a curveball but it's a good one and it is going to change my life" Madi replied with tears in her eyes. "Why do you need to leave?" Vanessa asked.

"I've learned from you guys and our lesson this morning that you should make an opportunity out everything" Madi replied but this time a tear fell down her face "Madi please don't leave" Carly said with tears falling out of her eyes "Come here" Madi said before Carly ran out of her chair and into Madi's arms. "Listen guys, I understand how much Madi has made an impact lately on everyone. Me included when she leaves everything is going to be different, but she hasn't been here long and we have already forgot what it is like to be without her" Mr Stevenson said "Sir, don't make me cry please. I'm going to miss you so much. I'm going to miss all of you so much" Madi replied still with Carly hugging her "Madi can I have a hug please?" Vanessa asked, "Me too" Kit asked "Me three" Charlotte asked "Of course you can. Come here" Madi replied before the three girls jumped out their seats with tears rolling down their faces and ran towards Madi.

"Mads, we need to go" Jodi said

"Yeah, right everyone I'll see you later bye" Madi replied as the girls let go of her

"Bye Madi" Vanessa said

"I'll let Madi take you once before she leaves okay guys" Mr Stevenson said

"Yay" Everyone cheered

"I would love to sir" Madi said

"I'll organise it for you lot" Mr Stevenson said

"Yay" Everyone cheered again

"Bye everyone" Madi said

"Bye Madi" Mr Stevenson replied before Madi and Jodi left.

They headed down to Miss Edwards and Mr Stevenson office. "Aunt Cassie" Madi said "Hey Mini Marshmallow, you okay?" Cassandra asked "Yeah, I've got someone I want you to meet" Madi replied "Ooh who is it?" Cassandra asked "This is Jodi and Jodi this is my favourite Aunt Cassandra" Madi said "Nice to meet you Cassandra" Jodi replied as she put her hand out to shake "Call me Cassie and give me a hug. Any friend of Madi's is family to me" Cassandra replied before she gave Jodi a hug. "Madi she is amazing" Jodi said "I know, I got lucky" Madi replied "No I was the lucky one, I got you" Cassandra said.

"Come on, let's have a seat so I can tell you about my other family members" Madi said before her, Jodi and Cassandra sat down "Get prepared Jodi we have a big family" Cassandra said.

"Okay so Aunt Cass is my mum's sister and then on my side we have my Aunt Lexie, Aunt Amelia and my Aunt Kelly. We also have my Uncle Tyler, Uncle Chris, Uncle Eli and Uncle Harrison and on my dad's side. I have my Aunt Kate, my Aunt Clara, my Aunt Callie, my Aunt Casey, my Aunt Caydence and my Aunt Caitlin.

Then I have my Uncle Finn, my Uncle Cameron and Uncle Cole" Madi said "Wow a lot of Aunts and Uncles" Jodi replied "Now it's time for my cousins" Madi said. "Now there is a lot, so be prepared because a lot of them are twins or triplets" Cassandra said "Okay, here we go so on my mums side we have Abby, Ashely, Annie, Ayden, Allie, Blake, Bonnie, Bryson Bellamy, Bree, Carmen, Colette, Diana, Destiny, Derek, Dakota, Emmy, Everly, Faith, Fallon, Grace, Gwen, Grey and Hope.

Then on my dad's side we have Theo, Thomas, Lucas, Lincoln, Leo, Lewis, Payton, Leilani, Summer, Marley, Ivy-May, Liberty-Grace, Kendall, Kevin, Kennedy and Kass" Madi said, "Wow a lot of girls on your mum's side" Jodi said "Yeah and there is like seven girls on my dad's side" Madi replied "So who is your favourite Aunt and Uncle on your mum and dad's side" Jodi asked "My favourite Aunt and Uncle on my mums side is my Aunt Cass and my Uncle Tyler and my favourite on my dad's side is my Aunt Callie and my Uncle Cole" Madi replied.

"What about cousins" Jodi said "Umm…on my mums side Dakota, Emmy, Bellamy, Hope and Grey and on my dad's side Payton and Theo" Madi replied. "Who are you the closest to on each side" Jodi asked "I'm the closest to Everly, Grace and Faith on my mum's side and I'm closest to Payton on my dad's side" Madi replied.

"Okay I can't believe I never knew you had a big family" Jodi said "Well I don't really talk about them because they are a bit complicated and most of them are annoying" Madi replied. "You need to tell her about Christmas last year when your mum and dad hosted it and we all came and all your dads side came that was fun" Cassandra said "Oh yeah, so it was my mum and dad's turn to host Christmas dinner and my god it was awkward. All the Aunts had an argument, all the Uncles were talking about football, all the little cousins all were crying and being annoying and the older ones were sitting on their phones or just ignoring everyone" Madi said. "God how many were there" Jodi asked "There was forty cousins, me and my five sisters, my mum and dad and there was ten aunties and seven uncles" Madi replied, Jodi's jaw just hit the floor "Exactly Jodi, exactly" Cassandra said. The bell rang for the end of the day "Are you two staying here or are you leaving?" Cassandra asked "I'll wait" Madi replied "Same" Jodi replied "Jods you can leave if you want" Madi said "Are you sure Mads?" Jodi asked. "Yeah" Madi replied as she looked at her Aunt "Okay, I'll see you soon" Jodi said before she left. "You have an amazing friend in Jodi" Cassandra said "I know, I'll be sad to leave her and the other girls, you need to meet them" Madi replied. "Well I'll speak to Miss Edwards and maybe tomorrow I can treat you all to McDonald's" Cassandra replied "You would do that Aunt Cassie" Madi asked "Of course I would Mads" Cassandra replied before Madi got out her chair and gave her Aunt a hug.

Just then Cassandras phone rang "Who is it" Madi asked "It's your Aunt Amelia, she's facetiming me" Cassandra replied before answering it. "Hey Cass, your kids wanted to speak to you" Amelia said.

"Umm…before I speak to my kids, looks who is here" Cassandra said before she handed Madi the phone "Hi Aunt Amelia how are you?" Madi asked "Oh my god Madi, Hi sweetheart I'm good, how are you?" Amelia replied "I'm okay, I miss you" Madi said. "I miss you too" Amelia replied "Now can I see my kids" Cassandra asked while laughing "Yeah here you go" Madi replied before she handed the phone back.

Cassandra kids were Emmy (13), Dakota (13), Bellamy (11), Grey (9) and Hope (2) "Hey babies, mama misses you" Cassandra said "Mummy I miss you" Hope said.

> "I'll be home soon baby with your big cousin" Cassandra replied
>
> "Cousin Madi is coming to stay with us" Hope said
>
> "Yeah baby, she's coming to stay with us" Cassandra said
>
> "Yay I love Madi" Hope replied
>
> "Hey mama" Grey said
>
> "Hey buddy, how are you" Cassandra replied
>
> "I'm good mama" Grey said
>
> "Have you been good" Cassandra asked
>
> "Yeah mama" Grey replied
>
> "Hey mama" Bellamy said
>
> "Hey Bell-bell, have you been good" Cassandra replied
>
> "Yeah mama and I've helped Aunt Amelia around the house and helped with
>
> the younger two" Bellamy replied.

"That's my Bell-bell" Cassandra replied "Emmy, Dakota come speak to your mum" Amelia shouted "Coming Aunt Amelia" The two girls shouted "Hey my twins" Cassandra said. "Hi mum, I miss you" Emmy said "I miss you too Em" Cassandra replied "Hello mum, when are you coming home" Dakota asked "I'll be home soon Kota" Cassandra replied.

"Okay mum, I'm in the middle of rehearsing my dance" Dakota said "Okay princess I'll speak to soon" Cassandra replied "So your kids are fine, I haven't killed them okay" Amelia said while laughing "I knew they were fine, I just wanted to speak to them because they are my babies" Cassandra replied "Well I'm going to feed these children and I'll speak to you later" Amelia said "Bye" Cassandra said before she hung up.

Then Miss Edwards walked in "Hi you two" Miss Edwards said "Hi Miss Edwards Madi said "Hi Molly" Cassandra said "Madi, are you okay now?" Miss Edwards asked "Yeah, I'm better now that I've spent time with my Aunt and spoke to my other Auntie" Madi replied. "That's the girl I know, a family girl" Cassandra said "Madi I love to see you smiling so keep it up" Miss Edwards said "Oh Molly, I was wondering if tomorrow I could buy Madi and her friends a McDonald's" Cassandra asked "Of course" Miss Edwards replied.

"Thank you Miss" Madi said "You deserve it before you leave" Miss Edwards said "Right Mads I've got a question, are you staying in the schoolhouse or do you want to come and stay in a hotel with me tonight" Cassandra asked. "I'll stay in the schoolhouse as it will be one of the last times I see everyone" Madi replied "Rebecca is in the schoolhouse remember" Miss Edwards said "I know but I'm not going to let one girl wreck my last few days here" Madi replied before Miss Edwards and Cassandra smiled "That's my girl" Cassandra said.

"Do you want to go with your Aunt or me" Miss Edwards asked "Umm…Aunt Cass would you mind if I go with Miss Edwards?" Madi replied "No of course not, I'll meet at the schoolhouse" Cassandra said. "Right are we ready and we'll go now so your Aunt Cass can get to her bed, she's been travelling all day" Miss Edwards said "Yeah let's go" Madi replied before she grabbed her school bag and her Aunt Cassie's hand and headed out the office and out the school to the parking lot.

They arrived at the schoolhouse and walked in "Hi Miss Madi" Miss Davis said "Hi Miss Davis" Madi replied "Hi Miss Edwards" Miss Davis said "Hi Miss Davis" Miss Edwards said "Miss Davis, this is my Aunt Cassandra" Madi said. "Call me Vanessa" Miss Davis said as she put her hand out for Cassandra to shake "So is Madi nice to you as she is to everyone else" Cassandra asked, "Yeah she's a lovely girl, I'm sad to see her go" Miss Davis replied as she put her hand on Madi's arm.

"Don't make me cry miss, I've done enough crying" Madi said. "Oh sweetie, listen why don't you take your Aunt through to the living room where the girls are" Miss Davis asked "Yeah" Madi replied before her and Cassandra left Miss Edwards and Miss Davis by the front door and headed into the living room.

"Hey girls" Madi said "Hey Mads" Addison said "This is my Aunt Cassandra" Madi said "Nice to meet you Cassandra" Savannah said "Please girls call me Cassie, what are all of your names" Cassandra replied, "I'm Addison." "I'm Savannah", "I'm Morag", "I'm Paige", "I'm Brogan", "I'm Abby", Nice to meet you girls" Cassandra said "Yeah, so this is who I'm going to stay with when I leave" Madi said while fighting tears "About that Mads, we got you something" Jodi said "Is everyone trying to make me cry today" Madi replied before the girls laughed.

"Here" Jodi said while handed Madi a bag, Madi opened it and inside was a photo frame with a picture of all the girls from one of Madi's first days at the school, a necklace with Madi's name and her favourite sweets which were skittles "Thank you so much girls I love them" Madi said with tears streaming down her face "Group hug" Addison said before all the girls made a circle for a hug.

"I'm going to miss you all so much, you don't understand how much you have changed my life in a short amount of days" Madi said with tears "We are all going to miss you too Madi, you have changed us for the better. We have thought of things we would never have thought of before" Savannah said with tears as well "Listen girls" Cassandra butted in "Yeah Cassie" Paige said "How about I buy you all McDonald's tomorrow" Cassandra asked "Wait you would do that?" Jodi replied "Yeah like I said any friend of Madi's is family" Cassandra replied before the girls cheered "Thank you Cassie" All the girls said.

Miss Davis and Miss Edwards walked in "Madi, there is someone at the door for you" Miss Davis said "Okay, I'm just coming" Madi replied with confusion before she headed out the living room and saw her cousin Payton standing and the door with baby Cole "Hey Madi, told you I would visit" Payton said before Madi ran to hug her. "Oh my god this isn't happening" Madi said with shock "Yeah it, I came to see you" Payton replied "Can I hold Cole please?" Madi asked "Yeah" Payton replied before getting him out his buggy and handing him to Madi "Hi baby, you are getting so big. Payt come meet the girls" Madi said before her and Payton walked into the living room. "Girls, this is my big cousin Payton and her baby Cole" Madi said "Hi" The girls replied.

"Cass" Payton said with shock "Payt" Cassandra replied "It's so good to see you again" Payton said "Same, your little boy is so cute" Cassandra replied "Thank you" Payton said while her and Cassandra admired Madi who was holding Cole.

"Payton, do you have two minutes" Madi asked "Yeah" Payton replied before her and Madi and Cole headed out to the hall "Umm…I'm kind of glad you visited today because it means everyone is finding out at the same time" Madi said.

"What is it Madi" Payton asked "I'm moving to Frostford to live with Cass" Madi replied "I am so happy for Mads" Payton said "Wait you are?" Madi questioned "Yeah you deserve to have a happy ending without your parents but that will only happen if you go live with your Aunt Cass" Payton replied "Thank you Payton and thank for letting me see this little man again" Madi said before kissing Cole on the head "Let's go back into the living room" Payton said before they headed back into the living room.

Madi ran right over to her aunt Cassandra and gave her a hug "I love you so much Aunt Cass" Madi said "I love you more Mads" Cassandra replied. "Can I move in sooner please" Madi asked "How about you move in next Monday instead of two weeks' time" Cassandra said "Yeah please" Madi replied.

Cassandra and Payton and baby Cole left to go to their hotels. Madi ran upstairs and went straight to her bedroom and slid down her door and sat there with her knees up at her chest "I don't think I would ever have happy ending without my mum and dad" Madi thought to herself before someone came to the door. "Madi it's Miss Davis and Miss Edwards can we come in please?" Miss Davis asked "Yeah, yeah just a second" Madi replied before standing up and wiping away her tears "Just tell us when we can come in" Miss Davis said "In you come" Madi said before Miss Davis and Miss Edwards walked in.

"Are you okay" Miss Edwards asked "Yeah, everything is just happening so fast and I just need a minute to breath and catch up" Madi replied. "Listen, this will be good for being with someone who is related to you and is a close figure to your mum I know it will be hard to adjust but like your Aunt said it can be a trial period it doesn't have to be permanent" Miss Edwards said "Thanks Miss Edwards" Madi replied.

"We will always be here if you need any help with absolutely anything and we mean anything" Miss Davis said "Thank you Miss Davis" Madi replied "So are you excited?" Miss Edwards asked "Oh yeah I cannot wait. I mean I get to be with people that love me" Madi replied "So what cousins will you be living with when you move" Miss Edwards asked. "It will be my cousins Dakota, Emmy, Bellamy, Grey and Hope" Madi replied "What ones are they again?" Miss Edwards asked "These one" Madi replied before handing the two teachers a picture frame "Aww yeah, the cute ones" Miss Edwards said. "Miss, all my cousins are cute, they got the beautiful blue eyes from my mums side" Madi replied "They are cute though" Miss Davis said "Yeah they are" Madi replied.

"Are you still going to your ex foster parents tomorrow" Miss Edwards asked "I think so I'll give them a phone before I go to bed and I want to tell them about me moving before I tell the girls tomorrow" Madi replied. "Well we just wanted to make sure you are okay and that you know that even when you move, you can contact us whenever" Miss Edwards said "Thank you Miss, you are making me not want to move now" Madi replied. "Trust me, do this and you feel so much better honestly Madi, I'll miss you so much but you need to do what's best for you" Miss Edwards said.

"Miss Edwards, Miss Davis before I move can I please sing for my friends and the teachers" Madi asked "Yeah of course Madi, I want to hear your voice" Miss Davis said. "You know, I've seen her dance and run but never sing"

Miss Edwards replied "I'll sing as soon as I know what song" Madi said "I'm going to go but I'll see you tomorrow Madi" Miss Edwards said, "Bye Miss Edwards" Madi said "I'll come back up Madi okay" Miss Davis said "Okay Miss Davis" Madi replied before Miss Edwards and Miss Davis left Madi's room and headed downstairs.

Madi decided to phone her ex foster parents, just to get it over with. She got up of her bed and phoned Olivia "Hey Madi, everything okay" She asked "I have two questions and something to tell you" Madi replied "Okay" Olivia said kind of confused.

"Questions first, one is it still okay if I come for dinner tomorrow and two how are the girls" Madi asked "One, yes of course and two, the girls are good. Summer has been a little upset but you obviously know why" Olivia replied "Okay that's perfect I'll speak to her tomorrow" Madi said "What did you have to tell me?" Olivia asked.

"Oh umm…can you please not tell the girls I want to tell them tomorrow but I am moving to Frostford to live with my Aunt Cassandra because she doesn't see the point of me living here when I'm just in a schoolhouse so she wants me to have a second chance somewhere else" Madi replied. "Aah Madi that's amazing I'm so happy for you and I won't tell the girls" Olivia said "Thanks Olivia" Madi replied "I will see you tomorrow" Olivia said "See you tomorrow" before she hung up the phone. This was starting to get in Madi's head but she decided to get into her pyjamas and go to her bed, she fell asleep in a matter of minutes, Miss Davis walked in and saw Madi sleeping. She left and headed back downstairs.

Chapter 7 - Thursday

⁺◆◆◆◆⁺

The next morning Miss Davis was doing her usual rounds to wake everyone up "Madi time for school" Miss Davis said "I'm up" Madi replied "Can I come in please" Miss Davis asked "Yeah of course" Madi replied before Miss Davis walked in. "You were in bed early" Miss Davis said "Yeah I was tired and things were getting in my head and I just needed to sleep" Madi replied, "So the big day, are you still going to see your sisters today?" Miss Davis asked.

"Yeah" Madi replied "How are you getting there?" Miss Davis asked "I think either Simon or Linda or my Aunt Cass might take me I'm not fully sure" Madi replied "Okay well come get breakfast and then you can you get dressed" Miss Davis said "Okay Miss" Madi replied before her and Miss Davis left and headed downstairs.

"Morning Madi" Jodi said "Morning Jodi" Madi said "Come sit with us" Jodi said before Madi walked over to the table where Jodi, Addison, Savannah and Morag were sitting "What do you want for breakfast Madi?" Savannah asked "I'll get it Sav" Madi replied "Come on let me get it before you leave please Madi please" Savannah said. "Okay, toast and strawberry jam please" Madi replied "Okay I'll be right back" Savannah said before she left the table and headed into the kitchen.

"She's been making everyone's breakfast this morning" Jodi said "Is she okay?" Madi asked "She is taking you leaving really hard, I think it's because her older sister left to move elsewhere to have a second chance with her auntie" Morag replied. "She never said anything" Madi said "She doesn't like discussing her family" Jodi replied "So don't say anything" Addison said, "I won't" Madi replied before Savannah walked out with toast for Madi and fruit for everyone else "Here you go Mads" Savannah said.

"What do we have today" Madi asked "Umm…history, PE, double English and double maths" Addison said "I hate double maths" Morag said "Same" Jodi replied "That toast was amazing Sav, thank you" Madi replied before she left the table and headed upstairs.

She didn't know if she was ready to tell her sisters that she was leaving them, they needed their big sister as much as she needed them, but this was her second chance and she needed to take it. She felt so guilty and wished her mum and dad were still here, so she didn't have to do this. There was a knock on the door "Mads it's me, can I come in please" Jodi said "Yeah in you come" Madi replied before Jodi came in "Are you okay" Jodi asked "Yeah" Madi replied "Mads don't lie to me please" Jodi said "I feel so guilty, I don't want to leave my sisters but this is my second chance but I so wish my mum and dad were here so I didn't need to do anything" Madi replied.

"Mads you have nothing to feel guilty about because you are doing this for you and no one else okay, yes your sisters might take it hard but Mads you are doing this for you" Jodi said "Thank you Jods, I am going to miss you so much" Madi replied. "You have given everyone advice so my turn" Jodi said "Well I need to get ready but I'll meet you at the front stairs so we can walk together" Madi replied "Okay" Jodi said before she left Madi to get dressed.

Madi got dressed into her uniform, she fixed her tie and her skirt and decided to put her hair in French braids, just as she was starting to braid her hair her phone rang it was Payton.

"Morning Mads" Payton said after Madi answered it

"Morning Payt, morning mister Cole" Madi replied

"Can you say Madi, Cole" Payton said

"Ma...Ma...Madi" Cole said

"Well done baby" Payton said

"Well done Cole" Madi replied

"What are you doing" Payton asked

"I'm braiding my hair for school because I've got PE and I don't want to have a boring ponytail" Madi replied "Are you ready" Payton asked "Yeah I just need to do my hair and sort my bag" Madi replied as she finished her first braid. "Looking good and what classes are you in today?" Payton asked "History, PE, double English and double maths" Madi replied "So an okay day really" Payton said "Yeah I guess so" Madi replied as she finished her second braid. "Also I'm going with Cass for lunch to get you and your friends McDonalds and I'll bring Cole" Payton said, "Okay Payt, listen does this look alright" Madi asked as she pulled a sport headband on "Yes you look beautiful" Payton replied "Thanks Payt" Madi said before there was a knock on the door.

"Mads it's me again" Jodi said

"In you come" Madi replied before Jodi walked in

"Do you have a minute" Jodi asked,

Madi could see she was really worried "Yeah, just give me a minute" Madi replied

"I'll see you later Mads" Payton replied

"See you later, bye Payt, bye Cole" Madi replied before she hung up.

"It's Sav" Jodi said

"What's happened?" Madi asked

"She's locked herself in the bathroom and she won't come out and we don't know what to do" Jodi replied "I'm coming" Madi said as she quickly got off her floor and left her bedroom. All the girls were standing outside the bathroom "Give me five minutes but please go finish getting ready so I can talk to her by myself" Madi said. "Okay" Addison and the other girls said before went into their rooms "Sav, it's Mads let me in please" Madi asked before the door unlocked "Madi" Savannah said with tears streaming down her face.

"Hey, hey, hey what's wrong" Madi asked as she wrapped her arms around Savannah "My big sister" Savannah said, "What about her?" Madi asked "She has fallen ill and I can't go see her because she lives in Astroford and I can't get a hold of her or my aunt or my uncle and I'm starting to worry" Savannah replied. "Why don't we go to my room because this floor is really uncomfortable" Madi asked "Yeah" Savannah replied laughing with tears still.

The two girls got up and headed into Madi's room, they sat on Madi's bed "Listen I know you don't want to but why don't you finish getting dressed and then I can do your hair for you" Madi said. "I just have my hair to do, I'm dressed and my teeth are done and my bag is sorted" Savannah replied "What do you want your hair style to look like?" Madi asked. "Can you do half-up half-down and plait the ponytail please if you don't mind" Savannah replied "No of course I don't, can you sit on the floor in front of the mirror" Madi said before Savannah sat on the floor. "Thanks Madi" Savannah said "It's okay Sav, I like doing people's hair" Madi replied before she and Savannah continued talking "Yeah so I am going to miss you" Savannah said "I am going to miss you too and your hair is done" Madi replied "Thank you Mads" Savannah said.

The two girls left Madi's room and headed downstairs where the rest of the girls were sitting and waiting "Sav, you okay?" Addison asked, "Yeah she's fine, aren't you" Madi replied before Savannah nodded "Come on, let's go" Jodi said before the girls left the schoolhouse and headed to school. The girls reached the school "Listen girls, me and Sav will catch you up, she's coming to see Miss Edwards with me" Madi said. "Okay, we'll see you in history" Jodi said before the two girls left the rest of the girls and headed to Miss Edwards office.

Madi knocked on Miss Edwards door "In you come" Miss Edwards said "Hey Miss, hey Sir" Madi said, "Morning Madi, you are in a good mood this morning" Mr Stevenson said "Yes I am Sir" Madi replied. "What can I do for you girls?" Miss Edwards asked, "I was wondering if I could talk to you please, well us" Madi replied as she gestured to Savannah "Yeah of course" Miss Edwards said. "I've got a class so I'll let you girls talk to Miss Edwards and I'll catch up with you in class later" Mr Stevenson said before he left.

"What can I help you with girls?" Miss Edwards asked "Miss I was just wondering if you could give me and Savannah a note because Sav isn't herself today" Madi replied, "What's up Savannah?" Miss Edwards asked "It's just family stuff" Savannah replied. "Come on you can talk to me, it's what I'm here for and if its making you this upset, then I need to know" Miss Edwards said "It's my big sister" Savannah replied "What about her?" Miss Edwards asked, Savannah looked at Madi, Savannah didn't want to say anything "Her sister has fallen ill and Sav can't go see her because she lives in Australia and she can't get a hold of her aunt or her uncle" Madi replied.

"Savannah, you should have just told me" Miss Edwards said "Miss, I couldn't say anything" Savannah replied "Savannah if you want you can work in here today and Madi can bring your work along, or I can give you a note that explains to your teacher the situation and that if you do get a bit upset that you are allowed to leave and that Madi can go with you" Miss Edwards said.

"Can I have a note" Savannah asked "Yeah of course and also if you leave then come here okay" Miss Edwards replied "Yes Miss, we will" Madi and Savannah said. "Here you go" Miss Edwards said before handing Savannah a note "Thank you Miss" Savannah said "Talk to me if anything happens please" Miss Edwards said "I will Miss" Savannah said as the two girls stood up to leave.

"Madi can I quickly speak to you, Savannah you can head to history" Miss Edwards asked "Yeah Miss, I'll see you in history Sav" Madi replied "See you in history Mads" Savannah said before she left the office and towards her history class. "Okay so, are you still going for dinner at your ex-foster parents tonight?" Miss Edwards asked, "Yeah I am Miss" Madi replied with a really sad voice "What's wrong?"

Miss Edwards asked. "What makes you think something is wrong" Madi replied "One when I asked you about your ex-foster parents you lost eye contact and two your voice went very sad so what's wrong" Miss Edwards said.

"I need to tell my sisters I'm leaving them when I see them tonight and I just feel so guilty I mean I am the last person that is family that is here and loves them" Madi replied still avoiding eye contact with Miss Edwards. "Hey look at me" Miss Edwards said before Madi made eye contact with her "Miss is this going to take long I need to get to history?" Madi asked "You still have 15 minutes before the bell rings so no, listen Madi you have nothing to feel guilty about, this is for you, you don't like it here so you need to leave and it's for you and you only Madi and you need to remember that, your sisters will be absolutely fine here" Miss Edwards said. "I know Miss, but my sisters are still very young and they will feel like I abandoned them" Madi replied.

"That might be the case but Madi I know you love your sisters, everyone knows you love them but Madi this is for you. Now get your butt to Savannah and I'll see you at lunch" Miss Edwards said before laughing "Bye Miss" Madi said before heading out the door "Bye Madi" Miss Edwards replied even though Madi had already left.

Madi arrived at history 15 minutes early, just for the fact that Sav was there "Hey Mrs Glen do you mind if I sit in here until class starts" Madi asked "No of course not Madi, in you come" Mrs Glen replied before Madi walked in and sat next to Savannah. "Mrs Glen what did you have for your breakfast this morning?" Madi asked "Oh I had some eggs, bacon, toast, orange juice and some coffee. How about you girls?" Mrs Glen replied "I had some porridge and banana" Savannah said "I had toast and strawberry jam" Madi replied. "Sound nice" Mrs Glen said "So Miss are you going to miss me when I leave" Madi asked "Of course I will Madi" Mrs Glen replied "Mads when do you leave, I know you changed it" Savannah asked. "I leave on Monday" Madi replied "That soon" Savannah said "Yeah, I know" Madi replied.

"Well Madi, how would you feel of doing your presentation a little early because you won't be here" Mrs Glen asked, "When will I do it Miss and how will I finish it because I need to see my sisters and I need to pack" Madi asked. "Well we are in history tomorrow so how about then and I will just allow you and Hunter to do a PowerPoint instead of a poster and I'll speak to Mr Vandelay and ask if I can take you and Hunter out of some of your classes today so that you can finish it before tomorrow how does that sound" Mrs Glen replied. "Yeah Mrs Glen, that's fine, can you say to Hunter as well please" Madi asked "Yes of course Madi" Mrs Glen replied before the bell rang.

Madi moved back to her seat and everyone else walked in "Right you lot, posters today. I need to speak to Hunter and Madi outside please, everyone else get into your pairs and start working" Mrs Glen said before Madi and Hunter headed outside "Miss, are we in trouble?" Hunter asked with panic in his voice before Madi laughed "No Hunter, you aren't in trouble" Mrs Glen replied with laughing. "Hunter you worry so easily" Madi replied with laughing.

"Why is everyone laughing, what have I missed?" Hunter asked, "Never mind Hunter" Madi replied while laughing. "So the reason I asked to speak to you was Madi is moving away as you know and you won't be able to do your poster so what I was suggesting to Madi earlier, you can do a PowerPoint instead and present it tomorrow if that's okay" Mrs Glen asked.

"Yeah that's completely fine and Madi still can't believe you are leaving on Monday" Hunter replied, "Wait I never told you I was leaving then and neither did Mrs Glen, how did you know?" Madi questioned "I overheard Miss Davis and Miss Edwards talking about it" Hunter replied "And you didn't think to check that it was correct" Madi snapped. "Madi, there is no need to snap" Mrs Glen said, "I'm sorry Hunter, it's just getting to me" Madi replied "It's okay Madi, I get it must be difficult" Hunter said "It is hard" Madi replied as a few tears rolled down her face. "Madi why are you crying" Hunter asked "Mrs Glen, can I go to the toilet please?" Madi asked "Yeah of course on you go" Mrs Glen replied "Thanks Miss" Madi replied before she ran to the toilet "Miss is Madi okay" Hunter asked "She will be fine, now back in" Mrs Glen replied before her and Hunter walked back in.

Madi reached the toilet, she cried some more and then washed her face before Miss Edwards walked in "I heard there is an upset Madi in here" Miss Edwards said "I'm fine Miss, I've calmed down" Madi replied. "I know you are in history but come with me" Miss Edwards said "Okay miss" Madi replied before her and Madi headed out of the toilet and towards the music room "Right Madi, this school is very fortunate to have a music room and a recording studio" Miss Edwards said as she opened the music room door.

"Miss why are we here?" Madi asked "Well I thought since running and dancing are ones I've seen you do, I thought I could hear you sing if that's okay with you" Miss Edwards replied "Miss I would love to" Madi said. "Right get in there" Miss Edwards replied before Madi walked into the recording studio with the microphone "Miss this is amazing" Madi said. "It is, what song are you doing" Miss Edwards asked, "When I look at you by Miley Cyrus" Madi replied "Okay time to sing" Miss Edwards said before she started playing the song.

Madi started to sing before Miss Edwards pulled out her phone and messaged Mr Stevenson "Come to the recording studio now if you don't have a class" The message said. At this point Madi was so into the song her eyes were closed and she was in her moment "Yeah, when my world is falling apart, when there's no light to break the dark, that's when I, I, I look at you…" Madi sang before Mr Stevenson walked in. Madi's eyes were still close and didn't realise Mr Stevenson was there "Wow, is there anything this girl can't do" Mr Stevenson said, "Honest this girl keeps everything hidden I'm surprised we even know what her interests are" Miss Edwards replied. "She is an amazing singer" Mr Stevenson said "Yeah, she kept this one quiet" Miss Edwards replied Madi finished singing and walked out of the recording studio.

"That was amazing Madi" Miss Edwards said

"Thank you, Miss, Hi Mr Stevenson what did you think?" Madi asked

"I loved it Madi" Mr Stevenson said

"Thank you, sir," Madi replied

"Okay Miss Madi, are you ready to talk" Miss Edwards asked

"Yeah I am Miss" Madi replied

"Okay let's sit here" Miss Edwards said before pointing at the chairs that were laid out from the school band rehearsal. "Okay miss" Madi replied before she sat down. Mr Stevenson went to leave "Where are you going?" Miss Edwards asked "I didn't think Madi would want me to be here for this" Mr Stevenson replied "Sir, come sit down I don't mind you staying" Madi said before Mr Stevenson sat down. "So why were you upset?" Miss Edwards asked.

"Well me and Hunter are doing our project tomorrow instead of Monday, but when me and Mrs Glen asked him if it was okay, he was like I still can't believe that you are leaving on Monday, but I hadn't told him that I was leaving on Monday and I asked him how he heard that and he said that he overheard you and Miss Davis talking about and I snapped.

I didn't mean to and he said that he understands that it is difficult but he doesn't, no one does and I feel alone and no one can understand how hard this is I mean I'm leaving my sisters who aren't even over the age of 10. I mean they won't understand and its starting to get too real to say the least" Madi replied, "I know you feel alone but you have loads of people here who care for you. I mean me, Mr Stevenson, Miss Davis, Mr Vandelay, Mrs Glen, even Mr Brown and many more and your friends god they care for you so much Madi.

You might feel alone with this, but you aren't, okay" Miss Edwards said as a tear fell down Madi's cheek "Aww Madi, don't cry" Mr Stevenson said "I will be crying so much tonight" Madi replied as she wiped the tear away. "Have you spoken to Olivia yet" Miss Edwards asked, "Yeah but I am not sure if what the plan is for me to get there"

Madi replied "I'll take you if you want and I'll pick you and then, I've heard what has happened and then I can prepare the staff for how you will be, how does that sound" Miss Edwards said. "You wouldn't mind Miss" Madi asked "No of course I wouldn't Madi" Miss Edwards replied, "Yes please Miss" Madi said.

"Okay I'll wait for you in the office and when you are finished come to the office and we will go" Miss Edwards said, "Okay Miss, thank you. Thank you, sir," Madi replied "Why are you thanking me I just listened" Mr Stevenson said before laughing. "You don't need to thank us Madi honest. It's what our job is" Miss Edwards said "I know but still I need to give you some thanks, which is why I have something for both of you in the schoolhouse" Madi said.

"Madi you didn't need to do that" Mr Stevenson said "I wanted to, I haven't been here long but I know amazing, supportive and caring teachers when I met them" Madi replied. "Aww Madi, we know an amazing pupil when we met her" Miss Edwards said "Thank you Miss" Madi replied, "Okay so how about we walk you back to history" Miss Edwards asked "Yeah please" Madi replied before her, Miss Edwards and Mr Stevenson left the music room and headed towards the history class.

They reached the history class and Miss Edwards knocked on the door, Mrs Glen then walked out "Madi are you okay?" Mrs Glen asked "I am now Mrs Glen" Madi replied "Mr Vandelay also says that it is fine that you go to a computing room to work on your PowerPoint and you are also allowed out during PE and one period of English and one period of maths if you don't get it finished" Mrs Glen said. "Okay Mrs Glen, also where is Savannah?" Madi asked as she looked in the class and noticed that Savannah wasn't there "She went to the toilet" Mrs Glen replied as Madi looked at Miss Edwards worried "On you go" Miss Edwards said "Thank you Miss" Madi replied as she ran away.

She reached the toilets, "Hey Sav, you in here?" Madi asked before she heard sniffles "Yeah" Savannah replied before she walked out the toilet cubicle "Hey what's wrong?" Madi asked "Here" Savannah replied before handing Madi her phone, Madi read the messages to herself and it was Savannah's aunt to say that Savannah's sister deteriorated really fast and unfortunately died. "Sav, come on, let's go to Miss Edwards office and you can phone your aunt", Madi said "I-I don't want to m-move. I can't m-move" Savannah struggled to say through her tears "Can I go Miss Edwards" Madi asked before Savannah nodded.

Madi ran quicker than she ever ran to the history class to where Miss Edwards, Mrs Glen and Mr Stevenson still were "Miss Edwards you need to come quick its Savannah" Madi said trying to catch her breath "What about her?" Miss Edwards asked "Her sister didn't…" Madi said before Miss Edwards interrupted "Okay, Jason you go get Vanessa because she is Savannah's parent figure, I'll go with Madi and see if I can get Savannah in the office and I'll message you where we are" Miss Edwards said.

"Okay message me where you are" Mr Stevenson said before he ran to get Miss Davis "Come on Miss" Madi said as she started to walk away "I'm coming Madi" Miss Edwards said as she started running to catch up with Madi.

They reached the toilet and Savannah was sitting on the floor sobbing "Sav, hey it's me and Miss Edwards" Madi said, so Savannah knew who was coming in "Hey Savannah,

I need you to take a few deep breaths okay" Miss Edwards said softly as she sat in front of Savannah "Can I go get her a bottle of water from your office please Miss" Madi asked.

"Yeah, you know where they are anyway" Miss Edwards replied before Madi walked out the toilets and towards Miss Edwards office. "Madi, are they still in the toilet?" Mr Stevenson asked "Yeah I'm just going to get Savannah a bottle of water" Madi replied "Miss Davis, you go ahead. I'll catch up" Mr Stevenson said "Okay" Miss Davis replied as she started to run down the corridor. Madi and Mr Stevenson entered the office.

"Madi, you seem upset. I know I'm not Miss Edwards, but you can talk to me" Mr Stevenson said "I'm fine sir" Madi replied as tears started to pool in her eyes "Madi, come on I'm on your side" Mr Stevenson said. "I feel exactly what Savannah feels every day. I miss my sister and my brother" Madi replied with her voice breaking "Madi, I understand that it can't be easy to help your friend when you went through something like it" Mr Stevenson said. "I want my mum and dad back" Madi replied with tears "I know, I know. Do you want me to get Miss Edwards" Mr Stevenson asked "Yeah please sir" Madi replied with more tears "Okay, wait here" Mr Stevenson said before he went to leave.

"Sir take a water bottle for Savannah please" Madi said "Yes of course" Mr Stevenson replied before he left leaving a very upset Madi in the office. Madi was trying not to cry when she was helping Savannah. Savannah was already upset; her crying wouldn't have helped anything. "Madi, I'm here, it's okay" Miss Edwards said as she took Madi in for a hug. "Miss, is Savannah okay?" Madi asked "Madi, you are some girl, you are upset and in tears and you are asking about someone else" Miss Edwards replied "I'm kind of trying to avoid talking" Madi said "You need to talk about it" Miss Edwards replied.

"I know but I really don't want to" Madi said "Come on, talk to me because this will be one of the last times I get to help you" Miss Edwards said, "Fine, I feel for Savannah, I was in her shoes with my brother he was only four days old and I was only three, I mean how do you think my parents felt when they had to tell little me that my little brother was going to die in like less than a week" Madi replied with tears.

"Madi, listen I understand that this hard but I mean you have helped Savannah so much today" Miss Edwards said before the bell rang "Hunter, my project" Madi said. "Hunter's working on it don't worry, he just wants you to be okay" Miss Edwards replied "Miss when will this stop happening, I mean nothing can set me off in tears" Madi asked "I don't know Madi, I honestly wish I did because I hate seeing you upset" Miss Edwards replied. "I can't wait until I see my sisters tonight, I have got them all a present" Madi said "That's the girl I know, a caring big sister" Miss Edwards replied before Madi smiled.

"Madi now that you have spoken to Miss Edwards, how do you feel?" Mr
Stevenson asked
"I feel a lot better, thank you Sir" Madi replied.
"Do you want to go catch up with Hunter?" Miss Edwards asked
"Yeah, where is he?" Madi replied
"In the computer room, next to Mrs Glen classroom" Mr Stevenson said

"Okay, thank you Miss, thank you Sir" Madi said

"Your aunt is bringing McDonalds here, so you and girls just head here at lunch"

Miss Edwards said

"Okay Miss, I'll tell the girls, bye" Madi said before walking out.

"That is one strong girl" Mr Stevenson stated, "Yeah it is" Miss Edwards replied.

Madi reached the computer room and took a deep breath "Hey Hunter, how's the project coming along?" Madi said "Yeah it's nearly done" Hunter replied, "Really" Madi said shocked "Yeah I work really fast and I've been working on for nearly an hour now" Hunter replied. "Sorry for leaving you" Madi said "It's fine, I understand" Hunter replied "Is my stuff still in history?" Madi asked "No, I brought it, here it is" Hunter replied, "Thanks Hunter" Madi said before Hunter handed her stuff. "So do you want to see the PowerPoint" Hunter asked "Yeah of course" Madi replied "Sit here" Hunter said before pulling the chair beside him out. "Thanks" Madi replied before sitting down "Okay here you go" Hunter said before running through the PowerPoint "That's amazing Hunter, well done, you can take all the credit for the presentation honest" Madi said "No thank you, it's our project" Hunter replied "Are you sure?" Madi asked "Yeah, as I will keep saying it's our project" Hunter replied "Thank you Hunter" Madi said.

The two finished up the project and started to rehearse it so they weren't reading off the PowerPoint, "Okay so you do the introduction and I'll do the conclusion just because you do the introduction better than me" Madi said. "Yeah that's perfect I like the introduction better than the conclusion" Hunter replied "Okay so I am going to ask Mrs Glen if she has any spare paper and we can make flashcards so we can read from them if you want" Madi said "Yes that's perfect" Hunter replied "Okay I'll be two minutes" Madi said before she left the computing room and headed next door to Mrs Glen's classroom. Madi knocked on Mrs Glen's door "In you come" Mrs Glen shouted before Madi walked in "Hey Mrs Glen, I was just wondering if you had any flashcards or paper so we can make flashcards so we can write down what we need for the project?" Madi asked.

"I do have flashcards actually, here's a bundle for you" Mrs Glen replied before handing Madi a pile of flashcards "Thank you Mrs Glen" Madi said, "Is the project done yet?" Mrs Glen asked "Yeah" Madi replied "Good I can't wait to see it" Mrs Glen said "I can't wait to do it but I better get back to Hunter so we can practise" Madi replied. "Well I'll catch up with you later see you later Madi" Mrs Glen said "Bye Mrs Glen" Madi replied before leaving Mrs Glen's classroom and heading back to the computing room.

"Have you got them?" Hunter asked "Yeah, here" Madi replied before handing Hunter half the pile "Okay so what slides am I doing?" Madi asked, "Well excluding the conclusion and introduction there is 10 slides so split it in half so you can do slide 3,5,7 and 9 and I'll do 2,4,6, and 8. How does that sound?" Hunter asked, "Perfect" Madi replied before they copied the slides they needed to do, by this time there was only 20 minutes till break "Do we go to PE?" Hunter asked.

"We only have 20 minutes I don't see the point but if you want to we can go" Madi replied "No let's just get to know each other better, I mean I know somethings about you but not a lot" Hunter said. "Do you want to play 2 truths and a lie" Madi asked "I love that game, you go first" Hunter replied "Okay so one I have four sisters, two my birthday is the 27th of April and three I really enjoy football" Madi said. "Number two is the lie" Hunter replied "No it's the three, I do enjoy it just not like it, like I enjoy running, dancing and tennis" Madi said "Your birthday is three days after mine" Hunter said "Your turn Hunter" Madi said.

"Okay one I sing, two my birthday is the 24th of April and three I have four older siblings" Hunter said "Number one is the lie" Madi replied "No it's three" Hunter said. "Wait you sing, no way" Madi replied "Yeah, I write songs and do covers I do enjoy it, I just don't tell many people because they wind me up about it" Hunter said. "Wow, I mean I wow. I thought you were a singer" Madi replied, "We should totally do a duet" Hunter said "Yeah, I need to speak to Miss Edwards about drama class so we might be able to do some sort of performance thing" Madi replied. "Yeah" Hunter said. The two talked about many different things until bell rang. "Break time" Madi said, "Finally, I am starving" Hunter replied, "Honestly same" Madi said as she pushed her chair "Let's go" Hunter replied as they left. Madi and Hunter walked together until Madi met up with Jodi, Addison, Morag, Paige, Darcy, Brogan and Abby.

"Hey Mads" Jodi said

"Hey, are you all okay" Madi asked

"Yeah, are you Mads?" Jodi replied

"Yeah, surprisingly. How was PE?" Madi asked

"It was so bad, we were running again, what were you doing" Addison replied

"Me and Hunter were working on our project and we got to know each other
better" Madi said

"So, do you like him?" Brogan asked

"No" Madi lied "She is lying, OMG she likes him" Darcy said

"Madi and Hunter up a tree" Addison said

"I don't like him, okay just drop it honestly" Madi replied before slamming her locker and running to the toilets "Look at what you lot have done" Abby said "I'll go" Darcy said "No I'll go" Abby said before she ran to the toilets to see Madi.

Abby reached the toilets and heard two people talking "You shouldn't get a second chance at a family; you shouldn't even be here. You are taking all the teachers attention and what for, so you can cry over your dead parents and siblings and get out of work" The two voices said before Abby walked in. "Rebecca and Jess I should've known" Abby said before Rebecca and Jess rolled their eyes "We didn't do anything" Jess said "Yeah, so it wasn't Rebecca saying that Madi shouldn't get a second chance at a family and she shouldn't be here" Abby said before crossing her arms. "It wasn't meant like that" Rebecca replied "Okay then, and Jess it wasn't you, who said that she gets all the teachers attention and what for, so she can cry over her parents and siblings and get out of work" Abby said.

"I didn't say that" Jess said "Whatever, you are both just bullies, come on Madi lets go" Abby said before Madi ran from behind the two girls and stood behind Abby. "That's it Madi, go cry about your dead parents and how we are bullying you" Rebecca said "Cow" Jess said as Madi and

Abby left. "Where do want to go and who do you need?" Abby asked, "I want Miss Edwards, please tell her I'm at the door and she should know what I mean" Madi replied. "Okay I'll go say and you go where you need to go" Abby said "Thanks Abby" Madi replied before her and Abby went their separate ways.

Madi ran up to Miss Edwards classroom and went to the stairs by the classroom where she went whenever she was upset. Madi had tears falling from her face, Miss Edwards came behind Madi and she didn't realise that Miss Edwards was there "Hey Miss Madi" Miss Edwards said giving Madi a small fright. "Hey Miss" Madi replied before wiping her face to clear the tears, "Sorry didn't mean to give you a fright but a little birdy told me you were upset and wanted me" Miss Edwards said before sitting down next to Madi. "It's fine and yeah" Madi replied.

"What's wrong?" Miss Edwards asked "Rebecca and Jess were picking on me again and saying that I don't deserve a second chance at a family and I shouldn't be here because I take all the teachers attention and I cry over my parents and my siblings just to get out of doing work." Madi said as her tears started to stream down her face "Oh Madi come here" Miss Edwards replied as she put her arms out for Madi came in for a hug "Addie, Brogan and Darcy were winding me up, but they didn't mean it" Madi said.

"What were they winding you up about?" Miss Edwards asked "Its fine" Madi replied "Come on tell me" Miss Edwards said before Madi broke out the hug "Fine, Hunter has a crush on me and we were getting to know each other better when we were working on our project and I have a slight crush on him and they were winding me up about it"

Madi replied. "Madi no way, he's such a nice boy, you would be a cute couple" Miss Edwards said "Well it can't happen anyway because I'm leaving" Madi replied.

"Well you will be back to see your sisters and you have facetime and phones" Miss Edwards said, "I know but then I don't know if he would like to long distance and I don't know if I want to either" Madi replied. "Well you can only shoot your shot" Miss Edwards said "I can't do that and I won't do that" Madi replied "Okay just don't get angry I'm just trying to help you" Miss Edwards said "I know I'm sorry Miss" Madi replied.

"Are you feeling better now because I want you to be able to enjoy your last few classes before you leave" Miss Edwards asked, "Yeah, also drama tomorrow can I do my singing thing for everyone" Madi replied "I will ask Mr Vandelay but I don't think he will have a problem with it but tomorrow will be an emotional day for you okay so everyone knows that" Miss Edwards said before the bell rang. "English time" Madi said before she stood up "Come on I'll walk you to the class and how about I take you and Hunter so you can talk to him" Miss Edwards said before she stood up. "Yes, Miss because you aren't going to let this one go are you?" Madi asked "Nope I am not" Miss Edwards replied as her and Madi headed towards Mr Stevenson's class.

Chapter 8 - Relationship

They arrived at the class "Mr Stevenson sorry for being a pest but would it be possible to borrow Hunter for two minutes" Miss Edwards asked. "Yeah of course, Hunter Miss Edwards wants you" Mr Stevenson replied "Madi is also coming with me so is it possible if she leaves her bag" Miss Edwards asked, "Of course" Mr Stevenson replied before Madi left her bag in the class and walked out to meet up with Miss Edwards and Hunter.

"Hunter you aren't in trouble don't worry. I just think you and Madi should talk about something so use my office" Miss Edwards said "Okay" Hunter replied before he and Madi headed down to Miss Edwards office. They both arrived at Miss Edwards office and took a seat "So what do we need to talk about?" Hunter asked "Well I heard a rumour that you had a crush on me is that true" Madi asked before Hunter looked away and his face turned red with embarrassment. "Yeah Madi, I like you and I have since the day you started" Hunter replied, "You don't need to be embarrassed" Madi said.

"Do you like me?" Hunter asked "Yeah I do" Madi replied "So the real question now that we have confessed how we feel about each other is. Will you be my girlfriend?"

Hunter asked "Of course I will" Madi replied with a huge smile on her face. "So are we going to tell people or not?" Hunter asked "Yeah of course we will but also you don't mind doing long distance" Madi replied. "I don't care I'm with my favourite girl" Hunter said "Come on you let's go find Miss Edwards" Madi replied before she pushed her chair in and headed out the office with Hunter behind her.

They started walking to Miss Edwards classroom to see if she was there. Hunter then grabbed Madi's hand.

"Hunter" Madi said

"What?" Hunter questioned

"Nothing" Madi replied before she let go of Hunters hand

"Excuse me" Hunter said

"What?" Madi asked

"You let go off my hand" Hunter replied before Madi playfully rolled her eyes

"You are so needy, come on" Madi replied before taking Hunters hand.

They arrived at Miss Edwards classroom and Madi knocked on the door "In you come" Miss Edwards said "Only us Miss" Madi said after her and Hunter walked in "So how did it go?" Miss Edwards asked "Umm...well" Madi replied as she grabbed Hunters hand "No way" Miss Edwards said smiling "Yip, we are together" Hunter replied. "I'm so happy for you guys" Miss Edwards said. "You are the first person we have told" Madi replied "I feel privileged, I can't believe it" Miss Edwards said. "We should get back to class" Hunter said, "Yeah we should, actually I need to speak to Miss Edwards about something else so you go and I'll be along in like five minutes okay" Madi replied "Okay babe" Hunter said before leaving.

"Did he just say that" Madi asked looking shocked "Yeah he did" Miss Edwards replied. "Wow, anyway, will I come to your office once I finish my maths class" Madi asked "Yeah" Miss Edwards replied "I need to stop at the schoolhouse so I can get the girls presents and get changed if that's okay with you Miss" Madi said. "Yeah how about I come get you early from maths so we can get you sorted" Miss Edwards asked, "Miss that would be amazing please" Madi replied, "Okay I'll come get you a little early. Now Miss Madi get back to English please" Miss Edwards said, "Thank you Miss, see you at lunch" Madi replied "See you at lunch Madi" Miss Edwards said before Madi left and headed back to English.

"Okay I need everyone to get into pairs and I will allow you to pick your own but I do want to pair certain people up which will be Jess with Rebecca, Madi with Hunter, Jodi with Darcy and Hudson with Brogan" Mr Stevenson said before everyone got into their pairs and Hunter came to sit with Madi.

"You do realise if Mr Stevenson didn't pair us I would pick to go with you anyway" Hunter whispered to Madi "Yes" Madi whispered back "Right, I didn't really need you to get into pair but I thought it would be more fun" Mr Stevenson said. "What are we doing sir?" Jodi asked "We are going to be talking about our families today because it was either write an essay or talk about them so I thought since we have just about a period and bit that is enough time to write them and hear some today and we will hear the rest on Monday." "Is that okay with everyone?" Mr Stevenson said before Madi raised her hand.

"Sir" Madi said "Yeah Madi", "Can I go first please?" Madi asked "Yeah tell me when you have finished writing it" Mr Stevenson replied "I will sir" Madi said before grabbing her English jotter and a blue pen. Everyone was working through their talks. This kind of thing was difficult for Madi, I mean what could she say. The more she thought about it the more she made herself feel sick, Hunter noticed that her hand and leg was shaking.

"Hey I know this is difficult but you have this okay I believe in you babe" Hunter whispered to Madi, "I just don't know what to write" Madi whispered back still with her hand shaking. "Hey, give me your hand" Hunter whispered before he put his hand out "Thank you baby" Madi whispered back before placing her hand in his. The pair continued writing with their free hands before Hunter noticed that Madi had stopped writing.

"You okay Mads?" Hunter asked "Yeah I'm done" Madi replied "Say to Mr Stevenson" Hunter said "Sir I'm finished" Madi said "Perfect, come to the front" Mr Stevenson said before the bell rang for the end of period three "Can I talk to you outside for two minutes sir before I do the talk?" Madi asked "Yes of course, everyone keep writing" Mr Stevenson replied before him and Madi walked outside. "I can't do this talk if Rebecca and Jess are in the class.

I already had a run in with them about family" Madi said, "Listen you can do this even if they are in the class because everyone else in that class believes in you especially Hunter" Mr Stevenson replied. "Did Miss Edwards tell you?" Madi asked "Yeah" Mr Stevenson replied. "Of course she did, actually sir can I see if she wants to listen to my talk please it would make me less stressed please" Madi asked "Yeah on you go" Mr Stevenson said before Madi ran to Miss Edwards class which was only down the corridor from Mr Stevenson's.

"Woah Miss Madi, where is the fire?" Miss Edwards said after Madi ran into her class "There isn't one but we are doing talks in English about family and I'm first and I was wondering if you would come and listen to it, please Miss" Madi said. "Of course, let's go" Miss Edwards replied before her and Madi headed back to the class. "Okay, first person doing the talks is Madi and want everyone to give her the undivided attention she deserves and also show her respect please" Mr Stevenson said before he went to sit at the desk behind Rebecca and Jess beside Miss Edwards.

"Hi, so Mr Stevenson asked us to write about our families and let's just say I had a difficult time putting my family on paper, but I am going to tell you what my parents were like and what my sisters are like. My parents were amazing, I don't know how they coped with me and my sisters because we were a bit of a handful but they both came from big families, they were the best parents I could ever ask for. I'm glad I got them, but from the day they died I have never been the same and neither have my sisters, but I am getting there and my sisters.

Now my sisters we have Summer, Autumn, Lilly and Grace and we also had Jessie but she died in the crash alongside my parents, Summer is nine and is a very sensitive and sweet girl, Autumn is seven and is a complete ball of energy and will always do anything she can to make you laugh and smile. Lilly is six and has the best smile and always gives you hugs and finally Grace who has just turned one and was Jessie's twin and is the baby of us. She just always giggles no matter what.

They live with my ex foster parents Olivia and Simon who are so nice. Now that's my family but I also want to really quickly mention my schoolhouse family, I love all of you guys so much. I can't believe I'm leaving you all but thanks to a lot of you I have been able to have another family and people I can turn to. I got a chance to meet my boyfriend Hunter so without you guys we wouldn't be together so yeah that my families. "Any questions?" Madi said "When did you and Hunter make it official?" Darcy asked "At the start of the period I decided that this would be the best to tell you all at the same time" Madi replied "I can't believe it, finally you both caved" Jodi said before Madi laughed "Yeah" Madi replied.

"Imagine not actually having parents at least with us we can go home and see our parents she can't because you know they died. Wow so sad" Rebecca said to Jess with a sarcastic tone "And she thinks Hunters going to stay with her. "Wow" Jess replied before the two laughed. "Rebecca and Jess, let's go for a walk to Mr Vandelay's office shall we" Miss Edwards said before the two girls rolled their eyes and walked out with Miss Edwards behind them. "That was amazing Madi, that took some real courage and confidence" Mr Stevenson said while smiling, "Thanks sir, I can't believe I actually done it" Madi replied before she went to sit back down.

"Do you lot know what, since Madi gave an amazing talk on something that is hard for her to talk about. How about instead of listening to other people's talks we have a break? We only have half an hour anyway" Mr Stevenson said "Can we please sir?" Jodi asked. "Yeah you can sit on your phones or do homework but I don't really want you all moving so please stay in the seat you are in" Mr Stevenson replied. "Thank you sir" Everyone said, "You lot deserve it because you have been working so hard lately and you haven't had much praise or treats for the amount of work a lot of you are putting in" Mr Stevenson said.

Madi and Hunter were sitting on their phones.

"Babe" Hunter said

"Yeah" Madi replied

"How about we take some pictures together" Hunter suggested

"Yes" Madi replied before the two were taking pictures of the two of them

"I am going to put this one as my lock screen because it's my favourite one" Hunter said

"Okay I'm going to do the same" Madi replied

"Madi come here a second" Mr Stevenson said before Madi got out her seat and walked to Mr Stevenson's desk "Yeah sir" Madi said. "Would you like to take my second years tomorrow?" I only have them for a period but I know they would love to see you Mr Stevenson asked, "OMG sir I would love to what period do you have them?" Madi replied. "I have them period 1 is that okay?" Mr Stevenson asked, "Yes sir, can I do any lesson I want with them" Madi replied "Yip" Mr Stevenson said. Madi went back to her seat smiling "I love your smile" Hunter said "Thank you" Madi replied before her and Hunter continued playing on their phones.

The bell rang for the end of the two periods "Right you lot, on you go and I'll see you on Monday for more talks and

Madi I'll see you first thing tomorrow" Mr Stevenson said "Yeah sir" Madi replied. "Bye sir" Darcy said "Bye Darcy" Mr Stevenson replied, "Bye sir" Madi said "Bye Madi" Mr Stevenson replied before Madi headed out the classroom where Hunter was waiting for her.

"You didn't have to wait for me" Madi said fixing her bag "Here give me your jacket" Hunter replied before Madi rolled her eyes "Fine" Madi said before handing Hunter her jacket. "Let's go for lunch?" Hunter replied before grabbing Madi's hand and headed down to the main area with all the lockers.

"Hey lovebirds" Jodi said joking "Shut up Jodi" Madi replied in a joking tone "You two are cute together" Abby said "Thanks Abby" Madi replied before Miss Edwards walked along "Girls, come get your lunch" Miss Edwards said. "I need to speak to my auntie so let's go and Hunter come with me" Madi replied before the girls and Hunter headed to Miss Edwards office.

"I just got chicken nuggets, cheeseburgers and chips" Cassandra said after everyone entered. "Aunt Cass, you got a minute?" Madi asked "Yeah always" Cassandra replied before her and Madi headed out to the lockers "Okay don't freak out but see the boy that's with Jodi well he's my boyfriend as of today but please Aunt Cass don't freak out" Madi said. "Does he make happy?" Cassandra asked "He does, he really does" Madi replied with a smile, "If he makes you happy that makes me happy, also he can stay for McDonalds I got too much anyway" Cassandra said. "Thank you, Aunt Cass," Madi replied before her and Cassandra walked back into the office.

"Why hasn't anyone had anything yet?" Cassandra asked "Miss Edwards and Darcy are away to get paper plates, cups, napkins and juice" Jodi replied. "Hunter come over here" Madi said before Hunter walked over to Madi and Cassandra "Nice to meet you Miss" Hunter said to Cassandra "Hunter call me Cassie or Cass please", "Nice to meet you Cassie" Hunter replied "Same to you, also hurt my niece, I hurt you" Cassandra said "Aunt Cass" Madi said sternly "Sorry" Cassandra replied before Miss Edwards and Darcy walked back in.

"We have plates and juice and cups and napkins" Miss Edwards said "Come on you lot dig in" Cassandra said before everyone grabbed a plate and helped themselves to the food. "So Mads, are you excited to go stay with Cassie?" Jodi asked "Yeah I actually am" Madi replied before Payton walked in with Cole. "Hey, Mister Cole was being fussy, so we were dealing with him" Payton said.

"You are here that's all that matters, can I hold Cole and feed him chips please Payt" Madi asked "Yeah of course, here you go" Payton replied before handing Cole to Madi. "Hi baby" Madi said to Cole while walking back over to where she was sitting which was with Hunter.

"Who is Madi sitting next to?" Payton asked "That's her boyfriend Hunter as of today" Cassandra replied "They look cute together" Payton said "They do don't they" Cassandra replied before walking out the office where everyone was. "Payt where did my Aunt Cass go" Madi asked "She left I don't know where she went" Payton replied. "Should I go get her?" Madi asked.

"How about me and you both go?" Miss Edwards replied "Please Miss" Madi replied "Or I go with Miss Edwards and you all stay here" Payton said "Yeah I'll watch Cole" Madi replied before Miss Edwards and Payton left. Madi just stood at the door with Cole in her arms "Mads, you good?" Jodi asked "Yeah, yeah I'm fine" Madi replied. "You sure" Jodi asked "Yeah, come Cole let's get chips" Madi replied before she walked back to where she was sitting.

"Baby are you okay?" Hunter asked "Yeah I'm fine, will you watch Cole for two minutes. I just need a little air" Madi replied. "I'll do it Mads" Jodi said "Thanks, I'll only be two minutes. Cole be a good boy okay" Madi replied "He will" Jodi said before Madi ran out the office.

She ran to a bench outside and sat down to compose herself, what if her Aunt didn't want her to come stay, what if she didn't settle in Frostford, what if she didn't like her new school, what if her and cousins have a fight, what if she couldn't see her sister. All these thoughts ran through Madi's head, she could feel her eyes filling with tears and her leg shaking and her breathing getting heavy.

Just then Mr Stevenson noticed Madi with her head in her hands.

"Hey Madi, you okay?" He asked

"Yeah" Madi replied still not looking at him

"Madi, come on look at me" Mr Stevenson said before Madi lifted her head with tears

streaming down her face

"Like I said sir, I'm okay" Madi replied while wiping a tear away

"Madi, you are crying so somethings wrong" Mr Stevenson said before sitting next to Madi

"My auntie walked out the office and I don't know why and all these thoughts ran through my head, like maybe my auntie doesn't want me to come stay, what if I don't settle, what if I don't like my new school, what if me and my cousins have a fight and what if I couldn't see my sisters" Madi replied.

"Hey, your auntie is so excited for you to come stay with her it's all she ever says to Miss Edwards and me and you settled fine here and you will love your new school, but remember you can do anything and it will be like being with your sister if you and your cousins have a fight and you will be able to come see your sisters on the holidays so don't overwhelm yourself" Mr Stevenson said. "Thank you sir, I better get back" Madi replied with a smile "I will see you bright and early tomorrow for your class" Mr Stevenson said "See you bright and early tomorrow" Madi replied before she headed back into the office.

"Hey Mini Marshmallow, you okay?" Cassandra asked "Yeah are you?" Madi replied "Yeah I am, come give me a hug" Cassandra said before Madi ran into her arms "Why did you leave?" Madi asked. "I just needed a little air, you are just growing so fast and I feel like I've missed a lot of your life" Cassandra replied, "I love you Aunt Cass" Madi said "I love you more, now go eat" Cassandra replied before Madi went back to where she was sitting and finished her lunch. The bell for the end of lunch rang "Right you lovely girls and Hunter, head to maths and I'll catch up with you all tomorrow because Madi is doing a performance and you are all invited" Miss Edwards said. "Bye Miss, thanks Cassie" The girls said "No problem girls" Cassandra replied with a smile "I'll see you all later, bye" Madi said "Bye Mads" Payton replied before Madi and Hunter headed out the office.

"I'm leaving early so I can get changed and get my sisters presents" Madi said, "At least you are getting to see them before you leave" Hunter replied "Yeah, it's going to break my heart to say goodbye to them" Madi said before they arrived at maths and joined the line of everyone else waiting to get into class. "You have my number don't you?" Hunter asked "Yeah why" Madi replied "If you need to message me at any time while seeing your sister, just message me and when you come back to the schoolhouse we can talk and cuddle how does that sound" Hunter asked. "That sound's perfect" Madi replied before Mr Skelton let everyone in.

"Right everyone, we are going to work through our textbooks does everyone have theirs" Mr Skelton said. "Sir I've left mine in the house" Brogan replied, "Okay Brogan I've got spare ones, anyone else" Mr Skelton said. "Brogan I've got yours, I forgot to give it to you" Abby said "Thanks sis" Brogan replied "Okay now that's sorted, we are going be doing algebra, so pages one hundred and five to one hundred and eight and I want everyone to at least complete the first three questions by the end of the first period" Mr Skelton said before everyone grabbed their textbooks and jotters out their bags.

Everyone was working through the questions "Sir can you help me with this one?" Katie asked "Yeah of course" Mr Skelton replied before he went over to help Katie. Madi's phone then started ringing it was Olivia "Sir can I please go take this please?" She asked "Yes" Mr Skelton replied before Madi grabbed her phone and walked out.

"Hey, Olivia is everything okay?" Madi asked "Kind of" Olivia replied "What do you mean kind of?" Madi asked "Well Summer, she punched someone at school today" Olivia replied "She did what" Madi said "Yeah and she's suspended for five days" Olivia replied. "When I come tonight, I'll speak to her if that's okay?" Madi said "Yeah, she will probably tell you why she done it" Olivia replied.

"Okay, well I'll speak to her then I'll tell the girls about me leaving" Madi said "See you tonight, also chicken unicorns for dinner is that okay" Olivia said. "That's fine and I'll see you tonight" Madi replied "Bye" Olivia said "Bye" Madi replied before she hung up the phone. Madi walked back in the classroom "Everything okay?" Mr Skelton asked "Yeah" Madi replied before she sat down.

The bell rang for the end of period 5 "Okay where are we at everyone?" Mr Skelton asked "I'm at the end of question four" Madi said "Same" Darcy said "Is everyone on question four or on five" Mr Skelton asked before everyone agreed. "Sir I'm really stuck I'm still on two" Jodi replied "Right everyone keep going and Jodi I'll come help you now" Mr Skelton said before he went over to sit next to Jodi to help her.

"Mads who phoned you" Darcy whispered

"Olivia, Summer decided to punch someone at school" Madi whispered back

"No way" Darcy whispered back

"Yip" Madi whispered

"Girls, focus on your work please" Mr Skelton said

"Sorry sir" Madi and Darcy replied.

There was a knock on the door "Come in" Mr Skelton shouted before Miss Edwards entered "Sorry to interrupt but I was just wondering if I could take Madi" Miss Edwards asked. "Yeah of course" Mr Skelton replied "Madi can you bring all your stuff?" Miss Edwards asked "Yeah" Madi replied before packing up her stuff "Thank you Mr Skelton" Miss Edwards said "No problem, bye Madi" Mr Skelton replied before Miss Edwards and Madi walked out the classroom.

"Miss, you got me really early I still have about thirty-five minutes left" Madi said. "Your Aunt wanted to talk to you so I thought I would come get you so that she could talk to you" Miss Edwards replied, "Okay miss and thank you honestly" Madi said "Come on you and stop thanking me it's my job" Miss Edwards replied. "But then I'm being rude so you know and I've always taught my sisters to be polite even though Summer punched someone today" Madi said "She did what?" Miss Edwards replied "Exactly what I said, I don't know why but I'll speak to her tonight" Madi replied before they reached the office.

"On you go first" Miss Edwards said before Madi walked in "Okay what do you need to talk to me about Aunt Cass" Madi asked "Well how would you feel if Payton was to come live with us?" Cassandra asked. "Wait really" Madi replied "Yip, there is nothing keeping me in Glasgow and there is a course I really want to do in a University in Frostford plus your Aunt Cass is just amazing" Payton said. "She is amazing and I would love that so much honestly" Madi replied with tears in her eyes "Oh don't cry, come here the pair of you" Cassandra replied before Madi and Payton both gave Cassandra a hug.

"I can't believe this, I am so excited" Madi said while smiling "Mads, you do realise that you moving to Frostford will probably be the best thing ever for you and I know you will worry about your sisters but they have a great set of foster parents and this is maybe what you need" Payton replied. "Yeah I just feel like it's my job to protect them now ever since my parents died" Madi said, "We know baby but you are fifteen, you deserve to be a teenager" Cassandra replied.

"Miss Madi, we better go" Miss Edwards said "Okay Miss, I will phone when I get back from seeing my sisters if that's okay Aunt Cass" Madi replied. "Yeah baby" Cassandra said before Madi and Miss Edwards headed out the school and towards Miss Edwards car. They got in the car and headed to the schoolhouse "Do you have your keys?" Miss Edwards asked "Yip" Madi replied before grabbing her keys out her pocket "Right, let's go" Miss Edwards said before turning off the engine and getting out the car.

"Miss, I don't know if I can do this anymore" Madi said as she unlocked the schoolhouse door "Yes you can" Miss Edwards replied before the two of them walked into the schoolhouse "What if I just move without telling them" Madi asked. "Madi, you can't do that, they need to know and they need to find out from you" Miss Edwards replied, "I know, right give me two minutes till I get changed and then you can help me grab my sisters presents if that's okay" Madi asked. "Of course, on you go" Miss Edwards replied before Madi ran upstairs to get changed into her outfit that she left out which was a pink casual top, a pair of leggings, her white trainers and her blue denim jacket.

"Miss, can you come help me?" Madi asked from the top of the stairs "Yeah coming" Miss Edwards replied as she walked upstairs and into Madi's room, "Can you open that suitcase for me please, so I can sort my hair?" Madi asked "Yeah, I love your outfit" Miss Edwards said as Madi was taking her hair out the braids she done this morning.

"Thank you Miss, how many gifts is there in the suitcase?" Madi asked as she scrunched her hair to make sure it was wavy, "There is nine" Miss Edwards replied "That's perfect" Madi said.

"Your hair looks amazing" Miss Edwards said "Thank you Miss, let me put these presents in a bag" Madi replied before grabbing a carrier bag she had in her room and putting the presents in it "Is that you sorted?" Miss Edwards asked "Yeah Miss, let's go" Madi replied before grabbing the bag with the presents in it.

They made their way downstairs "What time is it?" Miss Edwards asked "Just gone five past three" Madi replied "Right, let's head to Olivia and Simon's because the traffic will be mental" Miss Edwards said. "Okay, this is scary" Madi replied before the two of them left the schoolhouse and Madi locked the door.

"What is their address again?" Miss Edwards asked "88 High View Hill" Madi replied "Okay, let me put that into that sat nav and then we can go" Miss Edwards said. "I'll text Olivia and ask her if her and the girls are home" Madi said "Okay let's go" Miss Edwards replied before she started the engine and headed out the schoolhouse carpark.

They arrived at Olivia and Simon house at half past three and Madi messaged Olivia to tell her that she was outside, Olivia came out to the car to meet Madi.

"Madi, I'll pick you up at quarter to six if that's okay" Miss Edwards asked "Yeah that's fine, is that okay with you Olivia" Madi asked "Yeah, now come on these girls are so excited to see you" Olivia replied.

"I'll see you later Miss" Madi said

"Bye Madi" Miss Edwards replied before she drove off

Madi and Olivia walked into the house, "Girls look who is here" Olivia said as the girls came running into the living room, Madi hid behind Olivia "Who mama, there isn't anyone here" Lilly asked. "Are you sure about that Lil" Madi replied "MADI" Lilly shouted before running towards Madi for a hug. "Hey Lil, you okay?" Madi said as she grabbed Lilly and pulled her in for hug "I missed you Madi" Lilly replied. "I missed you too sweetie, now let me give your other sisters a hug" Madi said before she put Lilly down.

"Me next, me next, me next" Autumn said "Come here then Almond" Madi replied as she put her arms out for Autumn to give her a hug "I missed you sissy" Autumn said. "I missed you too munchkin" Madi replied. "Are you here to stay sissy?" Autumn asked "No, sorry Almond, I need to talk to you girls but first Sum I need to talk to you" Madi replied "Girls how about we go into the kitchen and let Summer and Madi talk" Olivia asked, "Okay mama" Autumn replied before her and the girls walked into the kitchen.

"Come on let's sit down on the couch" Madi said before her and Summer sat on the couch, "Let me guess Olivia told you about me punching someone" Summer replied. "Yeah baby, I am not going to get angry with you I just want to know why you done it" Madi said before Summer looked at the floor. "You will get angry" Summer replied "I would never get angry with you without a good reason, baby you know that don't you, now please tell me why" Madi said.

"She was picking on me and I just got angry, I'm sorry Madi" Summer replied, "Hey baby, don't be sorry, I just wish you had told your teacher or someone else, did you tell the headteacher" Madi said. "No, I couldn't she would think

I'm just making excuses" Summer replied, "Baby listen you should have told the headteacher or even better told Olivia and Simon, they both want to make sure you are okay" Madi said. "But they aren't my mum and dad" Summer replied "Baby, mum and dad are never coming back so Olivia and Simon are the closest thing to our mum and dad okay baby and you need to trust them and tell them things" Madi said. "Okay Madi" Summer replied "Promise me, you will talk to them" Madi said "I promise" Summer replied "Pinkie promise" Madi said with her pinkie out "Pinkie promise" Summer said while locking her pinkie with Madi.

"Can we come in now?" Olivia said while poking her head out the side of the kitchen door "Yeah in you come" Madi replied before Olivia and the girls walked out the kitchen. "Do you want to talk to the girls now while I go check dinner" Olivia asked "Yeah, girls come sit down" Madi replied "I'm only in the kitchen if you need anything, now girls please listen to Madi" Olivia said before walking into the kitchen.

"Madi what do you have to tell us?" Summer asked "Okay girls, you know how I live in the schoolhouse, well do you remember Aunt Cass" Madi replied. "Auntie Cass is my favourite Aunt" Autumn said, "Well, she lives in Frostford and well she wants me to go live with her" Madi replied. "Wait you are leaving us again?" Summer said before storming upstairs "Madi, why are leaving us again" Lilly asked "Sweetie, besides you lot nothing is keeping me here and I don't see you every day so living with Aunt Cass is my Simon and Olivia.

I will come see you lot whenever I can, please don't be mad" Madi replied with tears in her eyes "I'm not mad sissy, we have Simon and Olivia and you don't have anyone" Autumn said "I'm not mad either sissy, I'll just miss you" Lilly said "I'll miss you girls so much, now let me go speak to your sister and then I'll give you presents okay" Madi replied "Okay Madi" Autumn replied before Madi walked upstairs to Summers room.

"Hey baby can I come in" Madi asked while peaking her head around the door of Summer's room "Yeah" Summer replied before Madi walked in "Baby I'm sorry I'm leaving but I need to do this for me and I know you aren't happy with me moving but I will always, always love you so much okay" Madi said. "I'm just going to miss you because you are my big sister, you are who we depend on" Summer replied "I know baby and I will still be there to depend on but it's just I'll be somewhere else" Madi said.

"I'm going to miss you so much" Summer said with tears "I'm going to miss you too baby, now come on lets go open presents" Madi replied "Wait you brought us presents" Summer asked "Yeah they are downstairs come on, let's go" Madi replied. "Yay" Summer said before running out her room and downstairs to the living room.

Madi followed behind Summer "Who wants presents?" Madi asked "Me, me, me" Lilly replied "Right, I'll do Grace first. Where is she?" Madi asked "She's in the kitchen, I'll go get her" Olivia replied. "Okay, now girls Grace has more presents because I got her two birthday presents and one present for the rest of you" Madi said before Olivia walked back in with Grace, "Here she is" Olivia said before handing Grace to Madi. "Hi baby" Madi said before kissing Grace's forehead "Grace open your presents" Summer said while handing Grace one of her presents. Grace opened one of her presents which was a pink bunny teddy, she opened her next one which was Duplo blocks and her last one was a charm bracelet with a charm that says baby sister and a red jewel.

"Girls I want you to open your presents at the same time and I'm going to record your reactions" Madi said "Okay" Summer replied before she, Autumn and Lilly opened their gifts which were bracelets that matched with Grace. Summer's charm said middle sister with a blue jewel, Autumn's charm said little sister with a green jewel. "They are beautiful Madi" Olivia said. "I got myself one and it say big sister with a purple jewel, I just thought they would be a way of remembering that no matter what we are together" Madi replied before Simon walked in.

"Hey girls" Simon said "Daddy" Lilly said before running into Simon's arms "Hey princess" Simon replied as he picked Lilly up and swung her around making her giggle, "Put me down" Lilly said before Simon put her down "Simon" Madi said before jumping to give him a hug "Hey champ" Simon replied while giving her a hug.

"Right guys, dinner is ready" Olivia said

"Come on girls let's go" Simon said while all the girls walked into the dining room

"Thank you Olivia" Madi said

"No problem Madi" Olivia replied

"I've actually brought you and Simon a gift" Madi said

"You didn't need to do that Madi" Olivia replied

"It's just a thanks for taking on my sister" Madi said

"Actually Madi, I need to talk to you about something" Olivia replied

"Okay" Madi said.

They all finished dinner about twenty minutes "Girls, do you want to go play in the living room and I'll come play with you" Simon asked, "Yeah daddy" Lilly replied before the girls ran into the living room with Simon behind them. "I'll help you with the dishes Olivia" Madi said "You don't need to" Olivia replied "I want to" Madi said.

"I'll wash and you dry and put away is that okay?" Olivia asked "Yeah" Madi replied before lifting the plates off the table and putting them on the worktop for Olivia to wash. "So Madi, me and Simon were wondering if you would be okay with us adopting your sisters" Olivia asked "Y-yeah I don't mind" Madi replied with a stutter. "It's just we love your sisters and we are in no way trying to replace your mum and dad, we just think with everything that's been happening it's better if we do it now but we wanted to ask your permission first" Olivia said. "Yeah I get that, have you told the girls yet" Madi asked "No we wanted to ask you first and we wanted to tell the girls in a special way" Olivia replied "Yeah it's fine with me, I'm leaving anyway" Madi said.

They finished the dishes and came through to the living room where the girls and Simon were.

"You okay Madi" Simon asked

       "Yeah I'm fine, what you lot playing with" Madi replied

       "I'm playing with my barbies" Autumn said

       "I'm playing with Grace and her new blocks" Lilly said

       "What about you baby?" Madi asked

       "Nothing, I just want to sing a song Madi" Summer replied

       "What song do you want me to sing?" Madi asked

"The song you sang to us when mum and dad died"
Summer replied

"Lost Boy" Madi said

"That one" Summer replied

"Right let me get the song on my phone" Madi said

"Girls come sit on the couch so we can listen to Madi's singing" Olivia said before everyone sat on the couch besides Madi. "Do you want me to start the song?" Simon asked "Yeah please" Madi replied before handing Simon her phone. "You ready?" Simon asked before Madi nodded, Madi started to sing softly "Yay Madi" Summer said, "I am a Lost Boy from Neverland, usually hanging out with Peter Pan, and when we're bored, we play in the Woods, always on the run from Captain Hook…" Madi sang with a smile "That's it Madi keep going" Simon said as Madi continued to sing "Come on Madi" Olivia soon after Madi finished singing.

"I miss when you sing to us" Summer said "I used to sing them to sleep and then I always sang to them when we were in the care home" Madi replied. "You have an amazing voice Madi" Olivia said, "Thank you, oh here's your present and your present Simon" Madi replied while handing Olivia and Simon a gift each, they opened it.

"Wow Madi I love it, thank you so much" Olivia said "Thank you Madi, I'm going to take this to work with me" Simon replied "Mummy, daddy what is it?" Lilly asked "Your big sister got us mug that say world's greatest parents" Olivia replied. "Thank you Madi again" Simon said before giving Madi a hug "Thank you Madi I love it so much" Olivia said before giving Madi a hug.

There was a knock at the door "That will be Miss

Edwards, I never realised the time" Madi said "I'll let her in" Olivia said before going and opening the door. "It's only me, Madi you ready to go?" Miss Edwards said "Just give me two minutes to say goodbye" Madi replied "Yeah that's fine" Miss Edwards said. "Girls go give Madi a kiss and cuddle please" Olivia replied before picking up Grace "Okay", Autumn said before running towards Madi "I love you so much Almond okay don't forget it" Madi said as she picked up Autumn and pulled her into a hug "I won't sissy" Autumn replied as Madi put her down.

"Madi, Madi, Madi" Grace said "Come here bubs" Madi said as Olivia handed Grace to Madi "Me next" Lilly said "Okay Lil" before she handed Grace back to Olivia and kissed her on the cheek "Don't leave Madi" Lilly said. "Oh sweetheart come here" Madi replied before picking up Lilly "I don't want you to go Madi" Lilly said crying, "Sweetheart don't cry I need you to be strong for me and your sisters okay" Madi replied while wiping Lilly's tears away "I'll try" Lilly said while sniffing "I love you so much sweetheart okay" Madi said "I love you too sissy" Lilly replied before Madi put her down.

"Can I get a hug Madi?" Summer asked "Of course baby, come here" Madi replied before Summer ran into Madi's arms "Please don't go" Summer said while crying "Baby I need to, but I love you so much and this means that you become the oldest because I won't be here, can you do that and remember our pinkie promise" Madi said. "I'll try, I love you too" Summer replied with sniffles "Right baby I need to go now" Madi said "No please no" Summer replied while tightening her grip on Madi.

"Summer, Madi needs to go" Simon said "No" Summer

replied, "Summer, either let me go or Simon will take you off me" Madi said "No" Summer replied before Simon fought to get her off Madi "Come here, it's okay, it's okay" Simon said as Summer was sobbing into his chest. "I love you all so much, bye Si, bye Olivia, bye girls" Madi said "Bye sissy" Autumn and Lilly said "Bye Mads" Simon said as Miss Edwards and Madi headed out the door.

They got into the car and Madi just started sobbing "I didn't cry in front of them" Madi said while sobbing, "Come on, let me get you to the schoolhouse" Miss Edwards replied before starting the engine and driving back to the schoolhouse. "They broke my heart; I mean Grace didn't know what was going on and they call Olivia and Simon mummy and daddy" Madi said, as they were getting out the car. "You knew it wasn't going to be easy but come here" Miss Edwards replied before Madi ran to give her a hug "Olivia and Simon want to adopt the girls and asked me if it was okay and I just agreed" Madi said while they were walking into the schoolhouse.

Hunter was waiting for Madi, he was sitting in the kitchen watching the door "Baby, you okay?" Hunter asked "No" Madi replied before breaking down again "Come on, let's go into the living room, it's empty" Hunter said as he took Madi's hand and took her into the living room. Miss Davis was also in the kitchen waiting for Madi and Miss Edwards to return "She's going to break my heart" Miss Davis said standing with Miss Edwards.

"You should have seen her sisters; they were so upset" Miss Edwards replied "I bet they were, do you want a cup of tea or are you going to head home" Miss Davis asked. "I think I'll head, Madi will be okay won't she" Miss Edwards replied "She's with Hunter, she will be perfectly fine, on you go and I'll see you tomorrow" Miss Davis said. "I'll see you tomorrow" Miss Edwards replied before heading out the schoolhouse and her car.

Back in the living room with Hunter and Madi "Hey it's okay let it out, let it out" Hunter said as he was holding Madi and cuddling her into his chest "I...I...I...can't... breathe" Madi replied as she lifted her head off Hunter's chest. "Madi, I'm going to sit in front of you and I want you to name five things that can see" Hunter said before sitting in front of Madi and taking her hands "I...can see...the pillow...the TV...the bookcase...the grey blanket and you" Madi replied while catching her breath a little.

"Can you name me four things that you can feel" Hunter asked "I can feel...the couch...the blanket...your jumper... and your hands" Madi replied. "Now can you name me three things that you can hear" Hunter asked "Umm...I can hear...my voice...your voice...and your music from your phone" Madi replied.

"Now can you name two things you can smell" Hunter asked "I...I...I can smell...your aftershave...and my perfume" Madi replied, "Last one can you name me one thing you can taste" Hunter asked "I...can taste tears" Madi replied with a little giggle "Well done baby, I'm so proud of you" Hunter said with a smile "Thank you babe" Madi replied.

"Do you want to talk now" Hunter asked "I do but can you get me a drink of water please?" Madi replied "Of course I can baby, I will be two minutes" Hunter replied before getting off the floor and walking to the kitchen for a glass of water for Madi. While Hunter was away, Madi decided to sing the song she had to sang to her sisters earlier, she put the song on her phone and walked over to the window and started to sing.

Hunter walked back but Madi hadn't realised that he walked back and just continued to sing. "I am a Lost Boy from Neverland, usually hanging out with Peter Pan, and when we're bored, we play in the Woods, always on the run from Captain Hook…" Madi sang while Hunter smiled, he hadn't heard Madi sing before and he absolutely loved it. "Madi" Hunter said before Madi started singing the next part of the song "Hunter, how much of that did you hear?" Madi asked turning around to see Hunter. "Like all of it" Hunter replied "Oh" Madi said while looking down, "Here's your water, come on let's sit on the couch and talk" Hunter said as he handed Madi her glass water and took Madi's hand and lead her to couch.

"Let's talk" Madi replied while sitting down "So what happened?" Hunter asked "They broke my heart, I mean they were crying and it was just so hard" Madi replied, "It must be hard, I don't know though because me and Hudson have always been together" Hunter said. "It made it even harder because Autumn, Lilly and Grace call Olivia and Simon mum and dad and I never thought that they would ever call anyone mum and dad besides my mum and dad, it made my heart break because it's just proving that the girls are coping better than me" Madi replied.

"It will seem that way but babe believe me, those girls know that you are struggling and they are trying to not show that they miss your mum and dad" Hunter said. "Olivia and Simon asked me if that they can adopt the girls, I said yes, I mean that makes me a bad sister because it means they won't be able to move to Frostford with me" Madi replied with pools of tears forming in her eyes.

"Hey, that does not and I mean that does not make a bad sister, you are just looking out for them and it's not as if you aren't allowed to see them" Hunter said. "Are you sure, I don't know if they will see it that way or will just seem that I'm just abandoning them" Madi asked "Yeah I'm positive babe" Hunter replied.

"I need to plan my lesson for second years" Madi said "Do you want help?" Hunter asked "No I think I'm just going to go facetime my Aunt and plan the lesson" Madi replied. "Okay then if you are sure babe" Hunter said, "Yeah, I am" Madi replied, "Okay, give me a hug then you can go upstairs" Hunter said. "Fine" Madi replied as she wrapped her arms around Hunter "I love you" Hunter said, "I love you more" Madi replied. "Now on you go my amazing girlfriend" Hunter said before he kissed Madi's forehead "Will you come say goodnight before you go to bed please?" Madi asked, "Of course I will baby" Hunter replied before Madi left the living room and headed upstairs to her room. Madi grabbed her phone and facetimed her Aunt Cassandra "Hey my princess, how did it go?" Cassandra asked "It went terrible, Summer had such a big meltdown" Madi replied, "Princess you know what she is like, she looks up to you so much and you are her big sister so of course she is going to be upset about it" Cassandra said. "I just feel so guilty Aunt Cass" Madi replied, "I know princess, I know but remember this is for your benefit, you haven't had a chance to be a teenager properly" Cassandra said.

"I need to plan my lesson for the second years tomorrow but I don't know what to do with them" Madi replied,

"Why don't you do posters with them?" Cassandra asked. "That's a great idea, I can do them on the poem they have been working on for the past few weeks" Madi replied, "Do you want me to stay on the phone or let you go to do that?" Cassandra asked "I don't mind" Madi replied "I'll stay on then you can bounce ideas off me how does that sound" Cassandra asked. "That's perfect, thank you Aunt Cass" Madi replied.

Madi and her Aunt Cass spoke for a good forty-five minutes "Anyhow Aunt Cass, I better get to bed" Madi said "Okay princess, I will speak to you tomorrow" Cassandra replied. "I love you Auntie Cass" Madi said "I love you more princess" Cassandra replied "Bye" Madi said "Bye-bye" Cassandra replied before hanging up.

Madi sat on her bed just staring at her phone. There was a knock at the door "Who is it?" Madi questioned.

"It's Miss Davis, can I come in?" Miss Davis asked
"Yeah Miss" Madi responded before Miss Davis walked in
"How are you feeling" Miss Davis asked
"A bit better, it's just hard. It feels like I've lost yet another part of me" Madi replied

"I get that but it will get easier and it may take a while but you are such a strong girl and I know you will get through it" Miss Davis said. "Oh Miss, I have a present for you" Madi replied "Madi you didn't have to do that" Miss Davis said "I want to Miss" Madi replied before getting up and grabbing a present from off her desk and handing it to Miss Davis.

Miss Davis opened the gift and it was a mug that said the world's greatest teacher "Oh Madi, I love it, thank you so much" Miss Davis said, "I just wanted to thank you and give you a gift for what you have done for me so far even though I haven't been here very long" Madi replied. "It's my job Madi, but I am so glad and so thankful that I have actually been able to be part of your life" Miss Davis said.

"Oh my I'm going to cry again" Madi replied before rubbing her eyes, "Come here" Miss Davis said while putting her arms out for Madi to give her hug "I'm really going to miss this place" Madi replied. "I'm going to miss you and I think a lot of the people here are going too" Miss Davis said, "Yeah I just can't believe I'm leaving on Monday" Madi replied breaking the hug. "Hey we still have three days together so let's make the most of them and give you memories from here" Miss Davis said, "Yeah" Madi replied "Anyway, it's time for bed" Miss Davis said "Okay Miss" Madi replied. "Is Hunter coming to say goodnight?" Miss Davis asked, "Yeah I think so" Madi replied "Okay, well I'll see you in the morning goodnight Madi" Miss Davis said "Goodnight Miss" Madi replied before Miss Davis shut the door.

Madi put her phone on charge and got changed into her pjs and lay in her bed before there was a knock at the door "Come in" Madi said before Hunter walked in. "That's me off to bed babe and I promised I would say goodnight" Hunter replied.

"Goodnight, see you in the morning" Madi said "See you in the morning" Hunter replied before giving Madi a kiss on the forehead. "I love you" Madi said "I love you more" Hunter replied before leaving Madi's room and heading to bed himself.

Chapter 9 - Friday

The next morning Miss Davis came round waking everyone up, she knocked on Madi's door "Madi, time to get up" she said "I'm up, I'm up" Madi replied rolling out of bed and walking to the door. "Breakfast time" Miss Davis said before walking downstairs with Madi behind her.

"Morning Mads" Jodi said

"Morning Jods, how are you?" Madi asked

"I'm good, how about you?" Jodi replied

"I'm good but I'm nervous" Madi said

"How are you nervous" Jodi asked

"I'm singing to you lot today and I've got to present my project to the history class with Hunter and I'm taking the second years this morning" Madi replied, "Don't panic everything will work out" Jodi said "I don't even know what song to sing" Madi replied. "I have the perfect one, hurry up eat your breakfast and then go get dressed and then I can tell what one it is" Jodi said as the two girls finished eating their breakfast and headed upstairs to get dressed.

The two finished getting dressed and Jodi headed into Madi's room, "Okay so I have three options so far" Jodi said "Which are?" Madi asked "Count on me by Bruno Mars, heart attack by Demi Lovato and have you watched the movie Annie" Jodi replied. "Of course I have watched Annie, it's one of my favourite movies ever" Madi said, "Okay, well you could sing the song opportunity from it" Jodi said.

"That song is perfect, well I could do more than one" Madi replied, "That's true" Jodi said. "What ones do you think?" Madi asked "Definitely opportunity and count on me" Jodi replied, "Okay then that's what I'm singing then, thanks Jodi" Madi said with a smile. "I can't wait to hear you sing" Jodi replied with a smile "Right go sort your bag because I know you haven't done that yet" Madi said. "Okay, meet you at the stairs in ten minutes how does that sound?" Jodi asked "Yip, meet you in ten, now go" Madi replied with a giggle before Jodi left and headed back to her room.

Madi lifted her bag off the floor to sort it out, she put the stuff she needed for today in and took yesterday's stuff out and then took her phone off charger and headed downstairs and grabbed her jacket off the coatrack. "Morning baby" Hunter said as he was waiting with the girls to walk to school "Morning babe, sorry it's been a very quick morning" Madi replied "It's okay, come on let's go" Hunter said as he put his hand out for Madi to take.

"Look at the lovebirds" Addison said, "They are so cute" Jodi said "You guys do realise we can hear you" Madi said "That was the point" Jodi replied "Madi be nice" Hunter said. "What, I was being nice, what do you mean?" Madi replied, "Come on, you need to go see Mr Stevenson and the rest of us need to not be late for drama or Miss Halfpenny will literally scream the face off us" Hunter said.

"I really don't want to go to drama" Addison said "What

are we even doing?" Jodi asked "Probably the improvisation things that we have been working on" Addison replied, "I don't like my group" Jodi said. "Who is in your group?" Hunter asked "Sage, Reagan, Scarlett and Jess" Jodi replied "Sage, Reagan and Scarlett are nice but not Jess" Addison said "I agree" Madi replied.

"Mads if you don't mind me asking, why aren't you coming into drama?" Addison asked. "No, I don't mind you asking, it's because of the way Miss Halfpenny actually spoke to me and she was calling me a liar and saying I was lying about Rebecca" Madi replied. "Oh yeah, is that why Rebecca is in detention for what she said to you?" Addison asked.

"Yeah and on top of that she has been bullying me so the teachers decided to give her detention" Madi replied. "Right enough question, Madi you need to go see Mr Stevenson and the rest of us will wait by the lockers" Hunter said, "I am so nervous for this" Madi said "Don't be, you will be amazing and the second years love you" Hunter replied. "Okay, I'm going to go now" Madi said before walking off to Miss Edwards and Mr Stevenson's office.

Madi knocked on the door "Come in" Mr Stevenson said before Madi entered.

"Good morning Miss Madi" Miss Edwards said with a smile

"Good morning Miss, good morning sir" Madi replied with a smile

"How are you this morning" Mr Stevenson asked

"I'm good but I'm nervous" Madi replied

"Don't be nervous Madi, they love you and I know that you will be amazing" Mr

Stevenson said

"Thank you, sir.

This whole day is just nerve racking and I finally choose what songs I am singing with helping with Jodi" Madi replied "What are you going to sing?" Miss Edwards asked. "Well if it's okay can I sing two songs" Madi said, "Of course it is" Miss Edwards replied. "I'm going to sing count on me and opportunity" Madi said "Nice choices, I can't wait to hear it" Miss Edwards replied.

"Madi what are you doing with the second years this morning?" Mr Stevenson asked "If it's okay I want to do posters with them about the poems because no offence sir the walls are pretty bare in your room" Madi replied with a giggle at the end. "Honestly they are" Mr Stevenson said while Miss Edwards giggled "Also I have your presents do you want them now or later" Madi asked "We will get them later" Miss Edwards replied. "Madi go get your friends and when the bell rings just head up to my class" Mr Stevenson said "Okay sir, see you soon" Madi replied before leaving the office and going out to the lockers to meet up with everyone.

"Mads you are back that was quick" Jodi said "Yeah I know" Madi replied "Baby come here" Hunter said "Okay" Madi replied before walking over to Hunter "I love you" Hunter said before kissing Madi's forehead. "I love you too, now what do you want?" Madi asked "I just wanted to tell you I love you is that okay" Hunter replied "You know I'm stressed don't you" Madi said, "Yeah but I do love you anyway" Hunter replied before the bell rang. "I love you too, now go to drama I'll catch up with you at break" Madi said "Break it up lovebirds" Addison said with a giggle "Bye baby" Hunter replied before walking away with the girls.

Madi headed up to Mr Stevenson's class and Mr Stevenson and Madi waited for the 2nd years to show up.

The 2nd years all showed up and were so excited to see Madi "Madi are you taking us" Vanessa asked "Yeah" Madi replied before all the pupils cheered "Right settle down and listen to Madi please" Mr Stevenson said before going to sit up the back of the room, "Okay so on your desks there is poster paper I would like you with the person next to you to create very colourful posters based on the poem" Madi said. "What do we need to put on the posters?" Carly asked "I would like you to include the poem name, the poet, what you think the poem is about, whether your liked the poem or not and why and what the poem has taught you" Madi replied.

"Can you write that on the board" Carly asked "Of course I can, now get started" Madi replied before turning to face the board and writing on the board the things that the 2nd years had to put on their posters. Mr Stevenson was sitting at the back marking tests that his 3rd years done, "Madi" Kit said as she put her hand up "Yeah Kit" Madi replied "Do you have any like coloured paper?" Kit asked "I don't know, Mr Stevenson is there any coloured paper" Madi asked. "No but Miss Edwards has some" Mr Stevenson replied "Right Kit come with me and can I trust you all to continue with your work" Madi asked "Yeah Madi" Everyone replied before Madi and Kit headed to Miss Edwards classroom.

Madi knocked on the door "Come in" Miss Edwards said before Madi and Kit walked in "Hi Miss, do you have any coloured paper that we could nick off you" Madi asked. "Yip of course I do, here you go" Miss Edwards replied before handing the paper to Kit, "Thank you Miss" Kit said before walking out the classroom. "Can I sit in here next period?" Madi asked "Yeah of course you can" Miss Edwards replied "Thank you" Madi said before walking out and catching up to Kit.

"Madi when do you leave" Kit asked "I leave on Monday but I'm not sure if I'm coming into school or not to just say goodbye" Madi replied "I'm going to miss you Madi" Kit said "I'm going to miss you too" Madi replied before they walked back in.

"Madi how does our look so far?" Vanessa asked "That looks really good, well-done girls" Madi replied as the girls smiled. She walked up the back to Mr Stevenson, "What time do they finish?" Madi asked "In twenty minutes" Mr Stevenson replied. "Can I pack them up early just to have a chat?" Madi asked "You are the teacher" Mr Stevenson replied, "Well since I'm the teacher can you please do the register please" Madi asked with a smile on her face. "Yes" Mr Stevenson replied before he went to the computer to complete the register.

"Right you lot, I would like to pack up a little early so we can have a little chat" Madi said "But we aren't finished" Vanessa replied "I know but I think Mr Stevenson will let you continue with them next lesson but put your names on the back and put them on Vanessa's table" Madi said before everyone got packed up and sat back down.

"I haven't known you guys long but you have all changed my life in some way and I am going to miss you all so much" Madi said "Madi, did you pack us up early for an emotional talk where most of us will probably cry" Vanessa replied. "Yes but the emotional part is already over and I just wanted to pack you up early" Madi said "What are you all in next period?" Mr Stevenson asked "PE" Kit replied.

"I don't want to go" Carly said "What's wrong with PE guys?" Madi asked confused "All we ever do is run and running games" Kit replied. "Running is well fun and do you do other things" Madi asked "We do dance sometimes and do games but it's running today" Vanessa replied before the bell rang "Right on you all go see you later" Madi said before everyone left.

"I'm going to head to Miss Edwards, I asked her earlier if I could sit in there this period" Madi said "Okay and well done on that lesson, you had done amazingly" Mr Stevenson replied, "Thank you sir" Madi said "See you later Madi" Mr Stevenson said "Bye sir" Madi replied before leaving the classroom and heading to Miss Edwards classroom. She reached Miss Edwards class and walked in.

"How was the lesson?" Miss Edwards asked, "It was really good but I think I want to be a social worker instead" Madi replied with a smile on her face "That is amazing, I mean you do still have two years left of school" Miss Edwards said. "Yeah, I wanted to be a English teacher but if I'm a social worker I can help kids in a similar position to me" Madi replied "That is amazing idea, I'm so proud of you" Miss Edwards said with a smile from ear to ear "Thank you miss" Madi replied with a small smile.

The two spoke for the rest of the period about anything and everything "Wow that period went really quick" Madi said as the bell rang "Yeah it did but we have spoken about a lot" Miss Edwards replied. "Yeah we did, I'm going to miss this" Madi said, "Me too, now on you go and get your break and go get your friends" Miss Edwards replied with a smile.

"See you later Miss Edwards" Madi said with a grin "See you later Miss Madi" Miss Edwards replied before Madi left.

Madi walked down to the lockers to meet up with the girls and Hunter. Hunter noticed Madi first and his eyes lit up again just like the first time he saw her. "Hey baby" He said to her while keeping eye contact. "Hi, how was drama?" Madi asked "It was good, Miss Halfpenny wasn't in so we got Miss Welch and Mr Stevenson" Jodi replied, "That's good" Madi said "How was your lesson baby?" Hunter asked. "It was really good, they got on with their posters and were really well-behaved" Madi replied "I'm glad, did it help you decide about teaching" Hunter asked "Yeah I want to train to be a social worker now because then I can help kids in a similar position to me" Madi said before everyone froze and looked at her.

"Baby, seriously" Hunter asked breaking the silence "Yeah, now why is everyone looking at me" Madi replied "We all thought that you would never relive that" Jodi said, "I've been thinking about it a lot lately and think I would be able to help kids who feel the same way as me and I will be able to help them a lot better than my social worker. Don't get me wrong she's amazing but she hasn't been through something like me" Madi replied while her eyes darted between everyone.

"We all just thought…" Addison said before Madi interrupted "Well you all thought wrong" She said before running off to the toilets. "Great guys, we done a great job" Hunter said before storming off somewhere "Are any of us going to go after Madi?" Addison asked "I'll go" Darcy replied before running off to the toilets to find Madi.

"Mads you in here?" Darcy asked before one of the toilet cubicles unlocked "Yeah I'm here" Madi replied, "Hey, come here" Darcy said before embracing Madi in a hug "I just needed one thing to go wrong and I would burst into tears" Madi replied in between sniffles. "Hey nothing has went wrong, I think everyone was just a bit shocked and surprised with it" Darcy said before breaking the hug with Madi.

"I just don't know what I want anymore. I mean I want to move but I don't. I want to be with my sisters but can't", "What do you mean you don't want to move?" Darcy asked with a little bit of shock in her voice "It's a big thing Darc, it's not something that is an easy decision and I'm moving on Monday of course I'm going to get cold feet a few days before" Madi replied with a lower voice almost like a whisper. "What do you mean you want to be with your sisters but you can't?" Darcy asked "Olivia and Simon are adopting them" Madi replied before Darcy wrapped her arms around her.

Hunter stomped round to PE. His eyes were filled with frustration, he went straight to Mr Newwall's office.

"Hunter, what's wrong?" Mr Newwall asked

"I've messed up big time" Hunter replied

"What with" Mr Newwall asked

"Madi" Hunter replied with tears in his eyes

"How" Mr Newwall asked

"I've upset her and I got angry at myself and I remembered that if I feel angry, I should come round here so I don't do or say anything I regret" Hunter replied. "At least you remembered what I said" Mr Newwall said before the bell rang. "Right I better go to history I need to present my project with Madi" Hunter said "Okay, come and see me at lunch" Mr Newwall replied, "Will do sir" Hunter said before leaving the office and heading to history.

Hunter arrived five minutes later than everyone else "I'm sorry I'm late" Hunter said "Come on Hunter, you and Madi have got the presentation" Mrs Glen said before Hunter walked over to his seat and sat down. "Why are you late?" Hudson asked "I was with Mr Newwall" Hunter replied in a whisper "Did you get angry again?" Hudson asked with his voice lowered "Yeah" Hunter replied with a whisper.

"Okay Madi and Hunter presentation time" Mrs Glen said before Madi and Hunter walked to the front "Was is it on your computer?" Madi asked "Yeah I'll log in" Hunter replied before logging into the computer. "Sorry for taking as long Mrs" Madi said "Don't worry about it, you two have as long as you need" Mrs Glen replied before Hunter loaded up the presentation, "Let's do this" Hunter said before Madi and Hunter started presenting their presentation.

They finished the presentation without any problems, "Well done you two that was amazing" Mrs Glen said while clapping "Thank you" Madi and Hunter both replied, "Right sit back down" Mrs Glen said before Madi and Hunter sat back down. Madi put her hand up "Mrs Glen" she said "Yeah Madi" Mrs Glen asked "Can I speak to Hunter outside please?" Madi asked "Yeah of course" Mrs Glen replied before the two of them went outside.

"Why were you late?" Madi asked with her arms crossed "I was with Mr Newwall" Hunter replied "Why" Madi asked "That's none of your business" Hunter snapped back "Why are you snapping at me" Madi replied back with an attitude "Drop the attitude" Hunter said "I've had enough" Madi replied before storming into the class.

"Madi, go take five minutes to cool down then come back, Hunter you do the same thing but stay away from each other" Mrs Glen said stopping the two from coming in "Fine" Madi replied before stomping off "Okay" Hunter said before also stomping off. Madi headed to Miss Edwards and Mr Stevenson's office and Hunter headed round to PE to see Mr Newwall. Madi got to the office to find Miss Edwards, she knocked on the door.

"Come in" Miss Edwards said "Hey just me, do you have two minutes?" Madi replied after walking into the office, "Of course I do, what's wrong" Miss Edwards asked. "Me and Hunter had an argument and I have really messed up" Madi replied with tears forming in her eyes "Hey, hey, hey don't get upset okay, I understand that you are frustrated but please, this is your last day. Don't get upset over a petty argument" Miss Edwards said.

"It's just annoying because he isn't talking to me and all I want to know is what is bothering him" Madi replied "I know you do; I know, and he will eventually tell you, all you need to know and focus on is this is your last day and you are leaving to start somewhere new" Miss Edwards said. "Okay I will" Madi replied, "How did your presentation go?" Miss Edwards asked

"It went really well" Madi replied. "Well done, I knew you would do good" Miss Edwards said "Thank you, well I better go back now" Madi replied, "Okay I'll see you period five and six for your singing" Miss Edwards said "Will I come here first" Madi asked "Yeah, come here at the end of lunch" Miss Edwards replied "Okay see you then" Madi said "See you later" Miss Edwards replied before Madi left the office.

Madi headed back to class unsure if Hunter would be in or not. She walked back into noticing Hunter wasn't there, Madi sat down in a seat up the back because everyone else was working on their posters. Roughly five minutes later Hunter walked in and sat at the back as well but the opposite side still not looking or trying to talk to Madi, he shut her out.

The two periods ended, and everyone was leaving "Madi and Hunter stay behind for two minutes please" Mrs Glen said "Okay" Madi said before everyone else left. Leaving Madi, Hunter and Mrs Glen in the classroom.

"What has happened between you two?" Mrs Glen asked, "He won't open up to me and all I want to know is what is going on" Madi replied. "We had an argument because Madi wouldn't drop her attitude" Hunter said "That is not true" Madi snapped back "Enough both of you, stop arguing. Madi this is your last day so why ruin it with a petty argument" Mrs Glen said stopping the two of them having another argument.

"I KNOW, EVERYONE KEEPS SAYING IT LIKE I FORGOT" Madi snapped with visible rage.

"Hunter you can go and Madi stay?" Mrs Glen said while looking at Madi "Okay Mrs, see you later" Hunter replied before leaving. "What is wrong, you snapped at Hunter and you snapped at me so just please tell me what's wrong" Mrs Glen said "I just don't know what I want anymore" Madi replied. "What do you mean?" Mrs Glen asked while tilting her head puzzled "I want to go stay with my Aunt of course I do but I really don't know what I want" Madi replied.

"Cold feet?" Mrs Glen asked "Yeah I think so, I mean yeah, I don't know" Madi replied "Don't let it get you frustrated and flustered, just think you get a new opportunity and a chance with your family" Mrs Glen said. "I will try Mrs" Madi replied "On you go get your lunch, I'll see you later" Mrs Glen said "See you later" Madi replied before leaving the class.

She headed out to the lockers where Jodi, Darcy and Addison were waiting for her to have lunch. "Where is everyone else?" Madi asked "No clue, we were waiting and then they disappeared" Jodi replied. "Okay then, they will probably appear again soon" Madi said "Yeah, anyway let's go get lunch" Darcy said before the four girls walked into the cafeteria.

They got their lunch, ate it and then headed back out to the lockers where they always hung around "So Mads, what songs are you going to sing" Addison asked. "Count on me by Bruno Mars and opportunity by Sia and from the movie Annie" Madi replied, "What's going on with you and Hunter?" Darcy asked "I don't know, he just fell out with me over an argument he started" Madi replied. "Don't break up, you guys are Hadi" Addison said "Hadi" Madi asked "Yeah, Hunter and Madi put together is Hadi" Addison replied grinning from ear to ear while the other girls started laughing.

The girls were sitting talking until the end of lunch "I need to go see Miss Edwards for my singing performance" Madi said as the girls stood up and walked towards the office "See you soon then" Addison replied. "See you soon" Madi said before the three girls started walking down to PE.

Madi knocked on the door of the office "Come in" Miss

Edwards said before Madi opened the door and walked in "It's only me, I am so nervous" Madi said fidgeting with her hands, "Don't be nervous, I've heard you sing and you are amazing and everyone will love your voice, trust me" Miss Edwards replied with a smile from ear to ear.

"Thank you so much Miss. I am honestly going to miss you so much" Madi said, "Don't worry about it and I am going to miss you a lot" Miss Edwards replied "You better miss me, Miss" Madi said before giggling "I will, don't you worry about it" Miss Edwards replied while also giggling. "I know I keep saying it but I am so nervous" Madi said "Come on, you will be fine" Miss Edwards said while her and Madi walked down to PE where she was doing her performance or so she thought. They reached PE and the dance studio was decorated with goodbye banners and there was a table with all of Madi's favourite sweets and presents for her.

"OMG, you didn't did you?" Madi asked while looking at everyone there who had huge smiles on their faces "We decided to throw a little going away party because we felt you deserved it" Miss Edwards replied. "Thank you so much everyone, honestly I don't think you all understand how much I will miss you all" Madi said.

"No we don't think you understand how much we will miss you. You haven't been long but you have made such a huge impact on everyone here" Miss Edwards replied, "Thank you for everything you have done for me over the past few days, I will forever be grateful" Madi said with a huge smile "Come on, let's have a party" Miss Edwards said before everyone cheered.

One period passed and everyone was talking and having the time of their lives "Madi" Miss Edwards said while signalling Madi to come over "Yeah Miss" Madi said, "You ready to do your performance the now" Miss Edwards asked. "Yeah, can I just get a few minutes to run through it" Madi replied. "Yeah of course, why don't you go into the changing rooms with someone and I'll come check on you in ten minutes, how does that sound?" Miss Edwards asked "Yeah that sounds perfect" Madi replied before walking towards Jodi.

"Mads, you okay" Jodi asked "Yeah, can you come with me for a few minutes" Madi replied "Yeah of course I can, what's wrong" Jodi said as her and Madi started walking out of the dance studio. "I'm doing my performance and you are coming with me so I can rehearse" Madi replied as her and Jodi walked into the strong body spray scented room.

"OMG, I have just had an amazing idea" Jodi said "What?" Madi asked "You know how you and Hunter have fallen out, well you could sing him a song as a way of showing how much you love him" Jodi replied. "What one though" Madi asked "Finally Falling from Victorious" Jodi replied, "Yes, I really want to sing more than two songs" Madi said. "You should sing the two we decided on this morning and then ask if anyone has any other requests, I don't think Miss Edwards would mind if you done that" Jodi said.

"I'll ask her when she comes to get us" Madi replied "Okay let's start practising. "What one are you going to sing first?" Jodi asked "I think I'll go with opportunity first and then count on me then finally falling and then if anyone else suggests any" Madi replied, "Good idea, now give me your phone for the music" Jodi said before Madi handed Jodi her phone.

Jodi went onto her music app and found opportunity on it and started playing it. Madi was singing her heart out and she sang better than she ever has before, the two girls loved this song, "Oh, now look at me and this opportunity standing right in front of me.

"One think I know it's only part luck and so I'm putting on my best show…" Madi sang while Jodi watched her proudly. She finished that song and Jodi put the next one on which was count on me by Bruno Mars. Madi sang her heart out again, she loved this song so much. Her parents used to sing her this song when she was younger, Jodi didn't know about how important this song was to Madi.

"You can count on me like one, two, three I'll be there and I know when I need it, I can count on you like four, three, two and you'll be there cause that's what friends are supposed to do, oh, yeah" Madi sang while Jodi kept looking at her proudly. She kept smiling at Madi and Madi smiled back even though inside she was freaking out so much, she finished singing that song and decided to get a drink of water because her mouth was like the Sahara Desert.

"I am so proud of you, that was amazing" Jodi said while Madi smiled "I just hope I don't freak out in front of everyone" Madi said, "You won't, I know you won't. You should just look at me throughout the performance and you will be fine" Jodi replied with a reassuring smile. "Is my aunt Cass coming, do you know?" Madi asked, "Do you want to ask Miss Edwards?" Jodi replied "Can you please" Madi asked "I will, give me two minutes and I'll be back" Jodi replied. "Okay" Madi said before Jodi left the extremely nervous Madi in the changing room.

Jodi found Miss Edwards "Hey, is everything okay" she asked "Yeah, Madi is just very nervous and we were wondering if she could do more than three songs, Madi was also wondering if her Aunt Cassie was coming" Jodi replied. "I actually need to talk about that so let's go" Miss Edwards said before her and Jodi left the dance studio.

They walked back into the changing room to find an extremely nervous Madi fidgeting with her fingers "Hey Madi, Jodi came and asked me about the thing you wanted to know and I don't care how many songs you do but I do need to talk to you about your Aunt Cass" Miss Edwards said causing Madi to look up from the floor.

"What's happened?" Madi asked while biting at her nails

"Look come sit down and I'll explain what has happened" Miss Edwards replied before her and Madi sat down on the bench in the changing room. "Something bad has happened hasn't it" Madi said while her leg bounced up and down, "She wasn't feeling too good and really didn't look good, so she went to the hospital just to get checked out and make sure everything is okay" Miss Edwards replied.

"So she isn't coming" Madi asked "No she isn't but she told me to tell you that you will be amazing and not to let your nerves get the best of you but Payton and Cole are coming" Miss Edwards replied "That's fine then" Madi said. "I know you are nervous but trust me I've heard you sing and you have an amazing voice" Miss Edwards said, "I am terrified, I do really want to do this but it is extremely nerve-racking" Madi replied. "You will be amazing, you can look at me or Jodi throughout" Miss Edwards said.

"I have one more song to practise then I'll come through" Madi replied before standing up "Do you mind if I stay here while you rehearse?" Miss Edwards asked "No of course not" Madi replied "This song is for Hunter" Jodi said, "Cute" Miss Edwards replied before Jodi started the music for Madi to sing. She was singing her heart out like she did earlier and Jodi knew this was the perfect song for Hunter and Madi, she knew Madi wanted Hunter to open up so badly but she knew him and knew it would take him a while before he opened up.

Miss Edwards was so proud of Madi and how far she had come in the past few days, she was really going to miss her because she had made such an impact on her and had experienced many things with Madi that she had never thought of before. "Suddenly I can see what I didn't before and I don't care what they say anymore cause I'm falling, falling. Finally falling, falling" Madi sang before the song finished.

"See, you have nothing to be worried about, you will ace this trust me" Miss Edwards said "I think I'm ready now, let's do this" Madi replied, "Let's go" Miss Edwards said before her, Madi and Jodi headed out of the changing rooms and back into the dance studio. "You've got this" Jodi whispered to Madi "Okay everyone, Madi as promised is going to sing a couple songs for us.

She will take any requests you all have so show her some respect and take it away Madi" Miss Edwards said as she handed Madi a mic that was linked up to the speakers alongside Madi's phone. Payton walked in just as Madi was about to start singing, she made sure Madi saw her before she started singing. Jodi started the song opportunity, Madi sang her heart out but she shut her eyes so she wasn't looking at anyone because that would make her nerves even worse.

Everyone was in awe they have never heard Madi sing before and were just completely taken back from Madi's voice. "Oh, now look at me and this opportunity standing right in front of me. One think I know it's only part luck and so I'm putting on my best show..." Madi sang before the song finished then everyone clapped.

"OMG Madi," Addison shouted,

"I decided to sing that song because I love that song and I am getting the opportunity so yeah," Madi said. Everyone stood just looking at her. "Next one, next one," Addison, Paige, Darcy and Brogan chanted. "You ready?" Jodi asked. Madi nodded. Jodi started the next song – Count on me by Bruno Mars – Madi sang while everyone still looked at her amazed.

Payton knew Madi loved to sing but she stopped soon after her parents died. Her parents always sang count on me to her, "You can count on me like one, two, three and I'll be there, cause I know when I need it, I can count on you like four, three, two and you'll be there." Madi finished and everyone cheered, the only person who knew the meaning behind the song was Payton. No one but Payton.

"For my last song unless anyone has any requests after it. I need Hunter to come to the front" Madi said before Hunter walked to the front and stood directly in front of her "Mads what you doing?" Hunter asked tilting his head puzzled. "I just wanted to say sorry for earlier and I love you but I didn't know how to put it into words so I found a song instead" Madi replied before Hunter smiled.

"You ready" Jodi asked before Madi nodded. Jodi started the song which was finally falling from Victorious, Madi sang and Hunter knew this was the girl he was going to spend the rest of his life with.

201

"Suddenly I can see what I didn't before and I don't care what they say anymore cause I'm falling, falling. Finally falling, falling" Madi sang then the song finished.

Everyone went mental and were cheering so loud. Everyone was so proud of Madi because they knew that she wouldn't normally do something like this. Hunter waited until she put the mic down and then he grabbed her into a hug and placed a small, short kiss on her lips. She was a bit a taken back and broke the hug and ran out the dance studio. "I'll go" Payton said to Miss Edwards. "Okay do you want me to watch Cole?" Miss Edwards asked. "Yeah please, I won't be long" Payton replied before walking quickly out the dance studio and towards the toilets.

She reached the toilets to find Madi pacing up and down muttering to herself, "Hey Mads" Payton said causing Madi to stop pacing and muttering and look at her. "Oh hey Payt, what's up?" Madi asked "I could ask you the same thing" Payton replied "That was rude" Madi said. "Why did you run out after Hunter kissed you" Payton asked "It was our first kiss on the lips and it was in front of everyone.

I panicked" Madi replied "I get that, honest I do" Payton said "I can't believe we are leaving on Monday, I mean I'm nervous but excited" Madi replied. "I know but at least we get to be together" Payton said "Yeah, what is it you are going to study again?" Madi asked, "It's a childcare and business course but it's different to the one here" Payton replied.

"We better get back and face everyone" Madi said "Once we are finished here, I'll take you to see your Aunt Cass. How does that sound?" Payton asked "Amazing" Madi replied "Let's get back now" Payton said before her and Madi headed out the toilets and back to the dance studio.

They walked back into the dance studio with massive smiles "Mama" Cole said while waddling to Payton "Hi baby, did you behave?" Payton asked "He was perfect" Miss Edwards replied while smiling "Thank you" Payton said while lifting Cole up "Hi my prince" Madi said while Cole put his arms out for Madi to take him.

Madi took Cole "Is it okay if I walk around with him?" Madi asked. "Of course," Payton replied, Madi started walking around with Cole. "Mads," Hunter said sounding intrigued. "Hey Hunter," Madi replied. "Why did you run away after I kissed you?" He asked. "I panicked, just drop it, I'm leaving on Monday so are we together or not," Madi said frustrated before storming off.

"Mads, what's up?" Jodi asked. "Hunter," Madi said fed up while fixing Cole in her arms. "He loves you so much, trust me, he just struggles to show it sometimes that's all," Jodi exclaimed. "How do you know him so well?" Madi asked. Cole started fussing in Madi's arms before she could get an answer. "Come on I'll take you back to your mama. Give me two minutes Jods, I will be back," Madi said before walking back to Payton.

"I'm back," Madi said "Now how do you know Hunter so well?" she asked "I grew up with Hunter and Hudson so we have known each other since we were babies. He helped me when my dad who was a single dad got put in prison so that is how I know him so well" Jodi said. "Wait your dad got put in prison?" Madi asked "Yeah, he wasn't a good guy" Jodi replied, "Anyway Mads you excited to start your new school?" Darcy asked.

"A little bit, I mean coming here was a great thing so maybe I'll get another Jodi, or another you. I am nervous of course but everyone gets nervous when it's a big thing" Madi replied. "Don't forget about us" Jodi said "I actually have something for all you guys but I'll give you them soon" Madi replied. "Are you staying in the schoolhouse over the weekend or with your aunt?" Darcy asked "I'm not sure actually" Madi replied before the music that was coming through the speakers stopped.

"Can I have everyone's attention please" Miss Edwards said as her voice echoed through the studio "So me and Miss Edwards have written a speech to say goodbye to Madi" Mr Stevenson said. "Oh sir, miss no please I don't want to cry" Madi replied, "Don't worry I cried writing it" Miss Edwards whispered to Madi.

> "Dear Madi, we are sad to see you go but we know you will be amazing and will do anything you can" Mr Stevenson said before passing the speech to Miss Edwards. "We haven't known you long but you have changed our lives and made an impact and I can't wait to see you flourish in life.
>
> Thank you for letting me experience things with you I never thought I would" Miss Edwards said before passing it back to Mr Stevenson.
>
> "Thank you Madi and don't forget to visit us. We will all miss you" Mrs Stevenson said.

"Thank you miss. Thank you, sir," Madi said "Come here and say something" Mr Stevenson said, Madi walked to where the two teachers were "Everyone I am so sad to be leaving and I am glad I got to meet you all" Madi replied. "Well everyone, we have 15 minutes till the end of the day so let's get this place spotless" Miss Edwards said before everyone started cleaning, the studio wasn't messy but had a little bit of rubbish.

"Everyone there is a bag with each of your names. Find the one with your name and take it, it's a present from me" Madi said as Mr Stevenson lifted a box from under one of the tables onto it, people grabbed their bags and headed out of the studio, once everyone left Payton got Cole sorted and Madi made sure she had all of her stuff.

"Well I guess it's time to go" Payton said "Yeah, yeah I guess so" Madi replied. "See you later Madi" Miss Edwards said "See you miss, bye sir" Madi replied, "Bye Madi" Mr Stevenson said before Madi, Cole and Payton headed out of the dance studio and to Payton's car but Madi made Payton stop at Miss Edwards and Mr Stevenson office so she could leave them their presents.

Payton took Madi's bag and Cole's bag and put it in the boot and Madi strapped Cole in his car seat to set off to the hospital "You sorted?" Payton asked "Yeah let's go" Madi replied before Payton started up the car and headed out the car park and towards the hospital. They arrived at the hospital and Payton unbuckled Cole and put his in the buggy and headed into the hospital, they found out which room Cassandra was in and headed to it.

"Hey princess" Cass said as she put down the book she was reading down "Aunt Cass are you okay?" Madi asked with her hands visibly shaking. "Come here princess" Cass replied while patting the bed, Madi climbed next to her and cuddled into her, "Listen to what you Aunt Cass says okay Mads" Payton said while taking hers and Cole's coats off.

"So the doctors done a whole bunch of tests on me and I'm just really dehydrated so they gave me an IV drip and said I would be discharged at some point tomorrow" Cassandra said.

"So it's nothing serious" Madi asked

"No princess it isn't, anyway how was your performance" Cassandra said

"It was really good expect Hunter kissed me on the lips" Madi replied

"I'm sorry I missed it and he did what" Cassandra said

"I know" Madi replied

"I got some videos of her singing if you want to see Cass?" Payton asked

"Of course I do" Cassandra replied before Payton handed Cass her phone with the videos.

She finished watching the videos and handed Payton her phone back to her "Thanks Cass" Payton said "What did you think aunt Cass?" Madi asked "I loved it and I'm so sorry I couldn't be there, and I can't believe that you done Count on me, I never though you would ever sing that again" Cassandra replied. "Neither did I" Payton stated "I didn't remember about mum and dad until I found a video of them singing it" Madi replied, "I am so proud of you sweetheart, I know you were panicking" Cassandra said "Thanks auntie Cass" Madi replied.

Payton, Madi and Cassie spoke for 2 hours until Payton said "I guess we better be going Mads" causing Madi to lift her head off her Aunt Cassie's shoulder "Yeah I guess so" Madi replied before giving Cassie a big hug. "Bye princess,

I love you so much alright" Cassandra said before kissing Madi on the forehead "Bye Aunt Cass, I love you too" Madi replied before heading out the room "Bye Cass" Payton said "Bye Payt" Cassandra replied before Payton followed after Madi.

They reached Payton's car and got buckled in and headed to the schoolhouse "You okay?" Payton asked Madi who was staring out the window not saying anything. "Yeah" Madi replied still looking out of the window "You sure?" Payton asked "Yeah I'm sure" Madi replied. Payton knew something was bothering but didn't want to pressure her into talking.

They finally reached the schoolhouse and Madi got her bag out the boot and headed in while Payton grabbed Cole, "Hey Miss Madi, how's your Aunt?" Miss Davis asked, "Hi miss, she's fine, she is getting out tomorrow" Madi replied. "That's good and Hunter wants to talk to you, he's in the living room" Miss Davis said, "Okay" Madi replied before walking into the living room.

"Something is up with her but I don't know what, she was really quiet the whole way back" Payton said "I'll keep an eye on her, you head to your hotel and put the little one to bed" Miss Davis replied. "Thank you" Payton said before heading out the schoolhouse and to her car. She waved to Miss Davis and headed off.

"Hey bubs, you wanted to talk to me?" Madi said

"Hey sit down" Hunter replied as Madi sat down

"What's up?" Madi asked

"You know I love you right?" Hunter replied

"Hunter what is going on, you are scaring me" Madi asked

"I can't do this; I'm done with our relationship" Hunter
replied with tears in his eyes
"You mean that I'm leaving in like 3 days and you are ending
this" Madi struggled to say getting choked with tears, "I'm
so sorry but I can't do it anymore" Hunter said. "You made
me happy when I was struggling and I thought you were
finally someone I could trust and tell everything to but you
chucked me away like rubbish" Madi replied before running
out the living room in tears and to her bedroom.

She ran past everyone, all the girls, Miss Davis, Hudson
and slammed her room door. She slid down her door and
sat with her knees at her chest sobbing. There was a knock
at her door "Hey Mads, open the door, it's me" Jodi said
"Jodi just leave her, give her a few minutes" Miss Davis said
"Okay miss" Jodi replied before walking back to her room.
"Madi whenever you're ready to talk I'm here okay, I'm going
to sit at the door", Miss Davis said "Okay miss" Madi replied
with a trembling voice. Miss Davis heard Madi's voice and
her heart broke for Madi. Around 10 minutes later Madi
opened her door "You ready to talk?" Miss Davis asked.
"Yeah" Madi replied "Okay, is your room okay?" Miss Davis
asked, "Yeah" Madi replied before Miss Davis walked in and
closed the door "What's wrong?" Miss Davis asked.

"Me and Hunter broke up" Madi replied before bursting
into tears again "Oh come here" Miss Davis said pulling
Madi into a hug. "I loved him so much miss and I finally
started to feel a little normal after my parents" Madi said
while wiping her tears away, "Listen he will come to his
senses but how about you go to bed and try to sleep you have
had a really long day" Miss Davis said. "Okay miss" Madi

replied "Give Payton a phone as well" Miss Davis suggested "I will miss" Madi replied.

"Do you want me to tell everyone to leave you alone tonight?" Miss Davis asked "Please" Madi replied "I normally get everyone up at 9 on weekends" Miss Davis said. "Okay miss and thank you for everything" Madi replied "That is what I'm here for" Miss Davis said before walking out of Madi's room and closing the door.

Madi wiped her eyes and grabbed her phone from her bed and messaged Payton

"Hey are you still awake?" She asked

"Yeah I am, what's up?" Payton replied

"Can you please phone me?" Madi asked before her phone rang

"Hey is everything okay" Payton asked

"No" Madi replied before bursting into tears again.

Payton heard her cousin on the other side of the phone sobbing and all she wanted to do was wrap her arms around her and hug her.

"What's happened?" she asked

"Hunter broke up with me" Madi replied with her voice breaking

"Mads, Mads listen tomorrow I am coming to see you and I can help you pack

and we can talk about this how about that" Payton asked

"Great" Madi replied while sniffling

"Go get some sleep and I'll see you tomorrow okay" Payton said

"Okay" Madi replied

"I love you, goodnight" Payton said

"I love you too, goodnight" Madi replied before hanging up the phone.

Madi got changed into her PJ's, put her phone on charge and curled up under her covers. She tossed and turned all night and kept crying.

She thought Hunter was going to be the one she spend the rest of her life with but things change. Eventually she fell asleep.

Chapter 10 - The weekend

- ◆ ◆ ◆ ◆ ◆ ◆ -

Miss Davis came to do her daily wake up, she knocked on Madi's door "I'm up miss" Madi said, "Breakfast in 5 minutes" Miss Davis replied before Madi opened the door "Okay miss" Madi replied with red puffy eyes that couldn't be hidden easily "Did you sleep alright?" Miss Davis asked.

"Yeah" Madi replied "Did you speak to Payton?" Miss Davis asked

"Yip, she is coming to see me and help me pack my stuff to put on the moving van tomorrow" Madi replied

"Okay well go get some breakfast" Miss Davis said before Madi headed downstairs.

"Madi" Hudson said "Hi Hudson" Madi replied "Listen I'm sorry about Hunter, he told me he broke up with you and I had an argument with him for it" Hudson said "It's not your fault but thanks anyway" Madi replied before walking into the kitchen. "Mads come sit here" Jodi said while pointing at a chair next to her "Okay, just let me get my breakfast first" Madi replied before heading into the kitchen to get her breakfast which was toast and jam as usual then sitting at the table with Jodi, Addison and Paige were sitting at. "How are you guys this morning" Madi asked trying to act as normal as possible "We are good" Addison replied "How are you Mads" Jodi asked "Amazing, perfect even" Madi replied and straight away all the girls knew she was lying but didn't say anything.

"What is everyone doing today" Paige asked "Payton is coming over to help me pack" Madi replied "I am going on a walk with a couple people" Jodi replied "I'm spending the day with Sav" Addison replied "Cool" Paige said "What are you doing?" Madi asked "Nothing" Paige replied "You can help me and Payton pack if you want" Madi suggested "I'll think about it" Paige replied "Okay well I need to start packing so I'll speak to you all later" Madi said before getting up and putting her plate in the kitchen and headed out the kitchen.

Hunter walked past "Hey Madi" he said "Bye" she replied before he grabbed her arm making sure she couldn't walk away "Why are you being like that" Hunter asked still gripping onto Madi's arm "One you are hurting me and two did you just magically forget what happened last night" Madi replied.

"I didn't think it would hurt" Hunter said as he released Madi's arm "You are so stupid, you didn't think you would hurt me, what made you think that" Madi replied, at this point everyone was listening "You were the one who ran out after I kissed you" Hunter snapped, "You know exactly why I ran out, you never gave me a reason why you were done with our relationship so why" Madi asked "I don't know, okay" Hunter snapped.

"Wow great answer" Madi replied "Right you two that's enough, Madi upstairs, Hunter breakfast and everyone back to what you were doing" Miss Davis said causing Madi to run upstairs not realising that everyone had been watching. Around half an hour later Payton arrived and came to straight to Madi's room "Hey it's only me" she said as she walked in to Madi's room.

"Payton" Madi said as she ran into Payton's arms.

"I'm here now okay" Payton stated as she hugged Madi tight.

"Where's Cole" Madi asked.

"With Paige, she said she will come up soon" Payton replied as Madi broke the hug.

"I am glad you are here" Madi said.

"Come on let's get you packed up" Payton replied.

"Is your stuff sorted?" Madi asked.

"Yeah, I got my mum and dad to pack everything up and send it to Cassie's" Payton replied.

"Oh, okay so it's just me that needs to get packed up" Madi asked.

"Yeah" Payton replied before Paige walked in with Cole in her arms.

The girls got boxes and started to pack everything away. They put on some music in the background, once they finished, they had a dance party because they had been at it for hours and they were knackered "We finally finished" Madi said "All that needs to be packed away is some of your clothes, your blanket and your teddy which you will put in your suitcase" Payton said "I'll do that tomorrow and then it's time to go" Madi replied.

"Can't believe you are leaving on Monday" Paige said "Neither can we" Payton replied. The girls spoke for another 2 hours "I'm going to go to the hotel and I will speak to you later okay" Payton said, "Okay and can you tell Aunt Cass about Hunter but tell her everything I told you I can't bring myself to tell her or talk to her right now" Madi asked "Of course I can Mads" Payton replied before her, Madi, Paige and Cole headed downstairs.

"It was nice to see you Payton" Paige said "Same to you" Payton replied while Madi put Cole in his car seat "That's Cole all strapped in for you" Madi said "I'll see you later okay, I love you" Payton said.

"I love you too" Madi replied before giving Payton a quick hug. Payton drove back to her hotel and Madi and Paige decided to cook dinner for everyone, they made macaroni and cheese because everyone loved that in the schoolhouse.

"Dinner time everyone" Miss Davis shouted before everyone came running downstairs "Me and Madi made dinner tonight" Paige said "Madi, Hunter with me" Miss Davis said. "What's up miss" Madi asked "Can I trust you two to eat at the same table without throwing food at each other" Miss Davis asked, "Yes miss" the two replied "Promise?" Miss Davis asked, "Promise miss" Madi replied, "Promise" Hunter replied, "Go get something to eat" Miss Davis said before the two sat down to have their dinner with everyone else in the schoolhouse.

Everyone finished eating and thanked Madi and Paige for making it "Who is on dish washing duty tonight?" Miss Davis asked "Madi and Hunter" Addison replied, "You two okay with that?" Miss Davis asked, "Yeah I'll wash, you dry" Hunter replied "Yeah" Madi replied before the two headed into the kitchen to do the dishes while everyone else done their own thing. They finished 20 minutes later without making eye contact or conversation, once they finished, they went in separate ways. Madi went to the living room and Hunter went to his room "Madi do you mind if we come wave you off on Monday?" Miss Davis asked, "Of course not" Madi replied "It will be everyone here, me and Miss Edwards and I think Darcy as well" Miss Davis said, "Okay" Madi replied.

Jodi, Addison, Madi and Paige were in the living room talking before Miss Davis interrupted "Bedtime I think girls" she said "It's not even late" Addison said "Addie, it's half past 10" Jodi replied "Bedtime" Addison said "Goodnight miss." The four girls said before heading upstairs to their rooms.

The next day the girls helped Madi put all her boxes on the moving van and then they spent the rest of the day playing games, watching movies and spending time together before Madi went to spend the night with her Aunt Cass for tomorrow. Madi's phone buzzed, it was her Aunt Cass messaging her "I'll be at the schoolhouse in 20 minutes to pick you up" she messaged "I need to make sure I've got everything because my Aunt Cass is going to be here in 20 minutes" Madi said "You want help?" Jodi asked "Yeah come on then" Madi replied before her and Jodi walked up to Madi's very bare room.

"Got everything" Jodi asked.

"Almost just need to put this picture frame in" Madi replied.

"What one is that?" Jodi asked

"Me and my sisters" Madi replied.

"Do you miss them" Jodi asked

"Every day and it doesn't help that Olivia and Simon are adopting them" Madi replied.

"Wait really" Jodi asked.

"Yeah I am so happy for the girls I mean all I wanted for them is to be adopted but I was kind of hoping that would have included me" Madi replied. "I know you do but you knew that it was going to happen" Jodi said "It just means that the girls can't come live with me" Madi replied. "I know but you can still see them can't you" Jodi asked "Yeah I just wished they could come live with me and I know that sounds selfish but they are my baby sisters" Madi replied, "That's not selfish, that's being a big sister" Jodi said "I'm really going to miss you" Madi said "I'm going to miss you more" Jodi replied with tears forming in her eyes

"Hey, no tears, not today" Madi said "I'm just going to miss you" Jodi replied.

"Come here" Madi said before giving Jodi a hug.

"Madi, your aunt Cassie is here" Miss Davis shouted upstairs "Just coming" Madi shouted back down "Time to go?" Jodi asked, "Yeah" Madi replied before grabbing her suitcase and heading downstairs "Hey princess" Cassandra said, "Hi Aunt Cass, you okay?" Madi asked "Yeah, yeah, are you ready to go?" Cassandra replied "Yeah" Madi said as Cassandra grabbed Madi's suitcase "You say goodbye and I'll put this in the car" Cassandra replied as Madi nodded.

"This isn't goodbye, this is see you later" Madi said "See you later Madi" Everyone replied "Bye Madi" Miss Davis said "Bye miss, see you tomorrow" Madi replied before heading out the schoolhouse with everyone behind her.

"See you later Mads" Jodi said.

"See you later Jods" Madi replied as she handed her schoolhouse key to Miss

Davis and then got in the car.

"Good to go" Cassandra asked.

"Yeah let's go" Madi replied as Cassie started up the car and drove away.

They got to the hotel and headed up to Cassie's room "What time is it?" Cassie asked "Half past 8" Madi replied "Go get your PJ's on" Cassie said "Okay" Madi replied lifting her PJ's out her suitcase and heading in the bathroom to get changed and do her teeth.

Madi finished everything and came out the bathroom and climbed on to the bed and cuddled into her Aunt Cass "Payton told me about Hunter, how are you?" Cassie asked "Heartbroken, strange, upset and hurt" Madi replied while her Aunt Cass stroked her hair "I can't believe him" Cassie said "It is what it is" Madi replied.

"That's my strong girl" Cassie said noticing Madi was falling asleep "You can go to sleep it's okay" She said before Madi fell asleep.

The next morning Cassie got Madi up at half past 7.

"Morning princess" Cassie said.

"Morning" Madi replied.

"Breakfast and then we will come get sorted" Cassie said as she pulled a jumper

and threw Madi a jumper too.

They met up with Payton and headed downstairs, Madi had her usual which was toast and jam. Once they all finished their breakfast, they headed back to their rooms to sort their stuff out. They headed out the hotel and towards the airport. Everyone from the schoolhouse was there along with Miss Edwards and Darcy. "Madi" Jodi said as she pushed past everyone "Jodi" Madi replied giving her a huge hug "Listen, I need you to listen to what he says" Jodi said as Hunter walked behind Jodi "No I can't" Madi replied "Please Mads for me" Jodi said "Fine" Madi replied.

"I made a stupid mistake; I should have never broken

up with you. It was a really stupid mistake, but I love you so much and want to be with you no matter what because you are my rock, my world, my everything. So, will you please take me back" Hunter said as he pulled out a small box.

"What is that" Addison interrupted.

"It's a promise ring" Hunter replied "Please Madi, I promise I will never hurt you again" He said looking back at Madi "Hunter, you are my everything so of course I will take you back" Madi replied as everyone from the schoolhouse cheered. "That's for you" Hunter said handing Madi the promise ring "Thank you, it's beautiful" Madi replied putting it on and giving Hunter a hug "Your auntie is giving me the death stare" Hunter whispered "She won't hurt you don't worry" Madi whispered back before laughing.

"Mads, we have to go" Cassie said "Okay, bye everyone" Madi said "Bye Madi" Everyone replied while waving as Madi, Cassie, Payton and Cole heading to the check in. They finished with check in and headed to security, once they finished with security, they headed to their gate to wait for the plane. The whole process took roughly 3 hours. They got on plane, Madi sat at the window, Payton sat at the aisle with Cole on her lap and Cassie sat in the middle.

Their flight was 4 hours long. Madi sat on her phone and did some writing for the journey, Payton entertained Cole and watched a movie when Cole fell asleep and Cassie read a book, she has been desperate to finish "We are here" Cassie said "Finally, my legs feel like jelly" Madi replied, the flight attendant done the announcements for landing before Madi, Payton, Cole and Cassie got off the plane.

Chapter 11 - Frostford

"I can't believe we are finally here, I can't wait to see Aunt Amelia, Aunt Lexie, Aunt Kelly and the kids" Madi said "Aunt Amelia is going to pick us and your Aunt Lexie and Aunt Kelly are watching the kids" Cassie replied "I'm so excited" Madi said jumping up and down. "Calm down" Cassie replied whilst her and Payton giggled, her auntie Amelia pulled up to the airport entrance where Cassie, Payton, Cole and Madi were standing "Hey you lot" Amelia said after getting out the car and opening the boot for them to put the suitcases in.

"AUNT AMELIA" Madi shouted as she ran into her aunt Amelia's arms.

"Hey Mads, I've missed you" Amelia said as she hugged Madi tight "I have missed you more" Madi replied "Hi sister" Cassie said "Hey Cass" Amelia said as she let go off Madi and hugged Cassie "Hey Amelia" Payton said "Hi Payton, is that Cole?" Amelia asked "Yeah, this is Cole" Payton replied "He is so cute" Amelia said "Thank you" Payton replied "Hurry up I want to go see my children" Cassie said "Demanding much" Amelia said as they got in the car and headed to Cassie's house.

They arrived at Cassie's and Lexie, Kelly, Dakota,

Emmy, Bellamy, Grey, Hope, Everly (15), Faith (15), Abby (9), Fallon (3), Grace (14), Colette (12), Bryson (8) and Bree (8) came out into the front garden. "MUMMY" Hope shouted as she ran to Cassie "Hey baby" Cassie replied as she picked Hope up for a hug "MADI" Everly, Faith and Grace shouted as they ran to give her a hug "Hey girls" Madi said as she hugged them.

Madi caught up with everyone and then Lexie, Kelly, Amelia and all their kids headed home "I haven't finished sorting the room yet so you need sleep on the couch if that's okay with you two" Cassie said to Madi and Payton. "Yeah I don't mind" Madi replied "As long as I have somewhere to sleep, I don't mind" Payton replied "I've got a travel cot for Cole if you want it" Cassie said "Oh please, thank you" Payton replied before Cassie went and got the travel cot for Payton, Madi got into her PJ's, Payton got Cole changed then herself and Cassie set the travel cot up and got pillows and blankets for Madi and Payton.

> "Goodnight aunt Cass" Madi said as she hugged Cassie.
> "Goodnight, sweetheart" Cassie replied before kissing Madi's forehead.
> "Night Cassie" Payton said.
> "Night Payt" Cassie replied before heading to her bed.
> "Goodnight Payton" Madi said.
> "Goodnight Mads" Payton replied as she placed Cole down in the travel cot.

Madi got her blanket and teddy and got comfy on the couch, Payton switched the light off and headed back to the couch to go to sleep.

The next morning, Cassie walked into the living room to wake Madi up "Good morning Payton" Cassie said

"Morning Cassie" Payton replied as she was feeding Cole his breakfast "How did you sleep?" Cassie aske.

"Really good thanks" Payton replied "Sorry about your room, I will definitely have it done today" Cassie said "Don't stress about it honest" Payton replied "I'm going to get her up now" Cassie said pointing at Madi "Good luck" Payton replied while giggling.

"Madi, time to wake up" Cassie said "No it's too early" Madi replied "It's half past 10, come on" Cassie said "Fine" Madi replied opening her eyes "What do you want for breakfast?" Cassie asked.

"Can I have an apple please" Madi asked.

"Of course you can, is that all you want" Cassie replied.

"Yeah" Madi replied.

"Okay, here you go" Cassie said handing Madi an apple.

"Thanks Aunt Cass" Madi replied before eating her apple.

"Where are the other kids Cass?" Payton asked

"The four oldest ones are at school and Hope is at Day-care" Cassie replied.

"That's what I'll need to look into for Cole for when I go University" Payton said.

"Wait did you get accepted?" Cassie asked.

"Yeah, I got my email this morning" Payton replied with a huge smile.

"Well done" Cassie replied.

"Thank you" Payton said.

"Congratulations Payton" Madi said.

"Thanks Madi" Payton replied.

Madi and Payton got changed into their outfit for the day and decided to help Cassie finish sorting the room for

Madi and Payton, they were turning the toy room into Madi, Payton and Cole's room. The three of them had been working on it all day and finished it at quarter to 3 and once they finished, they headed to pick the kids up from school and day-care.

Once they picked the kids up, they headed home "Mummy, mummy, mummy" Hope said "Yes sweetheart" Cassie said "Is Madi staying with us forever?" Hope asked "Yeah she is sweetheart" Cassie replied "Yay" Hope said before running over to give Madi a hug.

"Are you happy about me staying Hope?" Madi asked "Very" Hope replied cuddling into Madi more "When are you starting school Mads?" Dakota asked "Tomorrow I think" Madi replied "Yip, you start tomorrow" Cassie said "I'm nervous" Madi said "Don't be, even though we aren't in the same classes we can still sit together at break and lunch time" Dakota replied.

"Everly and Faith are in your classes I made sure of it so you will at least have a couple people you know in your class" Cassie said "Okay that makes me a little less nervous" Madi replied "Can we go help Madi pick out her outfit and sort her bag please mum before dinner?" Emmy asked "Go on then" Cassie replied before Dakota, Emmy and Madi headed into Madi's room.

They helped Madi pick out her outfit which was a plain white t-shirt, black leggings, white trainers and demin jacket, they also sorted her school stuff into her school bag. "Mum says it's time for dinner" Bellamy said peeking her head "Okay we are just coming" Emmy said before the four girls headed through to the kitchen, "What are we having for dinner?" Dakota asked "Spaghetti" Cassie replied before handing the girls their plates "Thanks aunt Cass" Madi said before sitting at the table "Thank you mum" Dakota, Emmy and Bellamy said "Once you finish eating I want you all to go for showers and then its bed time" Cassie said "Really" Dakota asked "Yes" Cassie replied before they all ate dinner.

Hope was first for shower then it was Grey then it was Bellamy then it was Emmy then it was Dakota and finally it was Madi's turn "Okay, you can all have 20 minutes of iPad time and Madi can I speak to you" Cassie said before the kids all started playing their iPad's and Madi went outside to speak to Cassie.

"What's up aunt Cass" Madi said "How are feeling for tomorrow, you can start in a couple of days there is no pressure honest" Cassie asked "Aunt Cass will you stop freaking out, I am excited but I am also nervous because it's a new school and new people so of course I'm nervous" Madi replied. "Are you sure you want to start tomorrow?" Cassie asked "Yes aunt Cass now please stop worrying about me" Madi replied "Okay, on you go" Cassie said before the two walked back in.

"You okay Mads" Payton asked "Yeah I'm fine" Madi replied before sitting next to Grey on the couch "Right kiddos, 5 more minutes before bed" Cassie said "Mummy" Hope said "Yes baby" Cassie said "Can Madi read me a story?" Hope asked "Me too mummy" Grey asked "Me three mum" Bellamy asked "Is that okay Madi?" Cassie asked "Yeah I don't mind" Madi replied "But you have to go to bed now for Madi to read you a story" Cassie said "Okay mummy" The three kids said before they ran to their rooms, Madi ran after then and went to Grey's room first and read his book and then to the two girls and read them their book.

"That's them all asleep, is it okay if I go to bed now" Madi asked "Of course it is" Cassie replied before kissing Madi's forehead.

"Night aunt Cass, night Payt" Madi said "I'll be in shortly" Payton said before Madi nodded and walked into her room and went to bed.

The next morning Cassie got her up at half past 7 "Morning Madi, time to get up and have breakfast" Cassie said "I'm up and I'm going" Madi replied before getting out of her bed and heading to the kitchen "Morning Mads" Payton said "Morning Payt, morning Cole" Madi replied before grabbing a bowl of cereal.

"How are you feeling?" Payton asked.

"I'm really nervous actually" Madi replied before eating her breakfast.

"Once you are done, go get dressed please and then it's time to go" Cassie said.

"Okay aunt Cass" Madi replied eating more of her breakfast.

She finished eating her breakfast and put her bowl in the sink and headed to her room to get her outfit on "Are you ready Mads?" Payton said to Madi "Yeah, in you come" Madi replied before Payton came into the room. "You look amazing and I love your hair" Payton said "Thanks I curled it" Madi replied.

"Well Cassie is waiting for you" Payton said "I'm just coming" Madi replied grabbing her bag and walking into the kitchen where Cassie was "You look so pretty Madi, here's your lunch" Cassie said handing Madi her lunch bag "Can I fill up my water bottle please" Madi asked "Of course you can" Cassie replied before Madi went over to the sink and filled her bottle.

"Okay let's do this" Madi said "DAKOTA, EMMY TIME FOR SCHOOL" Cassie shouted, "We are here mum" Emmy said "I'm dropping you off early today" Cassie said "Why?" Dakota asked "So that Madi can meet everyone and stuff. Now in the car please" Cassie replied. "I'm in the front" Dakota said "No it's my turn" Emmy whined "Madi is getting the front seat now go" Cassie said before Dakota and Emmy headed to the car.

"Have an amazing time, tell me all about it later" Payton said giving Madi a hug.

"I will" Madi replied before heading out to the car.

They got to school, Dakota and Emmy got out the car and headed into school.

"Changed my mind I can't do this" Madi said.

"You will be perfectly fine, trust me, you have got this. I believe in you

and always will" Cassie replied.

"Okay, I will see you later" Madi said before getting out the car.

"I love you" Cassie mouthed before driving off.

"Here we go. Another fresh start" Madi said before walking into school.